A RAMAZ

NO RULES APPLY

ISBN-13: 978-1-8381911-5-3

PRAISE FOR NO RULES APPLY

'No Rules Apply is a gripping slice of Georgian Noir, giving an enthralling glimpse into the criminal underbelly of Tbilisi. AJ Liddle writes with style and undoubted authority, and in Ramaz Donadze he's created a complex hero we can root for.'

-Craig Robertson

'From the shocking opening, No Rules Apply hits the ground running and does not stop. The contrast between the shocking yet tender opening and the tightly woven plot made this a book I did not want to put down.'

-Marion Todd

'A thoroughly authentic thriller that takes the reader behind the scenes of crime and punishment in modern-day

Georgia. Ramaz Donadze is an excellent addition to the cast of international fictional police detectives and I'm eager to read about what he gets up to next.'

-Mark Wightman

'A page-turning roller-coaster ride involving ruthless criminals and high-up corruption in a vividly evoked setting. Ramaz Donadze is Georgia's Rebus: maverick, insubordinate and determined to get his perp.'

-Marsali Taylor

'Detective Ramaz Donadze's third outing in No Rules Apply is his most exciting investigation yet, dragging us deep into the danger and intrigue of the Georgian underworld. From the terrifying opening the case gallops towards an intense and thrilling conclusion, will keep you compulsively turning pages!'

-GR Halliday

ALSO BY AJ LIDDLE

THE RAMAZ DONADZE THRILLERS

No Harm Done
No Way Back
No Rules Apply

For Karis and Lex, the best girl and the best boy in the world.

Yes, I will laugh despite my tears,
I'll sing out songs amidst my misfortunes;
I'll have hope despite all odds,
I will live! Away, you sorrowful thoughts!

— Contra Spem Spero!
Lesia Ukrainka

PROLOGUE

'I'm hungry, D*eda*,' Zaal complained as he dumped his school bag inside the apartment door.

Sophia used her foot to push the door shut behind them, knelt in front of her son and pulled him to her by his jacket lapels. 'You're always hungry,' she said, smiling into his beautiful face. 'Where's my hug?'

The boy frowned in contrived exasperation then leapt into her arms. She held him tight for the few seconds he allowed her then stood, straining under his weight. *Six*, she thought, *he won't be my baby much longer.* 'Let's get you something to eat,' she said, carrying him, legs swinging, towards the kitchen.

'A biscuit!'

'No, not a biscuit, an… apple!'

'No—a biscuit!' he squealed, playing their familiar game.

'How about… a nice juicy carrot?'

'A biscuit. I want a biscuit!'

'Ah, I know. A potato, a big, beautiful, delicious—'

'*Deda...*' the boy said, squeezing her neck, alarmed.

She turned. The man was big, dressed in blue jeans, a black leather jacket and black industrial boots. A silk balaclava covered his head and face, the slit for his eyes pasting a few strands of ginger hair onto his forehead. He was wearing latex gloves, a pistol held casually by his side.

'*Gamarjoba*, Sophia. Don't worry. I'm not going to hurt you,' he said in accented Georgian.

'*Deda*,' Zaal whimpered again, his face buried in her shoulder.

She stepped back, keeping her son shielded from the intruder. 'My husband will be home soon. What do you want?' she said in a tight voice.

'Koba will be a while yet.' His eyes crinkled, the balaclava hiding his smile. 'But don't worry, everything will be fine, you'll see.'

'You know his name...'

'I know everything about you and your family, Sophia.'

'There's money, my jewellery, cards, take what you want.' She shook her head and mouthed, *Please don't hurt us*.

'Let's go in there,' the man said, using his gun to gesture towards the lounge door.

'No,' she said, her heart pounding.

He pointed the gun for the first time. 'In the lounge, Sophia. Please.'

She took a step towards the door then stopped. The man's eyes crinkled again and he stepped back. 'After you,' he said.

The room had been prepared. The blinds over the

balcony door and windows were closed and a chair was placed against the radiator with handcuffs attached to its pipework.

'Sit there and put these cuffs on,' the man said.

'I can't, who'll look after Zaal…'

The boy was sobbing now, his tears soaking through the thin fabric of her blouse.

'Put the cuffs on—he can sit with you. Don't worry, he'll be fine.'

'You keep saying that,' Sophia spat. 'Just take what you want and go.'

'Please do as I say.'

'It's okay, Zaal,' Sophia whispered into the boy's ear as she carried him to the chair and sat.

The man nodded his encouragement.

'I'll do whatever you want,' she told him. 'Please don't make me put these on.'

'Sorry, but you have to.'

Sophia held his gaze for a moment then, with one arm around her son, she reached down to attach the free end of the handcuffs to her wrist. A helpless tear welled in her eye and she told herself, *No, stop that, stop it now!*

'Why are you here?' she demanded.

The man placed his gun on the worktop and took photographs of her and the boy with his phone. He showed her one then tapped and swiped the phone to send it somewhere. 'Sorry, it's not the most flattering,' he said.

Zaal had stopped crying and was shivering with fear, his face turned into her breast, his snot staining her blouse. 'Why are you doing this to him? He's just a boy!' she said, her own fear turning to anger.

She heard the man sigh through the balaclava's silk. 'Keep your son with you, I'll get him that biscuit.' He tucked the gun into his waistband. 'Keep him with you,' he repeated and left the lounge.

Sophia measured the distance to the open lounge door and estimated how long it would take Zaal to get out of the apartment—too long. She hugged him with her free arm and whispered assurance and love into his ear while silently beseeching God to keep them both safe.

The man returned with a plate and a glass of milk. He crossed to the chair, bent to place the snack at her feet then straightened and ran his hand down the back of the boy's head with his gloved hand.

'Keep your hands off him,' Sophia snapped, turning her son away from the intruder as best she could.

'Of course,' he said. 'Can I get *you* anything? Water, something to eat?'

'No, I don't want anything from you!'

'Okay, I understand…' He pulled a chair from the kitchen table, placed it near her and the boy and sat. His eyes smiled again. 'I won't be here too long, try to relax.'

'What do you want from us?'

'Your husband is helping with a business matter. This is just to make sure there are no problems. Everything's going to be fine.'

'The bank…'

'Relax, Sophia, it'll be better for you and the boy.'

'I don't want him here, *Deda*,' Zaal whispered.

'Don't worry. Daddy will be home soon, everything will be okay.'

The man placed his gun and phone at his feet and

folded his hands in his lap. 'Yes, everything will be okay,' he echoed.

Zaal was fidgeting on her knee. 'Are you alright?' she asked.

'I need to pee…' he whispered.

The man's phone buzzed and he picked it up and nodded.

'I need to take my son to the toilet.'

The man nodded again then stood, put his phone in his pocket and tucked his gun into his waistband. 'He can go on his own.'

'No,' Zaal wailed, clinging to his mother.

'I think the boy should go on his own,' the man said evenly, his eyes fixed on Sophia through the slit in his balaclava.

Her gut clenched.

'Zaal should go to the toilet on his own, Sophia.'

Tears welled in her eyes, unchecked this time. 'You're not going to hurt him,' she said, her words cotton wool in her mouth.

'No, I promise.'

She hugged her son with her free arm. 'Run to the toilet, Zaal.'

'No, I don't need to anymore.'

She closed her eyes and held him a moment longer. 'Zaal, I love you more than anything. Always remember that.' She took a deep breath and made her voice firm, 'Please do as I tell you. Go to the toilet.' She moved Zaal off her lap and used her free hand to release his grip on her neck. He stood, reaching for her. 'Hurry, go,' she said, stroking his face.

The man stepped back a few paces and the boy looked between him and his mother then ran through the lounge door, his footsteps light and rapid on the wooden floor.

The intruder crossed to the doorway and looked along the corridor. Sophia saw him fumble in his pocket then turn and stride to where she was huddled by the radiator. She recognised the device screwed to his pistol, any lingering hope now gone.

'Don't let him see me,' Sophia begged.

He raised the silenced weapon, shot her twice in the head then watched as her body dropped from the chair. 'No, I wouldn't do that, Sophia,' he said then left the room, locking the door behind him.

ONE

Lieutenant Ramaz Donadze glanced at his watch. He'd been on the stand for nearly an hour and his earlier nervousness had been displaced by fatigue and boredom. He stifled a yawn and jabbed his thumb nail into his finger, the pain helping to restore his focus.

The defence attorney made a show of consulting his notes then looked up from the podium to fix him with a predatorial smile, an expression designed to unnerve and probably rehearsed in the mirror, Donadze thought. 'Lieutenant, you told the court that a quantity of a substance, later identified as cocaine, was found in my client's apartment. Was that cocaine hidden or left in plain sight?'

'It was packaged and taped under your client's bed.'

'So hidden, then. Who found it there?'

'My partner and I.'

'Your partner was in the room with you when the cocaine was found?'

'No, I was on my own. My partner was searching another room and I called her through.'

The attorney smiled again. 'You called her through… So, in fact, it was found by you alone?'

'Yes.'

'How long were you *alone* in the bedroom before you called your partner through?'

Donadze had guessed where the attorney was going with his questions and took a moment to answer. 'Not long, maybe three or four minutes.'

'You didn't think the bed would be a more obvious hiding place and that would cause you to look there first?'

'No. We were doing a general search of the apartment. We weren't even certain there was anything illicit to be found. But it was logical to look in the dresser and the wardrobe first.'

The attorney frowned and shook his head, suggesting that approach was anything but logical. 'Was this the first time you've recovered cocaine from an alleged crime scene?' he asked.

'No.'

'Have you ever recovered *packages* of cocaine like that found in my client's apartment?'

'Yes.'

'What did you do with these packages?'

'They were processed and stored in the evidence room at Mtatsminda Station.'

'All of them?' the attorney asked.

'Yes, all of them.'

The presiding judge stirred. 'Please get to the point Mr Gelovani.'

'Yes, Judge.' He paused then turned his attention back to Donadze, smiling conspiratorially. 'You have something of a reputation, Lieutenant.'

'Objection!' the prosecutor snapped.

'Sustained. Please refrain from commentary, Mr Gelovani.'

'I apologise, Judge.' He hardened his tone. 'You'd like to see my client convicted and jailed, wouldn't you, Lieutenant?'

'Objection!'

'Sustained.'

Donadze kept his expression neutral; the defendant was a prolific drugs and arms dealer and he would—very much—like to see him jailed.

The attorney made a show of consulting his notes again. 'Please remind the court how much this pack of cocaine weighed.'

'One kilogram.'

'I see. A small package then?'

'It depends on how you define small.'

'Small enough to hide on your person?'

'Yes, if that's what you wanted to do.'

'Isn't that, in fact, what you did do, Lieutenant? You brought cocaine into my client's apartment and taped—'

'Objection!'

'Sustained. Consider this your last warning, Mr Gelovani.'

'My apologies, Judge.' He looked at Donadze and shook his head in apparent disgust. 'I have no further questions for this witness.'

The judge turned to the jury. 'The Defence has offered no evidence that Lieutenant Donadze acted improperly during the search of the defendant's apartment and you are to disregard Counsel's last question.' He waited a moment to be sure the jury understood his instruction then turned to Donadze. 'You may stand down,' he said.

Irina Jaqeli was waiting as he walked through Tbilisi City Court's columned entrance and into the bright spring daylight.

'We've got a call, Ramaz.'

'What?'

'Bank robbery on Kazbegi Avenue—one dead.'

'Let's get going then,' he said, picking up his pace and striding towards his car.

'You did well on the stand,' Jaqeli said as she lengthened her stride to match his.

Donadze shook his head, 'I don't know, Gelovani achieved his objective, didn't he?'

'Maybe, but you couldn't prevent that. You could only answer the questions you were asked.'

'The judge gave him too much leeway—he should have stopped him earlier.'

'Why didn't he?'

'He was probably bought off. But it's not just the judge—the whole system's corrupt and the sad thing is, everyone knows it.'

'Don't worry, it's a strong case, Ramaz. There's a limit to what even a corrupt judge can achieve.'

'I know.'

The chrome work on Donadze's SUV was reflecting bright sunlight as he unlocked the doors and took his place behind the wheel. He'd only had the car a few months, a wedding present from his bride, Tamuna.

Jaqeli caught his expression. 'You love this car, don't you?'

'Is it that obvious?'

'It is to me.'

He pressed the starter button but didn't release the brake, looking straight ahead, his hands caressing the wheel's soft cover. 'How about you, Irina? Any doubts about how that coke got under the bed?'

Jaqeli turned in her seat to appraise him. 'Did you have to ask me that?' she said.

Donadze nodded. 'Kazbegi Avenue, then. Twenty minutes.'

One side of the wide, tree-lined avenue had been barriered off by uniformed police. Cars crept past, their drivers craning to peer into the bank through its glass walls and doors. A group of pedestrians had gathered on the pavement opposite, some taking pictures on their phones for pointless social media posts, Donadze guessed.

The Kazbegi Avenue branch of the First National Bank was sandwiched between an electronics shop and a small supermarket. Six steps led from street level to its entrance.

'Not too far from your apartment, Ramaz,' Jaqeli said.

'No, about ten minutes. This street gets busy with cars and pedestrians. Not great for a daytime heist.'

A uniformed officer approached Donadze's car as he and Jaqeli got out. 'Hey, Irina,' he said.

'Hey, Gio. What do we have here?'

The officer scratched his white-stubbled chin. 'It looks

like the bank manager's family was held hostage at their apartment while he was forced to open the safe.' He checked his watch. 'We got the call about forty minutes ago.'

'A tiger robbery...' Jaqeli said.

'A what?'

'Tiger robbery. That's what it's called when someone is held hostage to force someone else to commit a crime. It gets that name because of the way the criminals stalk their victims.'

'Oh, well, it's been a long time since I was at the Academy.'

'Right. So what's happening with the family? Is someone checking on them?'

'Soso Chichua got here a few minutes before you. He's gone with the manager to his apartment, left the bank for you and the lieutenant.'

Chichua worked out of Mtatsminda Station and was Jaqeli's first partner after she had been promoted to detective rank. 'Should I call Soso?' she asked Donadze.

'No, he'll call us when he's ready,' Donadze said. He turned to the officer. 'What's the manager's name?'

He pulled a notebook from his jacket pocket. 'Koba Brachuli.'

'What are we going to find when we go inside?'

'You've got one dead.' He glanced at his notebook again. 'Vano Chedia, one of the tellers, shot.'

'Have you spoken to anyone yet?'

'We had a quick word with Brachuli before he left to check on his family.' He pointed to his patrol car. A young woman was in the back seat, a blanket over her shoulders.

'And we spoke to her as well—Nana Pachulia—another teller. She's pretty upset, understandably.'

'Keep her there until we've had a look around. What about Forensics?'

'On their way, Lieutenant.'

'Good. Okay, Irina, let's see what we have here.'

The officer's partner was standing behind the control barrier, stamping his feet to keep warm. He nodded to the detectives and moved the barrier to let them through. Donadze pulled on latex gloves, feeling an immediate chill as he stepped out of the sunshine and into the shadow cast by the building.

It was a small branch with three tellers' desks and two ATMs: one inside and another on the outside wall. Donadze turned to look through the glass onto Kazbegi Avenue. 'This is pretty public,' he said.

'Yes, but maybe not so public through there,' Jaqeli said, pointing to two rooms at the back of the bank, both of their doors lying partially open. She walked to the first door and pushed it fully open with her foot. 'The saferoom,' she said. 'It looks like it's been cleared out.'

'Let's check the other room.'

An aluminium name plate indicated the office belonged to Koba Brachuli – Branch Manager. Donadze used the knuckle of his gloved hand to push the door, steeling himself for what he knew he would find inside.

He immediately recognised the butcher shop tang of fresh, violent death, the coppery stink of torn flesh and spilled blood. The dead man lay on his back, his arms outstretched as though trying—pointlessly—to break his fall. His white shirt was stained vivid red and dark, tacky blood had pooled around his chest and head. The left side of his skull had been shattered, ejecting blood, brain matter and bone onto the blue-carpeted floor.

Donadze followed Jaqeli into the room and they stood over the body.

'Two shots,' she said. 'Chest and head. This looks like an execution. Did it happen before or after the safe was opened?'

'That's what we're going to find out.' He paused a moment then crouched to stare into Chedia's devastated face. 'We'll find who did this to you, Vano. I promise.'

Donadze and Jaqeli left the bank and stopped at the top of the steps. Word of the robbery and murder had spread and more pedestrians had gathered on the opposite side of the avenue. Ill-tempered traffic was queuing in both directions to get past the police barriers. A TV news crew had arrived and the reporter shouted a string of rapid-fire questions at Donadze, all of which he ignored.

'We should close the street,' Jaqeli said.

'No need. Something new will happen and they'll move on soon enough.'

A black Mercedes SUV pulled up alongside the police barrier, its uniformed driver ignoring the incredulous gestures and horn blasts from the cars he was blocking. He jumped out of the SUV to open the door for the passenger in the rear.

The passenger stepped onto the pavement, took a moment to straighten his suit jacket then approached the officer controlling access to the bank. A few words were exchanged and the officer pointed to Donadze then opened the barrier to let him through.

Donadze watched as the man came up the stairs. He smiled and nodded to Jaqeli and held his hand out to Donadze.

'*Gamarjoba*, Detectives,' he said in accented Georgian. 'I hope you don't mind me being here?' He was about fifty, tall, slim and *expensive* looking, Donadze thought: expensive suit; expensive shoes; expensively cut salt-and-pepper hair with a tightly trimmed beard and an easy, expensive smile.

'Yes, in fact, we do mind. This is a crime scene. Who are you?'

The man reached into his jacket pocket and took a business card from his wallet. 'Christoph Maier, CEO of the First National Bank. I wanted to come here and offer my personal support, such a terrible thing.'

'The murder of one of your employees, you mean?'

'Yes, of course, that's what I meant.'

Donadze looked at the business card. 'Christoph Maier—you're from Germany?'

Maier offered his easy smile again. 'Given my job, most people presume Switzerland. But no, I'm Austrian. I've been in your beautiful country for just over two years.'

'Well, we appreciate your support. But this is a crime scene and you shouldn't have been allowed past that barrier.'

'No? In that case, I'm sorry,' he said, showing no sign of leaving. He gave a self-deprecating shrug. 'I should explain something to you, Detectives. Banking has been my life. I started working as a management trainee in Vienna—

something like thirty years ago, now. And do you know what that experience taught me? What I've come to learn is every bank's most important asset?'

Donadze judged Maier's question to be rhetorical and didn't answer.

'Reputation, Detectives, reputation. Reputation builds confidence. Customers need confidence, investors need it, regulators need it. But reputation is fragile and easily damaged. It's my job to protect it.' He smiled at Donadze. 'And you, Lieutenant, can help me do that...' He paused, waiting for the obvious question which Donadze declined to ask.

'By providing information, of course,' Maier continued, answering his own question, his tone hardening. 'I'd be very grateful, Lieutenant, if you would provide me with early and regular updates as your investigation proceeds.'

'Updates?' Donadze said. 'Of course, we always provide updates to victims.'

Maier allowed himself a look of disappointment. 'I suspect you are being a little obtuse, Lieutenant. I think you know I'm requesting slightly more than that. I need to be the first to hear if you uncover any weaknesses in our systems, for example. You know what I'm talking about: areas where our security could have been compromised, where one or more of our employees might have—'

'You'll have to excuse us,' Donadze interrupted. 'One of these employees is dead and we've got work to do.'

'Of course.' Maier's smile didn't reach his eyes. 'Your Colonel Meskhi is a friend. I'll let him know how helpful you've been.'

'Okay, Herr Maier. You do that.'

Donadze's phone buzzed, Soso Chichua was calling.

Maier nodded and turned to walk down the stairs.

Donadze watched him for a moment then swiped to take Chichua's call. 'Yes, Soso?'

'I'm at Brachuli's apartment, Ramaz. You'd better get over here.'

TWO

Nana Pachulia, the bank teller was still in the back of the patrol car. Donadze didn't want to keep her waiting and asked Jaqeli to take her statement while he drove to the Brachuli family's apartment. He arrived and pulled up behind Soso Chichua's car then walked to the entrance and buzzed apartment number twenty-four.

'Yes?' Chichua's distorted voice came over the small speaker.

'It's Donadze.'

There was a buzz as the door unlocked. 'Level six, Lieutenant. You don't need a code for the elevator.'

Donadze entered the building and let the door close smoothly behind him, the lock engaging with a click, its mechanism showing no sign of damage. The corridors and stairways were well-maintained and brightly lit. He called the elevator and took it to level eight, the top level in the block. He got out, noting an emergency trapdoor which gave access to the building's roof. The break-glass box was intact with the key inside. He crossed to the stairwell and walked down the stairs to the sixth level.

Chichua was standing by the apartment door. A big man in a badly fitted suit, his shoulders hunched, his eyes red.

'Are you okay, Soso?'

'I will be,' Chichua said. He let out a long sigh. 'It's just that sometimes...'

'Do you want to wait outside?'

'No, I'm okay. Let's go in.'

Chichua led the way to the lounge. 'Sophia Brachuli—she's in there,' he said, stepping aside to let Donadze enter.

Donadze stood inside the doorway. The woman lay on the wooden floor, her blood splattered against the wall and pooled under her body, her hand drawn back by handcuffs attached to a radiator.

Donadze rolled his head to ease the tension in his neck and shoulders as he approached the body.

'Two shots, Soso?'

'Yes, both to the head. It looks like an execution.'

'A second execution, then.'

'The bank?'

Donadze nodded. 'Who else lives here?'

'Sophia's husband and her son, Zaal. He's six.'

'Was Zaal here when this happened?'

'Yes, locked out of the room. At least he was spared seeing his mother like this.'

'Did he see the shooter?'

'Yes.'

'Is he with his father, now?'

'He took him to stay with Sophia's sister. I have her address.'

'Okay, we'll go there next. Anything else?'

'Nothing obvious, maybe Forensics will find something.'

'Maybe. I'm going to look around, why don't you get some fresh air?'

'Yes, okay.'

Donadze went from room to room, imagining how the Brachuli family had lived and how Sophia had died, her young son kept out of the room where her body had been left, chained to a radiator, her face and head devastated by the killer's bullets.

He completed inspecting the apartment and returned to the lounge. Standing over the body, he took a deep breath, welcoming the rage building in his gut. He closed his eyes and promised Sophia Brachuli, as he did all his murder victims, that he would find her killer.

The sun had set but the cool breeze had fallen away and the evening would—in different circumstances—have felt full of promise, of better times ahead. Of all the seasons, spring seemed to be the shortest, the transition from winter to summer brief and to be savoured. He imagined how pleasant it would be to return home in time to take an evening stroll with his wife and baby daughter but knew that couldn't happen anytime soon.

He had agreed to meet Jaqeli outside Sophia Brachuli's sister's apartment in Abashidze Street and she was waiting for him as he pulled-up on the wide, tree-lined road. He stepped onto the pavement to appraise the apartment block, a construction site when he'd last seen it. It had been erected on a generously sized plot, the outside space paved with smooth-concrete slabs and dotted with benches located beneath shade-providing trees. The architects had dressed the building in an attractive, white-concrete façade which would reflect sunlight without creating glare. He counted twelve levels, the apartments on each featuring tall, tinted windows and wrap-around balconies. Donadze felt a pang of envy when he considered his own modest apartment on Kandelaki Street.

Jaqeli joined him on the pavement. 'Nice,' she said.

'Did you speak to the teller?' Donadze asked.

'Nana Pachulia. Yes, but she didn't have much to add. She's clearly very upset that Chedia was killed and thought she could have done more to stop it happening. But she wasn't even aware anything was going on until she heard the shots. She described the noise, a silencer, I think. She was confused and didn't know what to do. It was only when the shooter came out of Brachuli's office that she knew for sure what was happening.'

'She raised the alarm?'

'Yes, she pressed it from her desk then ducked out of sight.'

'She looks young.'

'She's twenty two but looks younger. This was her first job. Lives at home with her parents. Her father came to pick her up.'

'Did she get a good look at the shooter?'

'No, she doesn't think she'd be able to give an accurate description.'

'How well did she know Chedia?'

'They'd worked together for about two years. They got on well enough but they weren't friends as such. There's quite a big age difference.'

'What sort of impression did you get. Do you think it's possible she's part of this, somehow? Passing information to a boyfriend, maybe.'

'It's possible, but no, I didn't get that impression at all. She struck me as being shy, a bit young for her age, probably. But there was nothing about her to make me suspicious.'

Donadze looked at his watch. 'It's getting late. Let's see what Brachuli can tell us.'

Jaqeli checked her notebook then pressed a button on the security door.

'Yes?' a female voice was heard over the speaker.

Jaqeli looked into the CCTV camera while raising her ID. 'Amelia Nanava?'

There was no response and a moment passed before a buzzer sounded and the door unlocked. Jaqeli shrugged and pushed it open.

Amelia hadn't provided the elevator's security code and they crossed the lobby and took the stairs to the fifth level. She was standing by her apartment door, waiting as Donadze and Jaqeli stepped into the corridor. She was tall, slim, attractive and in her early thirties, he guessed. Her highlighted brown hair was gathered into a ponytail and she was casually but stylishly dressed in denims and a white cotton top.

She let the door close behind her. 'It's late, can't you come back tomorrow? Koba and Zaal are devastated and Zaal needs to sleep. Surely this can wait.'

'We're so sorry for what happened to Sophia,' Jaqeli said. 'We know how difficult this must be for all of you, but we do have to speak to Koba and to Zaal. You can stay with Zaal if you think that would help.'

The apartment door opened again. Koba Brachuli was carrying his son, his face pressed into his shoulder. '*Gamarjoba*, Detectives,' he said. 'It's alright, Amelia. These officers have a job to do.' He offered Jaqeli a tired smile. 'Please come in.'

Brachuli was in his mid-thirties and was tall and fit-looking—defying banking stereotypes, Donadze thought. He was wearing suit trousers and a business shirt but his thick, dark hair was dishevelled and his face waxen and heavy, his eyes bloodshot. He nodded his thanks as Donadze offered his standard consolation.

'You'd better come through to the lounge,' Amelia said.

'Would you take Zaal to the bedroom, please?' Brachuli kissed the boy's head and handed him to his aunt. He fretted as he watched her carry him away. 'He's barely speaking, hasn't even cried. I don't think he'll ever get over this,' he said, his words tight in his throat, his eyes misting. He sniffed and wiped tears away with his fingertips, forcing a smile. 'Sorry.'

'There's nothing for you to be sorry about,' Jaqeli said. 'And try not to worry too much about Zaal; children are much stronger than we think.'

'Yes. Well, how can I help you?'

'May I record this conversation?' Donadze asked, noting Brachuli's shrug of approval. 'You told the officer at the bank that the robbery occurred around four thirty?'

'Yes, about then.' He shook his head. 'I was in my office when Vano called to tell me my customer had arrived. I went to meet him and take him through. He was there to discuss a business loan—or so he said when the appointment was made. Loans were never discussed, of course… He sat down in my office and handed me his phone. There was a picture of Sophia and Zaal… In our apartment…' Brachuli swallowed hard and blinked several times.

'Can we get you anything?' Jaqeli asked. 'Water or coffee?'

'No. Let's just get this over with.' He took a deep breath. 'Sophia was on a chair, in our lounge, Zaal was on her knee. She looked terrified… I didn't have to be told what was happening, I knew what it was… I just didn't think it would ever happen to me, to us…'

'Do you have an alarm in your office.'

Brachuli looked up, his eyes flashing. 'Why—do you think I should have used it?'

'No, of course not. We just need all the facts.'

'Well, in that case; yes, there was an alarm and no, I didn't use it.'

'Okay, what happened next?'

'He said my family would be safe if I cooperated. All he wanted was the bank's cash. He knew I couldn't open the safe on my own and he told me to call Vano through.'

'You need two people to open the safe?'

'Yes. One for the combination and one for the lock. I had the combination, Vano had the key.'

'And he called Vano by name?'

'Yes, he said, "Call Chedia through."'

'So you called Vano and he came to your office?'

'Yes. I told him my family was being held hostage and we were going to open the safe.'

'Are all your tellers authorised to open it?'

'No, Vano is—was—a senior teller. Kazbegi Avenue is a small branch, I don't have a deputy.'

'How did he react when you told him?'

'I could see he was scared but he just said, "I understand."'

'Okay, so what happened next?'

'We were given a bag and told to fill it. We went to the safe and opened it.'

'Was the bank still open, the doors unlocked?'

'Yes, I think so.'

'Any other customers?'

'No, not that I saw.'

'How about Nana Pachulia. Was she at her desk?'

'Yes. I told Vano not to speak to her, I didn't want her setting off the alarm.'

'When you say *we* went to the safe—did the robber go with you?'

'No, he waited in my office. We were gone about five minutes.'

'So you emptied the safe. Do you know how much cash was in it?'

'There would have been about a quarter of a million *lari* and fifty thousand US dollars.'

Donadze did a quick mental calculation. 'So, the equivalent of about four hundred thousand *lari*?'

'Yes, that's about right.'

'It doesn't seem much.'

'I told you, we're a small branch.'

'So you emptied the safe and took the bag back to your office?'

'Yes.'

'Then what happened?'

Brachuli dropped his head.

'Take your time, Koba.'

'We returned to my office, I was carrying the bag.' Brachuli cleared his throat. 'He—the man—was sitting at my desk. He told me to put it on the floor. And then he stood... He was holding a gun. It had a long barrel, a silencer like you see in the movies... And he just shot Vano. Didn't say anything, just shot him... He picked up the bag, walked up to Vano and shot him again... Shot him in the head... And then he left, didn't look back.'

'When did you call the police?'

'I didn't. As far as I knew, Sophia and Zaal were still being held. Nana must have heard the shot or maybe she saw the man leaving with the bag. Anyway, she must have known something was wrong and set off the alarm.'

'Do you have any idea why Vano was killed?' Jaqeli asked. 'Had he behaved in any way that the shooter might think was somehow disrespectful or challenging?'

'No, as I said, he went along with it. Hardly said anything, kept his eyes down all the time, avoided eye contact.'

'How about you, Koba? How well did you see the shooter?'

'Quite well. He was tall, well-built, dark hair, beard. You'll have him on the bank's CCTV.'

Donadze nodded but knew there might have been padding under his jacket and that the beard was probably false or had already been shaved off.

'How about his accent?'

'He didn't say more than he had to. But he did speak a little strangely. Like he was choosing his words carefully. Like Georgian wasn't his first language...'

'Okay, thanks Koba,' Donadze said, stopping the recording. 'We'll probably want to speak to you again.'

'Yes, I expect you will. Do you need to see Zaal, now?'

'Yes, we're sorry to have to put him through this,' Jaqeli said.

As Brachuli left the room to collect his son, Donadze stood and crossed to a wall hung with framed photographs. He recognised Zaal, his aunt, his father and what he presumed was his mother in several of the shots.

A few minutes passed and Brachuli returned to the lounge with the boy, his face again buried in his father's shoulder, his arms tight around his neck. Amelia followed behind, her arms crossed, her mouth a tight, white line.

'These police officers are here to help,' Brachuli spoke to his son, his voice soft. 'They just need to ask you a few questions about what happened to you and *Deda*. Don't worry, I'm going to be here with you, all the time.'

Jaqeli crossed the room and tentatively placed her hand on the boy's head. 'Zaal,' she said, her voice low and even, her fingers sliding down his head and neck to gently rub his back. After a moment the boy turned his head to gaze at her, his face set, his eyes unblinking.

'You're safe, Zaal,' Jaqeli said. 'No one can hurt you now.'

She patiently got the little boy to recount what had happened in his family home: how a scary man had been there after *Deda* had picked him up from school; how he'd pretended to be nice; how *Deda* had been brave and tried to get him to leave. But *Deda* had made him go to the toilet and when he came out the man was gone and he couldn't get into the room to see her. He knew something bad had happened and he'd run to the lady next door for help. Jaqeli coaxed a description of the intruder from the boy including his observation that the few strands of hair the man's balaclava hadn't covered were red.

Jaqeli looked at Donadze and he nodded, they had all they needed from the little boy.

'We're so sorry to put you all through this,' she said.

Donadze stood. Amelia was watching him, her bitter tears flowing unchecked. 'We'll find the people responsible for this. I promise you,' he told her.

She nodded almost imperceptibly and turned her gaze onto Jaqeli.

'Yes, Amelia,' Jaqeli said. 'We will find them.'

It was almost midnight before Donadze returned to his apartment in Kandelaki Street. He winced as the door lock clunked open, certain the noise would waken his mother, a light sleeper. He entered the apartment and pushed the door closed behind him, the dull, steel-on-steel contact impossible to mute. A dim light was glowing in his and Tamuna's bedroom and he crossed the hall to look in.

'Ramaz?' Tamuna whispered.

'Yes.' He crossed to their bed and kissed her forehead. 'Were you awake?'

'Not really. Is everything okay?'

'Yes, no problem. Go back to sleep, I'll see you in the morning.'

He kissed her again then turned off her bedside light and left the room.

Donadze wanted—more than anything—to see his baby girl, to know that she was safe and secure.

Eka was ten months old and Tamuna had insisted her cot should be moved to the apartment's third bedroom. The blackout blinds successfully shut out most of the external light and Donadze took a moment to let his eyes adjust then walked towards the baby monitor's dim LED. He stood over the cot for several minutes, watching and listening to his little girl's soft breathing and inhaling her sweet, baby smell, praying the horrors he endured would never encroach upon her world.

'Sorry I was late home, *chemo gogona*,' he said, his fingers transferring a kiss to her forehead.

He told himself he should go to bed but his mind was racing and he knew sleep wouldn't come easily. He made himself a coffee and took it to the balcony, grateful that the door slid silently open and closed behind him.

It would be another six hours or so before sunrise and the air was chilled and as fresh as it would ever be. He threw a cushion onto his favourite wicker armchair and sat, cradling his coffee on his chest, the steam warming his face. He listened to the perpetual buzz and wail of the city while he considered the limited information he had gathered to date. On the face of it, a nasty but efficient robbery of a small branch of the country's main bank. But the method used—a tiger robbery—was relatively sophisticated as it had to be coordinated across two different locations.

He thought its confident execution and the use of silenced weapons indicated the work of professionals and he wondered why professionals had found it necessary to kill two people. Perhaps murdering Sophia Brachuli and Vano Chedia had just been the safest and most expedient option; the removal of potential witnesses—but then why leave Koba Brachuli alive?

He also wondered about the branch which had been targeted and the relatively small sum of money taken. But he could see why overcoming security would be easier at a smaller branch and he knew people had died for much less than four hundred thousand *lari*.

Donadze took a sip from his coffee and grimaced, the dregs were cold. He glanced at his watch—one fifteen. He pulled himself out of the wicker chair and manoeuvred his way through the unlit apartment to the bedroom, dropping his clothes on the floor and sliding into bed where his wife lay sleeping. He turned his face into his pillow and closed his eyes, forcing his thoughts away from the horrors of the day until—finally—his consciousness blurred and he slipped into uneasy sleep.

THREE

Donadze pulled up outside Misha Arziani's apartment block and called Jaqeli to tell her he'd arrived. Arziani was a detective lieutenant based at Mtatsminda Station and he and Jaqeli had been together for about six months by Donadze's reckoning.

They left the building together. The two men hadn't seen each other for several days and Donadze glanced at his clock and reluctantly got out of his car.

'Looking good, Ramaz,' Arziani said. He was wearing his usual stylish clothes and open, friendly smile as he shook hands and slapped Donadze on the shoulder.

'Really?' Donadze felt anything but good. He had forgotten to set his alarm and had got up late, shaved carelessly and dressed quickly, getting in the way of Tamuna as she prepared for work and his mother who was fussing over Eka and insisting they all ate breakfast.

Arziani laughed. 'Well, not really. But I've seen you

looking worse.' He paused. 'You and Irina got the bank murders, then?'

'Colonel Meskhi wanted his finest on it.'

'You're talking about Irina?'

'Who else?'

'Okay, I agree—you're both hilarious,' Jaqeli said. She and Donadze got in the car. 'Where first, Ramaz? Chedia's wife?'

'Yes, Chedia's widow,' he said.

Eliso Chedia's home was on Kirim Street, a short distance from the sprawling Kukia Cemetery, Tbilisi's oldest graveyard and one of the few to escape destruction or re-purposing during Soviet Georgia's attempt to impose ideological collectivism on its citizens. The house was small and sat in a modest garden, its fruit trees and vines waiting impatiently for the summer sun to arrive.

Eliso opened the door, squinting in the bright morning light. The case file noted she was thirty-three but she looked older. Her dark, shoulder-length hair was unbrushed and her eyes were red and shadowed. She was bare-footed and dressed in joggers and a hoodie printed with an American university logo. It was too big for her, probably belonging to her dead husband, Donadze thought, her ability to keep him with her certain to fade over time.

'Police,' she stated, turning and walking back into her house.

Donadze nodded to Jaqeli and they followed her into her lounge. The curtains were still drawn but light shone through the thin material, spilling over the rail they hung from.

'Please sit down,' she said gesturing towards a couch.

She looked around distractedly then placed a small, wooden table in front of them.

Jaqeli smiled at the woman. 'There's no need, Eliso.'

'Just water, please,' Donadze said, knowing distressed people often find comfort in routines.

She shuffled into her kitchen and returned with a jug of water, two glasses and a plate with bread and cheese.

Donadze put his business card on the table. 'Irina and I have been assigned to Vano's case, Eliso. If there's anything you need, any questions you want to ask, call me on this number.'

Eliso twitched her lips to smile but made no effort to pick up the card.

'We'd like to ask you a few questions,' Jaqeli said, receiving an indifferent shrug in response. 'Did Vano enjoy working at the bank?' she continued.

'I suppose so. It's all he'd ever done. He had a job and he was doing okay. He was a senior teller and probably would have been promoted to deputy manager soon. He was happy enough, I think.'

'How did he get on with his boss, Koba Brachuli.'

Donadze watched Eliso choose her words carefully. 'Koba and his wife, Sophia? We saw them socially a few times after Koba was appointed as branch manager—but we didn't have a lot in common. They got on well enough, but they weren't friends.'

Donadze looked around the small room. The decor was faded and the furniture worn. 'Do you work, Eliso?'

'Yes, at a florist my friend owns. It's popular with people buying flowers for the cemetery,' she said, frowning. 'Why did you ask me that?'

'No real reason, we're just trying to fully understand your circumstances.'

'My circumstances are that my husband was killed doing his job, Lieutenant.'

'Yes, we understand and we're sorry,' Jaqeli said. 'Was anything worrying him? Did you notice any changes in Vano's behaviour recently?'

Eliso turned her angry gaze from Donadze. 'I'm not sure,' she said eventually. 'He seemed a bit distracted the last few weeks, but I thought he was worrying about me and the baby.'

'You're pregnant?' Jaqeli asked.

She unconsciously rubbed her belly, her smile unforced for the first time. 'Yes…'

'That's wonderful, Eliso,' Jaqeli said.

'We'd been trying for more than three years. But Vano will never see his son now…'

'You're having a boy?'

'Yes, he was so happy…'

'We're very sorry, Eliso,' Donadze said. 'But we will find the man who did this to your family.'

Eliso shrugged. 'I hope you do. But that won't bring Vano back, will it, Lieutenant?'

Donadze watched Eliso as she opened the curtains in her lounge, hoping that was some kind of metaphor for her future. She noticed him and raised her hand in acknowledgment. He raised his own hand then started his engine and drove off.

'She'll be okay,' Jaqeli said.

'I hope so. Maybe having a baby will help.'

'Why did you ask if she had a job?'

'I was trying to understand her circumstances. And her husband's...'

'Their financial circumstances?'

'Maybe...'

Jaqeli fell silent when Donadze declined to elaborate.

'What did Soso tell you about the CCTV footage?' he said at last.

'Not much, just that it's ready to view.'

'Okay.' He glanced at his clock. 'Tell him we'll be there in thirty minutes.'

Captain George Rapava, the Mtatsminda Station commander, was huddled with a group of fellow smokers as Donadze and Jaqeli approached the station entrance. The area was blackened with stubs which had been ground into the concrete, their empty packets blown or kicked into the borders. Donadze could see two civilians waiting in Reception for the Desk Sergeant to finish his cigarette.

'My favourite detectives,' Rapava said, giving them his warm smile, his eyes lingering on Jaqeli.

Rapava was in his mid-forties but looked younger. He was about one metre eighty tall, slim and smartly dressed in tan chinos and a blue shirt, the sleeves rolled back a couple of turns on his wiry forearms. He had been divorced twice and station rumour had it his current relationship was in trouble. He smiled at Jaqeli again, took a deep drag of his cigarette then pinched its tip and dropped it onto the concrete where it joined its comrades. 'Let's go in,' he said, leading the way to his office.

One of the first changes Rapava had made on being appointed station commander was to extend his office into the detectives' bureau. Two work stations had been lost to the extension but Donadze thought it a better overall use of space.

'Sit down,' Rapava said, taking his own seat at the small conference table. 'Tell me about your case.'

'Sir.' Donadze summarised the early work they had done on their investigation while Rapava sat, nodding pleasantly.

'Okay, that sounds good.' He paused. 'Colonel Meskhi wanted you on this one, Ramaz. It's important to him and that makes it important to me.'

'Yes, sir. Understood,' Donadze said.

'Okay, then you'd better find Soso.'

Chichua was waiting for them in an interview room.

'Hey, Soso,' Jaqeli said, smiling at the detective.

'I'm hoping you've got something for us to work on, Soso,' Donadze said, taking a seat.

'Judge for yourself, Lieutenant,' Chichua said. He leaned across the table to retrieve the projector's remote control, his face reddening with the effort. He jabbed buttons randomly and the projector eventually came out of stand-by to display a menu of options. He stared at it for a moment then resumed pressing buttons.

'The batteries probably need to be changed,' Jaqeli said. 'Let me see if I can do it.'

Chichua handed her the control and a moment later the video started. It lasted fourteen minutes, starting from the time the killer approached the bank to when he escaped onto Kazbegi Avenue.

'What do you make of this, Soso?' Donadze said.

'Professional job—fast, efficient and cool.'

'And ruthless,' Jaqeli added.

'Yes, certainly ruthless,' Donadze said.

They watched the footage three more times. The killer appeared to have been aware of the cameras and had kept his head down. Donadze told Chichua to pause the video at the clearest image they had of the man. He crossed the room and stood in front of the screen, the projector's focused beam lighting-up his back and head, dust sparkling in the air around him.

'Ramaz?' Jaqeli said after a moment.

Donadze turned, the light dazzling him. 'He's out there, Irina. Let's find him,' he said.

Donadze always enjoyed the long, twisting drive over the hills from Tbilisi to Shindisi, the temperature cooling and the air freshening with rising altitude, his mood lifting. He pulled onto the unsurfaced road leading to Gloveli's house and parked on the rough ground outside his garden. The sun was shining, the sky clear but a cool breeze was blowing as he and Jaqeli got out of the car. He looked up to see white smoke spluttering from the flue poking through the timber and corrugated-plastic roof of the ramshackle home, evidence that the stove was lit and it would be warm inside.

Veronika Boyko opened the door, hugged Jaqeli and gave Donadze a peck on his cheek. Veronika was a nineteen-year old Ukrainian who had been a material witness in a case Donadze and Jaqeli had recently investigated. Her life had been at risk before the trial and Donadze had placed her under the protection of his friend and mentor, retired police officer, Major Levan Gloveli. The case had been successfully tried but she had met a boy in the village and stayed on in Shindisi. They were engaged and had planned to marry in Ukraine, but the Russian invasion and ongoing war had forced them to change their plans and to marry in Georgia instead.

'How are your mother and sister, Veronika?' Jaqeli asked in Russian. 'I saw that there was fighting in Mykolaiv. Are they still at home?'

'They're safe at home for now, thank you,' Veronika replied in faltering Georgian and occasional Russian. She spoke fluent Ukrainian and Russian but, having decided to stay in the country, was now learning the language of her new home. 'I'd like them to leave but it's too dangerous to travel. And my mother is old...'

'It must be a terrible worry for you.'

'I try not to think about it.' She forced a smile. 'How is Misha?'

'He's good—most of the time.'

'Ah.'

'Yes, *ah*,' Jaqeli said, both women laughing.

Gloveli was standing by a chair which he had placed close to the stove, the heat soothing his aching joints, Donadze thought. He was pleased to see his old friend smartly dressed and cleanly shaved, his hair and unruly eyebrows trimmed and tidy—Veronika's continuing good influence, he guessed.

Jaqeli crossed the small living area and gave Gloveli a warm hug. 'It's nice to see you, Levan.'

'And you, Irina. Still not managed to shake Donadze off, yet?'

She shrugged. 'He's not as bad as everyone says.'

'*Gamarjoba*, Major,' Donadze said, ending their fun. 'Thanks for seeing us.'

'Since when do you have to thank me for that?'

'Can we talk?' Gloveli had retained an interest in police work and Donadze routinely visited his former commander to obtain a different—but trusted—perspective on his investigations.

'You're not in a hurry, are you? Veronika's made us a meal, let's eat first.'

Gloveli limped to a small wooden table which was covered with food, a jug of wine made from his own grapes, bottles of mineral water and soft drinks. He held out a chair for Jaqeli, then sat down heavily, groaning with the effort the others contrived not to notice. 'It's been a long winter,' he said.

The meal—consisting of various Georgian and Ukrainian dishes, including potato pancakes—was excellent.

Donadze put his hand over his glass as Gloveli tried to give him more wine. 'Can we talk now?' he said.

Gloveli sighed and turned to Veronika. 'Could you give us a few minutes? Donadze wants to discuss police business.'

'Yes, of course.' She smiled and crossed to her bedroom.

Gloveli turned his attention to his guests. 'The Kazbegi Avenue bank heist…' he stated.

'Yes.'

The old man stretched his legs while Donadze

summarised their investigation to date. 'What do you think, Major?' he asked.

'I think the killings are what make this stand out,' he said. 'Both brutal and apparently—'

'Unnecessary.'

'Yes, apparently unnecessary—and therefore not smart. Armed robbery is one thing, cold-blooded murder something else. Why would these people invite public outrage and more pressure from the police?'

'So, if they were unnecessary—'

'I said *apparently* unnecessary. If this was a professional job—and I think it was—then professionals wouldn't normally make that kind of mistake.'

'You're saying the murders were planned?'

'No, I'm not saying that. I'm saying, keep an open mind. At least *one* of the murders might have been planned. But maybe both were.'

'Sophia was killed first…' Jaqeli said.

'What does that tell you?' Gloveli asked.

'It could be *her* murder was planned. Then, having killed her, killing Chedia wouldn't bring a lot more pressure from the police and it might even have been useful—getting rid of a potential witness.'

'Yes, that's a possibility, but if that was the reason it would have made more sense to kill Brachuli—he spent more time with the shooter and would have made a better witness. There's another possibility, isn't there, Donadze?'

'Yes, there is.' Donadze paused. 'Maybe Chedia was involved. But he was a weak link and could have led us to the killers. He had to be taken out.'

'That's why you asked Eliso if she had a job, you

wanted to know if she and Chedia had money problems,' Jaqeli said.

Donadze shrugged, 'It's something we'll look into. The shooter asked for Chedia by name and he knew he was needed to open the safe.'

'Yes, but that's probably standard procedure and getting his name wouldn't have been difficult.'

'You're both right,' Gloveli said. 'But if Chedia was involved, it's possible killing him was part of the plan.'

'They killed Sophia but let Zaal live…'

'A six-year old wouldn't make much of a witness,' Donadze said.

'These people are scum, Irina. If the boy wasn't killed, it's because they didn't see him as a threat.'

There was a moment of silence then Jaqeli said, 'Chedia has a baby on the way, babies are expensive…'

'Don't get carried away,' Gloveli said. 'Remember, keep an open mind.' He filled their glasses. 'What else are you looking at?'

Donadze lifted his glass and sipped the wine distractedly. 'We need to figure out if the killers were working on their own or acting under orders.'

Gloveli drained his glass and seemed to contemplate pouring another. Instead, he rose to his feet, holding the back of his chair for support. 'You've got plenty to think about,' he said. 'I'll walk you to your car.'

Veronika came from her room and took Jaqeli's arm as they crossed the garden.

Donadze sensed Gloveli wanted to say something more and he slowed his pace to match the old policeman's.

'When am I going to see my goddaughter, Ramaz?'

'Soon, I'll bring her to see you.'

'Good.' Gloveli stopped walking. 'Listen Ramaz, I know Irina can look after herself…'

'No doubt about that, Major.'

'Yes.' He started walking again. 'But I want you to warn her about something, about someone; tell her to be careful around George Rapava.'

'You know Rapava?'

'I know everyone. But yes, he was in my command for a year or so. He was a good detective, but I heard rumours...'

'What kind of rumours?'

'His dealings with women—women he came across during investigations and female colleagues.'

'What do you mean by dealings?'

'Abuse of his position: coercion of female subordinates; favours from sex workers…'

'Rape?'

'It depends on how you define consent.'

'So if he was in your command, why didn't you do something about it?'

'I told you, they were only rumours, there was no evidence. In my own mind, I knew what was happening but there wasn't anything I could do—officially at least.'

'So, what did you do—unofficially? Did you speak to him?'

'Something like that.'

Donadze stopped and turned to face Gloveli. 'You beat him up?'

'I explained my position to him—forcibly. But forget that. I want you to have a word with Irina.'

'Why not speak to her yourself?'

'She'd be embarrassed if it came from me.'

'No, she wouldn't.'

'Okay, Donadze. Do you need me to say it? *I'd* be embarrassed. Just have a word, would you?'

FOUR

Donadze cleared the rutted drive, throwing dust and gravel into the air behind them as he accelerated onto the road back to Tbilisi.

'So what were you and Levan talking about?' Jaqeli had turned in her seat and was watching him.

He settled into his own seat and adjusted the car's temperature control, taking a moment to think. 'You don't miss much, Detective.'

'I try not to. So what were you talking about?'

'We were talking about you, Irina,' Donadze said. 'Gloveli asked me to warn you about George Rapava.'

'Why, what's he done?'

'He was in Gloveli's command. There were rumours about him, about how he treats women.'

Jaqeli paused for a moment. 'Yes, I've heard these rumours as well,' she said, her voice flat.

Donadze turned to glance at her. 'What? He did something to you?'

'No...'

'He tried to do something?'

'No. It was just talk: innuendo; suggestion...'

'You didn't report him?'

'No, I can deal with him.'

'Are you sure?'

'Yes, I know his type.'

'Well, Gloveli wanted me to pass on the message.'

'Okay, that was kind of him.' She paused again. 'You know I don't need your protection, don't you, Ramaz?'

'I know you don't.'

'Ramaz...'

'What?'

'Please don't discuss this with Misha.'

Donadze nodded. 'Why would I?' he said.

They drove in silence for several minutes, Jaqeli looking out her window at the landscape and the views of Tbilisi lying in the haze below.

'Do you really think Chedia was involved?' she asked eventually.

'I don't know. It's possible.'

'So we'll look at his bank records, telephone call history, credit card statements...'

'Yes, we'll contact our finance investigators,' Donadze said. 'Let's see if anything stands out. And we might have to speak to Eliso again.'

'You think she's keeping something from us?'

'Possibly. She said Chedia was distracted, maybe worried about her and the baby. But maybe it was something else he was worried about and she knows what that was.'

His phone buzzed in its windscreen mount. He glanced at the caller ID and accepted the call. 'Donadze,' he said.

'Where are you, Ramaz?' Rapava asked, his voice booming through the car's speaker.

'We're returning from Shindisi, Captain,' Donadze said, lowering the volume.

'Shindisi?'

'Yes, Shindisi.'

Rapava hesitated, seemingly waiting for Donadze to elaborate. 'Well, come straight here. Colonel Meshki's on his way in, he wants an update on your case.'

'Okay, thirty minutes.'

'What can we tell him? Do you have any leads?'

'No, nothing firm.'

'That's a pity, he seems to have taken an interest in this one.'

Donadze didn't respond.

'Is everything okay, Ramaz?'

'What do you mean?'

'Didn't Levan Gloveli retire to Shindisi?'

'Yes, he did.'

Rapava hesitated. 'Come straight to the station.'

'Thirty minutes,' Donadze said and hung up.

'What was that about?' Jaqeli demanded. 'I told you—I don't need your protection.'

'And *I* told you—I know you don't.'

They drove in silence for several minutes, Donadze manoeuvring his car around the tight bends of the steeply descending road.

'Ramaz?' Jaqeli said, at last.

'Yes?'

'Thanks.'

Donadze nodded. 'Let's see what Meskhi wants.'

Soso Chichua pulled himself to his feet as Donadze and Jaqeli walked into the detectives' bureau.

'Hey, Soso,' Jaqeli said. 'Did you miss me?'

'Of course I did, Irina. How was Major Gloveli, Ramaz?'

'Pretty much the same,' Donadze said. 'A bit slower on his feet, but still sharp.'

'Yes, it's a pity we don't have a few more like him.'

Donadze searched Chichua's face for hidden meaning but saw nothing. 'You're right, Soso, they broke the mould after Gloveli,' he said.

'I'm glad you're here.' Chichua lowered himself back into his chair. 'We've got the ballistics back.' He squinted at the information on his screen then gave up and put on his glasses. 'So, it looks like our shooters have the same taste in guns—both the weapons used were Sig Sauer M17 pistols.'

'Military sidearms?'

'Yes, the US have them, our military as well. They're probably in use in lots of countries around the world. But the M17 *is* a military variant—based on the P320. And there's something else; we already knew a silencer was used by Chedia's killer but it seems Sophia's killer used one as well.'

'So both weapons were military variants, both fitted with silencers and both victims were killed execution-style,' Jaqeli said.

'As I told you yesterday, Irina, you're dealing with professionals; you need to be careful until you know who you're up against.'

'I'm always careful, Soso, you should know that.'

'Did these guns come up on the ENFSI database,' Donadze asked, referring to the European institute which exchanges forensic-related information between member states.

'No, there weren't any markings on the bullets to tie them back to any weapons they've ever come across.'

'I suppose that was to be expected.'

Donadze's phone buzzed a text from George Rapava. *Room 1 come here now.*

'Come on, Irina,' he said. 'We've been summoned.' He put his hand on Chichua's shoulder. 'Thanks Soso.'

'Ramaz...' Chichua hesitated. He nodded towards the station commander's office. 'I've wanted to say this for a while now... Everyone here thought you'd get that job—*I* thought you deserved it.'

'Thanks, Soso,' Donadze said, surprised by Chichua's uncharacteristically sentimental words. 'But that's probably why you'll never work in Personnel.'

Chichua grinned. 'Yes, you're right, I've never been a good judge of character.'

Donadze and Jaqeli walked to the interview room. Donadze knocked on the door and opened it. Rapava and Meskhi were sitting on either side of the metal table. Meskhi looked uncomfortable in the chair, which was too small for his tall, lean frame and—bolted to the floor—too close to the table for his long, thin legs. He was dressed in his trademark dark suit with white shirt and dark tie, his highly polished shoes and shaved head reflecting light from the interview room's harsh LED lamps.

'Come in, Donadze,' Rapava said.

'*Gamarjoba*, Colonel,' Donadze said, noting Rapava had dropped the use of his first name in Meskhi's presence.

Rapava attempted a disarming smile. 'Sorry, Irina. We only need Lieutenant Donadze.'

'I'd like Detective Jaqeli to join us, Captain,' Meskhi said evenly.

Rapava's brief frown flashed to a welcoming smile. 'Of course, take a seat, Irina.'

It had been several months since Donadze had last seen Colonel Meskhi when, summoned to his office at the Ministry of Internal Affairs, he had been informed that Meskhi's plan to establish a special unit to tackle criminality—by what he called unconventional means—was to be shelved. Donadze was to have led the unit but the circumstances of a case he had recently closed brought unwelcome political attention and Meskhi had deemed it prudent to suspend his plan.

'The bank robbery killings: what do we know so far, Lieutenant?' Meskhi asked, steepling his fingers under his chin and closing his eyes, a mannerism Donadze had become familiar with.

Donadze paused to gather his thoughts. 'A tiger robbery, sir. The bank manager's wife and his son held hostage while he and his senior teller opened the safe. But his wife was killed, as was the senior teller *after* the safe had been opened and the money handed over.'

'A relatively small sum of money, I believe?'

'A quarter of a million *lari* and fifty thousand US dollars.'

'Tell Colonel Meskhi about the weapons, Donadze,' Rapava said.

'Ballistics are back, Colonel. Both pistols were silencer-equipped Sig Sauer M17s.'

'Military weapons,' Rapava added.

Meskhi opened his eyes. 'I prefer to hear directly from my investigating officers, Captain.'

'Yes, sir. Of course.'

'Similarities with other robberies of this type?'

Donadze nodded to Jaqeli to pick up the briefing. 'We're looking into that, sir,' she said. 'It's not the first time something like this has happened of course: banks; businesses; jewellery stores. But this level of ruthlessness is unusual—two senseless murders.'

'You don't know they were senseless though, do you, Detective?'

'No, sir. I should have said *apparently* senseless. It's true, there may be a reason or reasons for the killings.'

'Why are you smiling, Detective?'

'Sorry, sir. It's just that Major Gloveli gave us similar advice.'

'That sounds like you've been discussing this case with Levan Gloveli, Detective,' Rapava said, straightening in his chair. 'Gloveli's retired, he shouldn't be hearing anything about this or any other—'

'I don't see that as an issue, Captain,' Meskhi interrupted. 'Carry on, Detective.'

'Yes, sir. The main conclusion Lieutenant Donadze

and I came to is that the robbery and murders were carried out by experts, by professionals; they knew what they were doing. If the shootings weren't senseless then understanding the logic and the reasoning behind them could help solve this case.'

'Yes, I agree. Make sure you don't lose sight of that as your investigation progresses.'

It was after eight in the evening when Donadze returned to Kandelaki Street. He took the elevator and was met by Tamuna as the doors opened. He stepped out and she let the doors close behind him.

'Hey, Ramaz,' she said. 'I was hoping to catch you before I left.'

Donadze caught a hint of her perfume as she leaned forward to kiss him. 'Well, I'm glad you did. Where are you off to?'

'I'm meeting Lela for a coffee.' Lela Tabagari was Tamuna's best friend and a colleague at the Medifirst Clinic where they both worked.

'It's a bit late for coffee, isn't it?'

'A little, but it's difficult to get her attention, just now.'

'Preoccupied with her boyfriend?'

'I don't know what it is but something's bothering her. Anyway, I'm running late, better go.'

'Your usual place? I'll give you a lift.'

'It's okay, I'll get a taxi.' She kissed him again and pressed the button to call the elevator back.

He opened the apartment door and stepped into the

lounge. His mother was watching television, the volume turned down to a murmur. She struggled to get up from the sofa to kiss him. 'Did you see, Tamuna?' she asked.

'Yes, briefly,' he said, noticing again the lines that had deepened around her eyes and mouth following her heart attack a year or so ago.

She appraised him carefully. 'You're not annoyed that Tamuna's gone out, are you?'

'No, of course not. It's good that she's seeing Lela. How's Eka been?'

'She's been wonderful. You can look in on her while I get your dinner out of the oven. But please don't wake her.'

He walked to Eka's room and spent a few minutes gazing at his daughter as she slept.

Cooking aromas were drifting through the open door and he realised how hungry he was. He returned to the lounge and sat on one of the stools located by the breakfast bar. His mother had laid out bread, cheese, salad and pork *shashlik* dressed with raw onion and pomegranate seeds. He tore off a piece of bread and transferred a slice of *sulguni* cheese to his plate to accompany the barbecued pork. She placed a glass beside him and filled it with rich, red *Mukuzani* wine. Donadze took a generous sip, held it in his mouth and let the liquid slide down his throat.

'Hard day, *Ramazi*?' his mother asked.

'A little.'

'How about Tamuna?'

'What do you mean?'

'Did *she* have a hard day?'

'I don't know, I didn't get a chance to ask her.'

'Well, I can tell you—she did. She had a very busy

surgery, had to work late to clear her patient list then came straight home to feed Eka and get her off to bed. She was tired but hadn't seen Lela for a while so decided to make an effort to meet her.'

'Why are you telling me this, *Deda*?'

'Can't you see, *Ramazi*? Tamuna told *me* about her day because you weren't here to talk to her.'

'Okay, I'll ask her about her day when she gets home.'

His mother looked disappointed. 'Come on, Ramaz. You know I only meant that as an example. I'm trying to tell you that you and Tamuna need to make more time for each other. You've only been married a few months, you shouldn't take each other for granted.'

'I'm not sure that's what we're doing, *Deda*.'

She rinsed out a cloth and began wiping down the kitchen surfaces. 'Well, that's what I *see* you doing.'

Donadze finished eating and considered the wine bottle and his empty glass. 'I have to go out again,' he said.

'Surely not, Ramaz. Tamuna won't be long.'

He stooped to kiss her cheek. 'I know.'

Tamuna and Lela's favourite coffee shop was a thirty minute walk or a five minute drive from the apartment. Donadze decided to walk. He arrived at the coffee shop and glanced through its tall windows. The women were on high stools, deep in conversation. He thought they'd be a while yet. He crossed the road, pulled up his jacket collar against the cool evening air and read messages and email on his phone while he leaned against a shop front and waited.

About twenty minutes passed before Tamuna and Lela left the coffee shop together. He stayed out of sight until Tamuna had kissed her friend goodbye and was pulling out her phone to call a taxi.

'Why don't we walk?' he said.

She startled. 'What are you doing here, Ramaz?'

He offered her his arm. 'I'd like to walk you home, if that's okay?'

'Is something wrong?'

'No, everything's fine.'

She looked at him strangely but took his arm as they walked in the direction of their apartment.

'How was Lela?' Donadze asked.

Tamuna took a moment to answer. 'I'm not sure; there's something worrying her, I think. But she won't admit it, just said she was tired.'

'You think it's more than tiredness?'

'Yes, she seems to have lost her spark lately, she's more subdued. But I can't help if she won't talk to me about it.'

'All you can do is be patient. She'll want to talk at some point.'

'I hope so. You remember we're meeting her and Niko on Friday?'

'Her boyfriend? Yes, I remember.'

They walked in silence for several steps. 'Why are you here, Ramaz? Are you sure there's nothing wrong.'

'My mother thinks we should make more time for each other.'

Tamuna hesitated a moment. 'Well, she's right.'

'I know,' he said. 'So, how did your day go?'

FIVE

'Coffee, Misha?' Donadze said.

Arziani looked up from his laptop. 'Yes, good idea.' He clicked a button to freeze the screen. 'Have you started this training yet?' He was referring to a set of police online training modules.

'Not yet, is it worth the effort?'

'I think so. Where do you want to sit?'

'Let's go outside.'

'You don't like the coffee here?'

'Does anyone?' He glanced towards the station commander's office. George Rapava was talking on his phone, his chair reclined, his feet on the table. Donadze was conscious of his growing antipathy towards his commander and knew that was neither healthy nor wise. He understood his own psychology, how his sister's brutal murder made him protective of women who are preyed upon by men. But understanding that psychology did nothing to lessen his dislike of men like George Rapava.

Arziani caught his expression. 'What?'

'Nothing, let's get that coffee. There's something I want to discuss with you.'

The two men left the station and walked in sunshine to a coffee shop on Besik Street. A young waitress came out to the patio to take their order, her brightest smile reserved for Arziani, Donadze noted.

Arziani retrieved a pair of designer sunglasses from his jacket pocket. 'So, what did you want to talk about, Ramaz?' he asked, turning his handsome face into the sun.

'Have you and Irina discussed our new case?'

'The bank murders. Yes, a little. Is there something I can help you with?'

'Just your opinion. What do you thinks happening here, Misha? The Kazbegi Avenue bank branch was robbed and four hundred thousand *lari* taken. There were two—potentially—premeditated murders. Do you think something that big could have been done without sanction?'

'Sanction by Otar Basilia, you mean?' Basilia headed up the Kaldani crime family. The family had been named after its founder, Zaza Kaldani and—although there had been different bosses since Zaza—the name had stuck, a form of tribute Donadze presumed. Basilia had recently been convicted of murder and rape and was serving his thirty-year sentence in Gldani prison, from where he continued to maintain control of his gang.

'Yes, Kazbegi Avenue is part of his territory.'

'It'd certainly be a bold move for a freelancer to muscle in on Basilia's turf that way. But it wouldn't be the first time. That *profession* is all about natural selection, the survival of the fittest.'

'Or the law of the jungle, maybe. Do you think Basilia would have had his own people do it?'

Arziani returned the waitress' smile as she placed their coffee and water on the table. He took a sip of the water while he waited for her to leave. 'It's possible,' he said. 'But bank robberies haven't been his thing in the past.'

'No. But his circumstances have changed. Maybe he needed some quick money.'

'I suppose being jailed is one way to describe a change in circumstances. It's possible he's got less control now, maybe he had to make concessions on what he'll allow on his territory.' Arziani blew on his coffee to cool it then took a sip. 'So you need to know if and how Basilia was involved; was it something he'd organised or at least was aware of and approved? If not, was it done on his patch without his sanction?'

'In which case, he must be pretty pissed off.'

'You'd think so. So how are you going to figure out what did happen?'

Donadze took a sip from his cup and tasted coffee grounds on his lips. He took a drink of water. 'Easy. I'm going to Gldani Prison to ask him,' he said.

Donadze hadn't been confident Otar Basilia would agree to the meeting. He'd communicated his request through the crime boss' lawyer and had been deliberately vague about its purpose, knowing Basilia would probably guess the reason anyway. The fact that he had agreed to meet told Donadze he had an interest in the bank robbery and murders.

Gldani Prison No. 8 had changed dramatically since Donadze had first visited in 2010. Back then, Georgia imprisoned more people per capita than any other country in Europe. Prison life for its unfortunate inmates was both degrading and dangerous. It was only when leaked video footage revealed the abuse and torture of prisoners by their guards that the government took comprehensive measures to reform the country's penal system. *And it all feels so civilised now*, Donadze thought as he checked in and was escorted to a secure room to meet Basilia.

Donadze was kept waiting for about ten minutes before a door opened and Basilia was shown in. He paused inside the doorway and Donadze stood, both men appraising each other. Basilia was slightly shorter but powerfully built with thick, muscular legs, bull-like shoulders and virtually no neck. His belly bulged under a grey sweatshirt and his head was shaved to a dark shadow; a formidable man whose menacing presence was somehow enhanced by his lumpy, red nose and full, almost sultry, lips.

Basilia held up his manacled hands. 'Off,' he instructed the guard, his eyes fixed on Donadze.

The guard hesitated, glanced at Donadze then fumbled with a key to remove the handcuffs.

'Wait outside,' Basilia said as he lowered his powerful frame onto the chair.

Donadze waited until the guard had left the room then took a seat opposite the gangster. 'Okay, I'm impressed,' he said. 'The guards do what you tell them. You're the top man around here, the boss.'

Basilia smiled. 'It's all about respect, Ramaz. About knowing your place in the overall scheme of things.' He rubbed red marks left on his wrists by the handcuffs. 'How have you been? Tamuna and Eka keeping well?'

'Do we really have to go through this routine, Otar? You ask for my family by name as if you know them, you imply you could hurt them if you wanted to and I tell you I'd kill you if you did. It all gets a bit repetitive and boring, doesn't it?'

Basilia smiled again. 'Well, I hadn't thought of it that way—but you're probably right. What *shall* we talk about, then?'

'The Kazbegi Avenue bank robbery. The murders of Sophia Brachuli and Vano Chedia.'

'Yes, I thought that's what it would be...'

'So, what can you tell me?'

Basilia leaned back in his chair and placed his hands in his lap. 'You and I don't have a good history, Ramaz. Why would I tell you anything?'

'Because you want to. You wouldn't be in this room with me now if you didn't.'

'Because I want to... That's good, Ramaz. Very *insightful*. You *are* an excellent detective. It makes me wonder why you keep getting passed over for promotion. Doesn't it worry you to have a man like George Rapava as your boss?'

'No, it doesn't and we're playing games again.' He leaned forward and locked eyes with the crime boss. 'Were you responsible for the Kazbegi Avenue bank robbery?'

'Would you believe me if I told you I wasn't?'

'In this room, here and now—yes, I would believe you. Were you responsible?'

Basilia's face hardened. 'No.'

'Did it go ahead with your sanction?'

Basilia shook his head slowly.

'Do you know who *was* responsible?'

The crime boss smiled through sensual lips. 'Not yet,' he said.

'But you're looking?'

Basilia stood and gazed down on Donadze, rolling his massive shoulders. 'What you should be asking yourself, *Ramaz,* is this: what kind of man would kill a young woman that way—her son on the other side of a door. And—with a man like that—if *you* got too close, what do you think he'd do to *you*?'

Donadze stood. 'Help me find them, Otar.'

Basilia let out a long sigh and shouted, 'Petre!'

The guard opened the door. 'Yes?'

Basilia held his hands out to be cuffed. 'Sorry, Ramaz,' he said. 'I don't think I want to do that.'

'Did you find anything, Irina?' Donadze said.

Jaqeli looked up from the documents on her desk. 'Yes, I think so,' she said. She straightened in her chair and rubbed her eyes. 'But I need coffee.'

'I'll get you one. Meet you in Interview Room One.'

'Okay, thanks,' she said, gathering up the documents and transferring them to a folder.

Donadze walked to the kitchen and found Jaqeli's mug and a clean mug for himself. He was adding hot water to the coffee granules when George Rapava appeared.

'Ramaz.'

'Captain,' Donadze said, stirring sugar into the coffee and picking up the mugs to leave.

'Wait a minute…'

Donadze returned the mugs to the work surface and turned to face Rapava.

'What's going on, Ramaz?'

'With what, Captain? The investigation?'

'No, not the investigation. With you. Running off to Shindisi to see Levan Gloveli. The way you spoke to me yesterday. The way you behaved when Colonel Meskhi was here. Do you and I have a problem?'

'*I* don't have a problem, Captain.'

Donadze watched Rapava's face redden. 'So I do, is that what you're implying? You need to be careful, Lieutenant. You've got a reputation, can't get along with anyone in authority. But you need to remember; you report to me—don't think Meskhi would protect you.'

'I'm very sure he wouldn't. But it's not me who needs to be protected, is it, sir?'

'What do you mean by that, Donadze?'

'Will that be all, Captain?'

Rapava stood, fists balled. 'Watch your back, Lieutenant.'

'Sir,' Donadze said, picking up the mugs and brushing past his commanding officer.

Jaqeli was waiting in the interview room, her documents transferred to the table. 'Are you okay, Ramaz?'

'Fine. Captain Rapava wanted a word.'

He handed Jaqeli her coffee and took a sip of his own, his hand shaking from the encounter. 'Did the finance people find anything interesting?' Donadze had raised the possibility that Vano Chedia was involved in the bank robbery and wanted to check if he had received any large or unusual sums of money.

'Finance *person*—a woman called Tina Ninua. She was pretty good I thought, very thorough.' Jaqeli smiled. 'And one of Misha's ex-girlfriends, it appears.'

'Sounds awkward.'

'Not for me. Or for Tina, I think.' She patted a short stack of documents. 'This is what she came up with.' She pushed the stack towards Donadze. 'These all belong to Chedia: bank statements from two accounts he held with First National Bank; credit and charge card statements; credit and debit slips he'd signed and the schedule for his home purchase loan. Nothing untoward there that Tina could see.'

Donadze noticed Jaqeli had held back a document. 'However…' he said.

'However...' Jaqeli pushed the document across the table. It was printed with a logo incorporating a coat of arms and was headed, *United Bank of Belize*. 'This was in a safety deposit box rented by Chedia. Belize is a popular place to hide money, apparently. Its banks aren't quite as discreet as Switzerland's used to be, but they're very private all the same.'

Donadze scrutinised the document. 'A receipt for thirty thousand dollars. Paid into the United Bank of Belize exactly two weeks before the robbery, account holder—'

'Eliso Chedia,' Jaqeli said.

'*Eliso* Chedia…' Donadze stressed.

'This has got to be connected to the robbery, hasn't it?'

'I'd say so. The question is: does Eliso know she has this money secreted away? Or was it deposited in her name, without her knowledge?'

'By Vano?'

'He's the obvious candidate. It's why we looked at him in the first place.' He thought for a minute. 'Okay, we need to speak to Eliso again—but not right away.' He placed his hand over the document. 'Let's keep this to ourselves for the moment—no one else needs to know we have it.'

'Are you sure? Shouldn't we ask her to explain how the money got there?'

'Yes, and we will. But it's enough that *we* know it's there—let's keep this one up our sleeves, for now.'

Donadze's mother and Tamuna were watching television news when he returned home. Tamuna was on the couch giving Eka her bottle, the baby girl dressed in her pyjamas and ready for bed. The news programme was covering the continuing war in Ukraine and both women seemed subdued. His mother dabbed her eyes with the handkerchief she kept up her sleeve before standing to give Donadze a tight hug and—holding his face firmly between her two hands—applying wet kisses to his face and forehead.

Released from her grip, Donadze kissed the top of her head, discreetly wiped his face then bent to kiss Tamuna. 'Can I take her?' he said.

Tamuna sniffed and passed the baby and bottle to him. Eka protested the transfer for a moment then settled into her father's arms to take the rest of her milk while he and Tamuna continued to watch television and his mother laid food on the breakfast bar.

'This war is awful, these poor people have lost everything…' Tamuna said.

'Yes, I know, it's terrible.'

The coverage switched to the studio where a commentator discussed the government's refusal to condemn Russia's aggression. That approach was at odds with the country's president who had publicly stated her solidarity with Ukraine. The government was also out of step with most Georgians, many of whom had been out on the streets to demonstrate their support for the occupied country.

'It brings it all back, doesn't it?'

'Yes, it doesn't seem that long ago.' Donadze had been conscripted into the army for national service, which had coincided with the 2008 war with Russia. It was a dramatically uneven struggle and Georgia had been quickly overrun, the Russian tanks halting their advance fifty kilometres from Tbilisi after pressure from the EU. Although lasting only five days, the war had resulted in over eight hundred deaths with more than thirty thousand Georgians displaced.

'Turn it off, Ramaz,' Tamuna said, getting to her feet to help prepare their meal.

Eka fell asleep drinking her milk and Donadze carried her to her room and laid her in her cot, making sure the baby monitor was on and properly positioned. Although professing to be non-religious, he stood over his daughter and said a silent prayer that there would be no war in Georgia during her lifetime.

Donadze tried and failed to lighten the mood over dinner. The family finished eating and he and Tamuna tidied up in the kitchen while his mother took herself through to her room. Without asking, he took a bottle of

Tsinandali from the fridge and poured them both a large glass of the dry, fruity wine.

Tamuna sat and he pulled her to him. She closed her eyes, took a sip of her wine and smiled for the first time since Donadze had returned home. 'That's good,' she said.

He took a sip from his own glass. 'Yes, it is.'

They sat in silence for a few minutes before Tamuna said, 'What's going to happen if Russia wins in Ukraine? Will it be Georgia's turn next?'

Donadze held the glass by its stem and swirled its contents, observing the wine's bright, greenish colouring. He took a sip while considering how best to answer. 'It could be,' he admitted. 'Our government thinks appeasing the Kremlin makes invasion less likely. But I don't think that factors into Russia's thinking. Putin wants to rebuild the Russian Empire with him as its tsar. He's Peter the Great. Ukraine's been a set-back for him and maybe it will make him rethink his plans. Maybe the people around him will decide enough is enough. We just don't know.'

'She put her glass on the table. 'What would *you* do if Russia invaded?'

'I'd probably be conscripted back into the army.'

'Yes, but would you wait to be conscripted?'

Donadze sensed Tamuna's anxiety as she waited for his answer. 'No, I'd pick up a weapon, do whatever I could to defend our country and our people.'

'That's what I thought,' Tamuna said. She took a sip of her wine. 'Let's pray that never happens.'

SIX

Amelia Nanava had, on this occasion, provided the elevator security code and was waiting by her apartment door as Donadze and Jaqeli approached.

'I'm glad you've come,' she said, offering them a smile.

Jaqeli exchanged a look with Donadze; Amelia's friendly manner was in stark contrast to the hostility she had shown when they had first spoken to Koba Brachuli and his son Zaal on the day of the robbery.

The detectives followed Amelia into her lounge. She had prepared a cafetiere of coffee and placed a plate of imported biscuits beside it. She lifted the cafetiere and looked at Donadze expectantly.

'Please,' he said.

'Koba and Zaal aren't here?' Jaqeli asked.

'No, they'll be back soon. I persuaded Koba to take Zaal for a burger. It's the first time they've been out of this apartment since…'

'We can come back. We're only here to update you on progress.'

'No, please stay. I'm glad you're here. There's something I thought I should mention. It's probably nothing...'

'Okay,' Donadze said. 'Why not tell us what it is and let us decide if it's important or not?'

Amelia finished pouring their coffee and flopped onto a chair. 'I don't know if I should even be mentioning this,' she said. 'It seems a bit disloyal.'

'We won't take notes or record our conversation if that helps.'

She seemed to come to a decision and sat up, pushing a loose strand of hair behind her ear. 'It's about Koba and Zaal. But it's mostly about Koba,' she said.

'Okay.'

She looked between Donadze and Jaqeli. 'You must understand; Sophia and I were different people. We weren't as close as some sisters are—but I loved her all the same and she loved me. We'd always help each other whenever we could. And now, helping Sophia means being here for Zaal. She would have expected that of me and—to be honest—I expect it of myself. I won't leave if he needs me.'

'You're going somewhere?'

'Yes, to London. At least, I'm *supposed* to be going to London.'

'To work?'

'I work in hospitality management, in marketing. My company operates the Biltmore Tbilisi, that's where I'm based now. But I've been asked to take a job in head office. It's a two-year posting, maybe longer. I'd be taking on global responsibilities: one hundred and forty hotels in twenty-four countries. It means so much that I've been selected for the role—and it's a one-off opportunity, I doubt if I'll be asked a second time.'

'Yes, I can see that would be exciting,' Jaqeli said. 'But you feel you can't go now, because of Zaal?'

'Yes, but it's not Zaal I'm worried about—it's Koba.' She shook her head. 'I know what he's been through: he's lost his wife—my sister; his bank was robbed; he watched one of his colleagues being shot in his office. Of course, he's devastated—who wouldn't be? But that doesn't explain what he asked me to do...'

'What *was* that?' Jaqeli said.

'Well, you can see how much he loves Zaal. He's a great father of course, devoted to the boy. And he's not let him out of his sight since that day... That's what makes this all the more strange...'

Jaqeli looked at Donadze and he shook his head slightly—better to let her tell it in her own time.

Amelia let out a long sigh. 'I told Koba I'm going to turn down the job in London, that I'll stay in Tbilisi and help him bring up Zaal for as long as he needs me.'

'I imagine he's very grateful for your offer.'

'You would think so. But he told me, no, I should go to London…' She hesitated a moment. 'He also said I should take Zaal with me.'

'Did Koba say why he wants Zaal to go with you?' Donadze asked.

'He said something about opportunities: he'd go to a good British school; learn to speak English like a native; travel outside Georgia. But I could tell he hadn't really thought any of that through, he was just trying to justify sending his son away…'

'If it wasn't about opportunity, why do *you* think he wants Zaal to go with you?'

'I just don't know,' Amelia said. 'But, sending his son three thousand kilometres to England—he must have a very good reason.'

Donadze was about to tell Amelia that he and Jaqeli couldn't stay any longer when he heard the apartment door opening, followed by Zaal running up the hall shouting his aunt's name. He stopped abruptly when he saw the detectives in the lounge.

'Hey Zaal, how was your burger?' Jaqeli asked.

Amelia stood and opened her arms, inviting the little boy to run to her. She spun him around, making him squeal with laughter.

Koba Brachuli came into the room a moment later. '*Gamarjoba*, Detectives,' he said, offering them a tight smile.

It had been three days since Brachuli had been interviewed and he looked terrible. He had swapped his suit trousers and business shirt for loose tracksuit bottoms and a mismatched hoodie, his trainers grubby from street dust and dried mud. He hadn't shaved and his pallor, and puffy, bloodshot eyes suggested he hadn't slept either.

Amelia put the boy down. 'Come on, Zaal, let's play in your room.'

'How have you been, Koba?' Donadze asked.

Brachuli raised his hands as though inviting inspection. 'I think you can work that out for yourself, Lieutenant.'

'Yes, I understand. And we're sorry for what you're going through.'

Donadze looked away as Brachuli wiped his eyes with the back of his hand.

'This coffee is good,' Jaqeli said. 'Can I pour you a cup, Koba?'

'Yes, please.' Brachuli coughed to mask the catch in his voice. 'What can I do for you?'

'We wanted to see how you are and to give you an update on our investigation, if that's okay?' Donadze said.

Brachuli nodded his thanks to Jaqeli as she passed him his coffee. 'Yes, that's okay, there's nowhere else I need to be,' he said.

'The first thing to say, Koba, is that finding the men responsible for what happened to Sophia and Vano has our highest priority.'

'Something didn't *happen* to them, Lieutenant. They were murdered.'

'Yes. We wanted to discuss that with you. The way they were murdered suggests their killers weren't just street thugs.'

'*Professionals*?'

'Yes, professionals.'

'That term suggests admiration, Lieutenant. Is that how you see them?'

'No, definitely not. But understanding the people we're dealing with will help us find them. These men, these *professional* criminals don't make many mistakes. The robbery of a small bank, a modest sum of money stolen would have had a relatively low profile. But by killing two people in such a heartless manner, the stakes go up dramatically. So, why would professionals do that?'

'Are you asking me that question, Lieutenant?'

'No, of course not. I'm just letting you see where our investigation is taking us.'

Brachuli shrugged. 'Okay,' he said.

'We're looking at several possibilities. You're probably aware of how criminals operate in this city, how they take territory and control it. Kazbegi Avenue is part of the territory run by a gangster called Otar Basilia. He's ruthless and certainly capable of crimes like this, but we don't think he's responsible for your bank or what happened to Sophia and Vano.'

'I've heard of Basilia. If my bank was part of his territory, how can you be sure he wasn't responsible?'

'We won't rule him out, but we're as sure as we can be at this stage that it wasn't him.' Donadze paused. 'You don't have many people working at your branch.'

'No, as I said, it's quite small. A couple of tellers: Vano and Nana Pachulia. I can call advisors in if customers want to discuss home purchases, insurance, that kind of thing. I also have access to temporary staff for holiday cover and sickness. But otherwise, it's just the three of us.'

Donadze wanted to question Brachuli about Vano Chedia but didn't want to tell him about the money deposited in the Belize bank. 'Please don't read anything into this,' he said. 'It's just something we need to ask: did you ever have reason to question Vano or Nana's honesty?'

'What do you mean?'

'Money going missing, possibly. Complaints from customers, audits raising suspicion.'

'No. That never happened.'

'Okay, thanks.' Donadze picked up his cup and put it down again when he saw it was empty. 'Amelia told us she may be moving to London,' he said conversationally.

Brachuli's brow furrowed. 'Yes…'

'She mentioned you suggested taking Zaal with her.'

Brachuli glanced towards the lounge door, leaned towards Donadze and lowered his voice. 'That's none of your business, Lieutenant,' he said. 'And please do not talk about it in front of my son.'

Donadze nodded to Jaqeli and stood. 'No, of course not. Thank you for your time, sir,' he said.

Amelia Nanava showed Donadze and Jaqeli to her apartment door and gave them a brief wave as they stepped into the elevator.

'So why do you think Brachuli wants Zaal to go to London?' Jaqeli asked as the elevator door closed.

'It might just be what he told her; he thinks there are better opportunities for the boy in England.'

'Yes, and there probably are. But we've seen how he is with Zaal. It would break his heart to send him away.'

'Amelia certainly thought it was strange. Strange enough for her to mention it to us. But parents often make sacrifices when they think they're in their children's best interests.'

'It's not something you would ever do though, is it?'

'Send Eka away? No, I could never do that.'

They walked to Donadze's car. His phone rang as he started the engine, the caller unknown. He pressed the car's talk button. 'Donadze.'

'*Gamarjoba*, Lieutenant. My name is Emzar Kesaria,

Executive Assistant to Christoph Maier. I believe you and Mr Maier have met.'

Donadze stopped the car's engine. 'What can I do for you, Mr Kesaria?'

'We heard you already have a lead on our branch robbery,' Kesaria said, his tone suggesting admiration.

'What lead are you referring to?'

'You have more than one?' Kesaria said, his laughter sounding false even over the phone.

'What lead are you referring to, Mr Kesaria?' Donadze repeated.

Kesaria got down to business. 'The money paid into The United Bank of Belize, of course. Thirty thousand dollars in our employee's wife's name.'

'Your murdered employee, Vano Chedia?'

'Yes. Vano Chedia. Our senior teller: he opened the safe for the robbers and then they shot him. I'm sure you agree that this looks suspicious, Lieutenant. But Herr Maier is concerned, he feels—'

'How did you come by that information, Mr Kesaria?'

'Is that relevant, Lieutenant?'

'I think so. Please answer my question.'

'Well, I'm not entirely sure. But all financial inquiries leave a footprint, even police inquiries and I suspect our security people picked up on it. Anyway, Herr Maier asked me to contact you and repeat his request for regular updates as your investigation proceeds.' Kesaria assumed a conciliatory tone. 'He had hoped you would have brought this information to him when you first uncovered it. However, he appreciates he may not have communicated his request clearly—Georgian not being his first language—

and he suggested I should be your main point of contact going forward. He feels you may find that more comfortable.'

'I think Herr Maier was very clear, Emzar, and I'll tell you what I told—'

He paused as Jaqeli put her hand on his arm.

He nodded to her then continued in an even tone. 'As I informed Herr Maier, we routinely provide updates to victims of crime—and that includes your bank. My update to you is that we are currently pursuing several lines of inquiry but have nothing specific to report at this stage.'

'I see. Well, I think Herr Maier will be disappointed with your response, Lieutenant. He may have mentioned that he and your Colonel Meskhi are personal friends?'

'Yes, I think he may have mentioned that,' Donadze said, ending the call.

'Take a minute, Ramaz,' Jaqeli said.

Donadze eased his grip on the steering wheel. 'Thanks,' he said.

'Do you believe that's how Kesaria got the information about the Belize bank; our inquiries left a *footprint*?' Jaqeli asked.

'I don't know, he skated over that question quickly, didn't he? But even if we did leave some kind of trail, someone must have been looking for it.'

'Or maybe Herr Maier has a source of information. Maybe one of our colleagues is keeping him updated.'

'It wouldn't be the first time,' Donadze said.

SEVEN

Donadze and Jaqeli parked a short distance from the Kazbegi Avenue branch. It had reopened the previous day, a bored security guard the only clue that murder had been committed on the premises. *Purely for show*, Donadze thought, judging that the unarmed, middle aged man would have little or no chance of deterring a killer with a gun.

Nana Pachulia recognised Jaqeli and came out from behind her desk to greet them. She offered them a quick smile, glancing at Donadze apprehensively. 'Was there something else you needed, Detective?'

Jaqeli had taken her witness statement and this was the first time Donadze had seen Nana close up. He knew she was twenty two but her short, slim, pixie-like stature suggested sixteen. Acne spotted her pretty, fine-boned face, reinforcing her appearance of youth. Her tawny brown hair was cut short and fringed across her forehead like a curtain on the world. Her slacks and fitted blouse were functional, her only jewellery a thin, silver chain, its cross hanging close to her heart in the true Orthodox manner.

'How have you been, Nana?' Jaqeli asked.

'Me? I'm okay, I suppose...'

'Nana, this is Ramaz. We have something to discuss with you.'

'Now?'

'Yes, it's important.'

She glanced towards the manager's office where a man was standing by the door watching them.

'Who's that?' Donadze asked.

'Mr Berishvili. He's been sent from head office to cover until Koba comes back. I'll have to ask his permission, he's quite strict...'

'Let me speak to him,' Donadze said.

He crossed to the office and showed Berishvili his ID.

'Lieutenant Donadze,' Berishvili said, offering his hand. 'I know who you are.'

'Have we met?' Donadze asked.

'No, but I was told you're investigating the robbery and Vano's murder.'

'Who told you that?'

'You would expect me to have been briefed before coming here, wouldn't you?'

'Yes, I would. Who gave you the briefing?'

Berishvili hesitated, seemingly considering whether to answer or not. 'Well, if you think that's important, I met with a colleague called Emzar—'

'Kesaria. I spoke to him earlier. What did he tell you?'

Berishvili raised a placatory smile. 'Amongst other things, he told me you are a difficult man to deal with. I think he used the term, *one dimensional...*'

'I've been called worse. What else did he tell you?'

Berishvili had had enough. 'Let me tell *you* something, Lieutenant. Any conversations I have with my colleagues are private. If you wish to pursue this line of questioning you may do so with the Bank's lawyer present.'

'Thanks, I'll bear that in mind. I hope you'll bear in mind that one of your colleagues is dead and another has lost his wife. I presume you want us to find their killers?'

'Yes, of course I do. We all want that and I *can* tell you Mr Kesaria made that very point. He wants us all to cooperate with the police as much as possible.'

'Good. We have some follow up questions for Miss Pachulia—I hope you don't have a problem with that?'

'When you say you have some questions, does that mean—'

'It means we have questions for her, nothing more.'

'Well, it's certainly not a problem. I can cover Nana's desk if necessary.'

'Thank you, we shouldn't be too long.'

Berishvili went into his office and Donadze returned to Jaqeli and Nana. 'He's happy for you to come with us,' he said. 'Let's talk in the car.'

Donadze helped Nana into the front passenger seat and Jaqeli took a seat in the back.

'Thanks for speaking with us again, Nana,' Jaqeli said.

'No, that's okay, whatever I can do…'

'That's what we want to talk to you about. We're going to tell you something. You can't discuss it with anyone, not even your family. And then we're going to ask you to do something for us. You can say no—but you might help us identify the men who killed Vano and Sophia.'

'Okay. What did you want to tell me?' she asked, her voice tight.

Jaqeli nodded reassuringly. 'There are things about this robbery we don't understand. The type of criminals who committed these crimes don't usually make mistakes. We don't understand why men like that would rob a small bank to steal what would be—for them—a small sum of money. And we also don't understand why they killed Sophia and Vano.'

'No,' Nana said in a small voice. 'It seemed so pointless.'

'Yes, it *seemed* pointless. But maybe it wasn't. This is the information you can't repeat.' Jaqeli waited until Nana had nodded her agreement. 'We think that Vano may have been killed for a reason. We think it's possible he was involved in the—'

'No,' Nana said, shaking her head. 'That can't be true.'

'We only *think* it's possible, Nana. We may be wrong.'

'But you shouldn't be making these accusations if you're not sure,' she said, her voice rising.

Jaqeli raised her hands in a calming gesture. 'It's the nature of police work, Nana; we have to investigate all possibilities. And we're not accusing Vano of anything yet, we just have to consider this is something he *may* have been involved in.'

'What about me? Do you think I was involved? Did you consider that *possibility*?'

'We consider all possibilities. And no, we don't think you were involved.'

'Then you must have a reason to think Vano *was*?'

'Yes, we do, but it's better we don't share that with you for now.'

There was a long moment of silence. 'What is it you want me to do?' she said at last.

Jaqeli nodded to Donadze to continue. 'As Irina said, there are things about this robbery that don't seem to make sense. So we'll have to dig a little deeper to see if something else is going on at your bank. We can't do that without leaving a trail, a *footprint* they call it—and we don't want to do that. So we need someone on the inside, someone who has access to account information, customer records, transaction reports…'

'You want me to spy on my bank?'

'Not to spy as such, more—'

'Yes, it's a form of spying,' Jaqeli interrupted. 'We know what we're asking.'

'But I'd be sacked if my managers found out. I need this job, I'm the only one in my family working…'

'We understand it could be difficult for you if your managers *did* find out—but no one needs to know that you're helping us.'

'Well, I'm not so sure of that. But what if Vano was involved? Is that what got him killed? Would that man come back for me?'

'There's no reason to think so—but we'd keep you safe, you'd be protected,' Donadze said.

'Why would I need protecting if you don't think he'd come back for me…'

Donadze had recognised the flaw in his logic before Nana pointed it out. 'Will you help us?' he asked, guessing her answer.

She paused a moment. 'No,' she said, reaching for the door handle. 'Find someone else.'

'I'm sorry, Ramaz. I shouldn't have contradicted you,' Jaqeli said.

'It's okay. Nana knew exactly what we were asking her to do and the risks she'd be taking. It would have been better if I'd been more straight with her; she might have believed me when I said the shooter wouldn't return.'

'You should have seen your face when she said, *no*.'

'You'd think I'd be used to that by now.' He glanced at his clock. 'What are you doing this evening?'

'Misha and I are going out for dinner—somewhere he's booked. What about you?'

'You remember Tamuna's friend, Lela? We're doing something with her and her boyfriend.'

'A meal?'

'Probably…'

'Probably? You're hopeless, Ramaz.'

'You've been talking to my wife?' He started the engine. 'I'll drop you off.'

'No, it's too much of a diversion, I'll get a taxi,' she said, opening the door. 'See you tomorrow.'

The traffic was heavy and it took him twice as long to drive the short distance to his apartment as it would have taken to walk. He took the elevator to the fourth level and opened his apartment door.

His mother was sitting on the couch watching Eka crawling across the living room floor. 'It won't be long till she's walking,' she said.

'How are you, *Deda*?' he asked.

'Perfect, *Ramazi*,' she said, looking up to receive his kiss. 'Tamuna's getting ready.'

Eka had stopped crawling and was sitting on her bottom watching her father. Donadze lay beside her on the floor and the little girl climbed onto his chest. He gave her a gentle cuddle, her body feather-light, her warmth and smell a joy. When she squirmed to be released, he kissed the top of her head and hoisted her—squealing—on outstretched arms, her little legs and arms flapping, a worried look on her gorgeous face. He lowered her for a comforting hug then stood and handed her to his mother. 'I'll see how Tamuna's getting on,' he said.

Donadze went to their room, sat on the bed and waited until Tamuna came out of the shower, a towel wrapped around her body, another wrapped around her hair. She crossed the room, leaving damp footprints on the carpet. He closed his eyes to absorb the scent of soap and warm skin as she leaned forward to kiss him.

'Are you okay?' she asked.

'Never better.'

He remained sitting on the bed as she plugged in her dryer and positioned herself in front of her mirror cabinet. She removed the towel from her head and shook her long, dark hair loose. 'Shouldn't you be getting ready?' she said to his reflection.

'Probably,' he said, making no effort to move.

'Ah, I've got an audience…'

'An appreciative audience.'

'You're a strange man, Lieutenant Donadze…'

'I know, it's been said before.'

She turned on the dryer and, glancing occasionally at his reflection, used her fingers and brush to style her hair, leaving it straight and glossy. She finished, turned off the dryer and stood to face him, the towel still wrapped around her.

'Do we have to go out?' he asked.

'Yes, we do.' She dropped the towel. 'But not right away.'

The restaurant was attached to a hotel in Kostava Street. Donadze hadn't eaten there before but knew it had a reputation for high quality, expensive, international food. Most of the customers in the reception area were speaking English, German and other foreign languages—tourists and business people enjoying favourable exchange rates against the *lari*, he thought.

Lela's boyfriend had reserved their table and Tamuna gave Niko Shaveis' name to the waiter. He and Lela were already there and they stood as Donadze and Tamuna approached, Lela hugging and kissing them both.

Shaveis' handshake was uncomfortably firm as the two men were introduced. Donadze guessed he was in his late thirties. He was tall and good looking with fashionably styled hair, tight stubble and shaped eyebrows, his close fitting jeans and tailored white shirt a shop window for the physique he'd developed lifting heavy weights in the gym, Donadze presumed.

'Good to meet you, Ramaz,' Shaveis said with a wide, white smile.

A waiter arrived with a bottle of French champagne and four glasses. 'This is on me,' Shaveis said. The waiter uncorked the bottle and poured a small amount of the wine for him to taste. He took a sip and nodded for the waiter to fill their glasses. 'Lela and I are celebrating,' he added. He reached to cover her hand with his own. 'Aren't we, babe?'

'Yes, six months together,' Lela said. 'Or rather, six months next week,' she added, pulling her hand free.

'Always a stickler for detail, aren't you, Lela,' Shaveis said, his brief frown transforming into an affectionate smile.

The waiter finished pouring the champagne and transferred the bottle to its ice bucket.

Tamuna picked up her glass. 'Well, we should have a toast,' she said. 'To Lela and Niko—happy anniversary!'

'Happy anniversary,' Donadze repeated. He took a reluctant sip from his glass—he didn't like champagne: neither French nor its Georgian equivalent. 'Where did you two meet?' he asked, trying to sound interested.

'At a party for one of Niko's friends. I think you were invited, weren't you, Tamuna?' Lela said.

'I really don't remember; the first six months after Eka was born passed in a blur. I barely had the energy to look after her, let alone go to parties.'

'Well, I'm sure you don't regret a minute,' Shaveis said. 'Children are wonderful; Lela will make a fantastic mother one day.'

Donadze observed Lela's tight smile as Shaveis leaned across to pat her arm. 'From what I know of Lela, she'd be fantastic at anything she does,' he said.

'She certainly has her moments,' Shaveis said, winking at Tamuna. 'What about you, Ramaz? Lela said you're a policeman.'

'I said Ramaz is a detective, Niko. A lieutenant detective.'

'Okay, but that's still a policeman, right Ramaz?'

'Yes, absolutely right, Niko. What about you?'

'Cars—buy them and sell them. Come and see me when you're ready, I'll give you a good deal.'

'Ramaz likes to run his cars into the ground,' Tamuna said. 'He only got rid of his last car when I gave him a new one as a wedding present.'

'German?'

'Japanese, I think.'

Shaveis grimaced. 'Well, I'm sure it's very reliable.'

The waiter arrived with menus and Donadze skimmed the list to find something he might enjoy. He hoped they could eat quickly and leave. Shaveis had other ideas and took his time perusing the menu, pointing out the dishes he thought Lela would enjoy. He insisted on paying for their wine and chose an Italian white and a Spanish red.

'Do you like *Rioja*, Ramaz?'

'Never heard of it,' Donadze lied.

The food and wine were good but the evening excruciating. 'Would you like a *cognac* with your coffee?' Shaveis asked.

'No, thanks. It's been a lovely evening but we'd better go home and rescue Ramaz's mother,' Tamuna said.

Donadze stood and helped Tamuna out of her chair.

'Okay, we'll stay for a nightcap. Don't worry about the bill, Ramaz, I'll get it.'

'That's okay, Niko,' Donadze said. 'It's paid.'

'Really? Well, that's very generous of you. I'll pay next time.' He stood, kissed Tamuna and held out his hand to Donadze.

Donadze stepped in close and gripped Shaveis' hand

hard, watching him wince. 'Enjoy your brandy.'

Tamuna exchanged a long, tight hug with Lela. 'I'll see you on Monday,' she said, looking at her friend worriedly before picking up her bag and taking Donadze's hand to leave the restaurant.

She waited until the door had closed behind them. 'What a horrible man,' she said. 'I don't know what Lela sees in him.'

'Is he hitting her?'

'What?'

'Is he hitting her?'

'No. Why would you think that? Anyway, Lela's not that type. She's much too strong.'

'There *is* no type and she's not strong with *him*. He's got some kind of hold on her. I've seen it before, too many times. Emotional or physical abuse, maybe both. If he's not hitting her now, he might start soon.'

'Do you really think so?'

'Yes. You can see it for yourself, how she was with him.'

'She's not been herself, I know that.'

'She needs to leave him.'

'Ramaz, you can't be involved in this.'

'What do you mean?'

'You know what I mean. Lela needs to work this out for herself. Stay away from that man.'

EIGHT

'Ramaz, wake up. There's someone at the door,' Tamuna whispered.

Donadze came out of sleep reluctantly. He blinked his eyes awake and checked his watch—four fifteen.

There was another quiet knock on the apartment's steel door. He swung his legs out of bed. 'Wait there,' he said.

He crossed the room to retrieve his pistol and stepped through the dark apartment to peer into the door's spy hole.

Jaqeli must have seen movement across the lens. 'It's me,' she said, her voice low.

He drew back the door bolts, turned the keys in their locks and pulled the door open, glancing past Jaqeli to check she was on her own.

'What's happened?' he asked.

'We've been trying to call you. Where's your phone?'

'My phone?' He returned to the bedroom. It wasn't in its usual place on the bedside cabinet.

Tamuna was sitting on the edge of the bed. 'Who is it?'

'It's Irina. She's been trying to call me but I've left my phone somewhere. Try to go back to sleep.'

She shook her head. 'Easier said than done.'

Jaqeli had moved to the living room and was standing by the breakfast bar. 'Is this what you're looking for?' she asked, holding his phone like a courtroom exhibit.

'Yes.' He took it from her and switched it off silent mode. 'You said *we've* been trying to call?'

'Captain Rapava and me. He called me when he couldn't get you.'

'What's happened?' he asked again.

'It's Otar Basilia—he's been found dead in his cell.'

Donadze paused. 'And not from natural causes, I presume?'

'No, from multiple stab wounds.'

'Well, he had plenty of enemies.'

'Yes, but it was only two days ago that you spoke to him—that seems too coincidental to me.'

'And to me. Have they moved the body yet?'

'Captain Rapava told them to leave it in case we want to take a look.'

'Do we?'

'I do.'

'Me too.' He realised he was only wearing shorts and a T-shirt. 'Give me a few minutes,' he said. 'Help yourself to coffee if you want one.'

Donadze returned to the bedroom. Tamuna was out of bed and getting dressed. 'You're not getting up, are you?' he said.

'What makes you think that, *Detective*?'

'It's going to be a long day if you get up now.'

'A long day for you as well. I was half-awake anyway. I couldn't stop thinking about Lela.'

'About me saying she's being abused?'

'Yes, and thinking why I hadn't spotted it myself. I've seen her and Niko together a few times; it should have been obvious.'

'It's not obvious unless you've come across that kind of thing before. There's a strange psychology going on; part of Lela knows what Shaveis is doing to her but part of her probably still loves him and can't accept the truth. She may be embarrassed she's let herself get into that position with him and that's why she doesn't want to confide in you.'

'You said he might be hitting her?'

'It's possible, now or sometime soon. Things progress: people like him—abusers—start by undermining their victim's confidence and self-esteem. They isolate them and keep them from their family and friends. You said yourself that Lela was more distant than usual. But they keep their victims off-balance by telling them they love them and want to protect them. They're looking for control and violence is often a way of achieving that.'

'I can't let that happen to Lela.'

'I could talk to Shaveis.'

'No, we both know what that means. It's not what she needs.'

'What *are* you going to do then?'

'I don't know.'

'She needs to leave him, Tamuna.'

'Yes, I realise that.'

He went to the shower room, brushed his teeth, splashed water on his face and head then returned to the bedroom and pulled on clean clothes.

Tamuna and Jaqeli were in the living room, talking together when he returned. 'Ready?' he asked.

Jaqeli took a last sip from her coffee cup. 'I'm always ready,' she said, putting the cup down and standing.

'Is everything all right, *Ramazi?*'

Donadze's mother was out of bed, her dressing gown cinched at her waist, her slippers slapping the wooden floor as she walked.

'Everything's fine, *Deda*. Something's come up and Irina and I have to go to work. I'm sorry I woke you. Why don't you go back to bed and try to sleep?'

His mother smiled. 'Maybe later, I'm awake now.'

Donadze looked at his watch—four thirty five. 'Well, we'd better go, Irina' A thought occurred to him. 'How did you get here?' he asked. 'Taxi?'

'I was going to take a taxi but Misha insisted on dropping me off.'

Donadze closed his eyes and let out a long sigh. 'Someone else losing sleep because of me,' he said, crossing to the door just as Eka started crying.

Gldani Prison No. 8 was stirring as Donadze and Jaqeli presented their IDs at Reception. They were kept waiting for about fifteen minutes before a prison officer arrived, the same officer who had escorted Basilia to his meeting with Donadze two days previously.

'Mr Basilia will see you in his cell,' he said with a bow and a conspiratorial grin.

Donadze declined to join in the fun. 'Hilarious,' he

said. 'Although you weren't cracking jokes about Basilia the last time I was here.'

The officer's face contorted as he struggled for a retort. 'Follow me,' he said sourly, turning to lead the way.

Basilia's cell was in a block within the general population, the designation given to most of the prison's inmates. Prisoners in this population were free to mingle or visit their neighbours—always subject to regular head counts and a return to their own cells overnight. But the murder had caused the block to be locked down, its steel doors bolted shut, its inhabitants furious at the loss of their limited freedom and excited by the real or imagined scent of Basilia's blood.

'Has anyone else been in here?' Donadze asked the officer.

'Just the guards who found him.'

'Forensics?'

The officer shrugged. 'How would I know?' He unlocked the cell's door and pulled it open. 'Make it quick,' he said. 'I want that scumbag out of here soon.'

It had been a messy killing: the bed's mattress and sheets were soaked in blood; the duvet kicked off in the struggle and lying bunched, red and wretched on the carpeted floor. A small wooden table had been knocked over and broken, the mobile phone, reading lamp, paperbacks and chocolate bar that had sat upon it now lying in the sticky gore. Basilia had put up a struggle but his life had ended on a prison mattress, gagging against a greasy kitchen towel, his cotton vest pulled back over his massive shoulders to reveal a patchwork of stab wounds and slashes across his broad, hairy back.

Jaqeli pointed at the footprints in the blood. 'That looks like the work of two men.'

'Not surprising, Basilia was strong. It would have taken at least two to get him onto the bed and hold him there.'

'Basilia told you the robbery had nothing to do with him?'

'That's what he said and I believed him. I still do.'

'He also implied he was looking for whoever *was* responsible. Do you think he found them and that's what got him killed?'

'It's possible.'

'Whoever did it must have already been in the prison. Staff or inmates.'

'Yes, they must have been.' He looked at Basilia's cut and bloody body. 'This is different from the bank murders—they were clean kills with silenced weapons. There's been a fight here and Basilia would have got some blows in. There's a good chance Forensics will recover DNA and—if inmates were responsible—we'll have them on our database.'

'But they must have known we could do that.'

'They probably didn't care.'

'Lifers?'

'I think so. But instructed by someone with enough clout to issue that kind of order. We'll speak to the prison director before we leave; make sure there's a search of the cells and common areas. He might be able to find the murder weapon or the clothes the killers were wearing. They'll be soaked with Basilia's blood.'

Donadze noticed a bottle lying behind the cell door. It was half-full of a golden liquid and he rolled it with his foot to reveal its label.

'Remember this?' he asked.

'Should I?'

'Basilia's favourite Scotch. He offered it to us when we visited him during the people trafficking investigation.'

'The investigation that sent him here. Yes, I remember it now.'

'"Eighteen year-old Macallan. Water, no ice, the way it should be drunk,"' Donadze said, imitating the gangster. He shrugged. 'Maybe Scotland will miss him.'

'Maybe.' Jaqeli took a last look at the murdered man. '*Gaumarjos*, Otar,' she said in mock salute.

Donadze unlocked his car and took his place behind the wheel, the stench and despair of Basilia's cell and Gldani Prison still tight in his nostrils. He tried and failed to stifle a yawn. He'd been up since four and it was now only eight but he was already tired and facing another long day ahead.

'I don't know about you,' Jaqeli said. 'But I'm hungry.'

'Eating's for wimps,' Donadze said, paraphrasing a line from one of his favourite movies.

'Maybe, but this wimp needs food.'

'Where do you want to go?'

'Our apartment, I've got plenty in. You can chat with Misha while I get something ready.'

'Okay, that sounds good.' He started the car's engine. 'When you say *our* apartment...'

'Yes, *Sherlock Holmes*. I'm giving up my own place and moving in with Misha. There's no point in paying two rents.'

'Absolutely. Well, congratulations.'

'*Congratulations*? We're sharing an apartment, Ramaz, nothing more.'

'I know, but that's a milestone, isn't it?'

'I don't know, it might be…'

'You'd like it to be?'

'Okay, that's enough of that conversation. It's me who's the psychologist, remember?'

'How could I forget?' he said, negotiating the prison junction and accelerating onto the road back to the city centre.

Arziani was on his leather chair, his phone on the armrest as Jaqeli and Donadze walked into the lounge. He winked at them by way of greeting and held up two fingers to indicate how much longer he would be on his call.

The lounge looked and felt different from when Donadze had last visited a few months ago. Back then, it had seemed minimalistic, masculine and starkly different from his own apartment where baby paraphernalia was strewn everywhere. Arziani's exercise bike and weights were still set up in a corner but the room had been softened with wall hangings, a rug, framed photographs and a tall, ceramic vase containing a display of dried pampas grass.

'Looks great,' he said to Jaqeli.

'Thanks. It's a beautiful morning, let's eat on the balcony.'

Donadze glanced at his watch as Jaqeli retreated to the kitchen, already resenting the time away from their investigation. The air was a little fresher and cleaner on the fifteenth level and he leaned over the balcony rails, oxygenating his blood and admiring unobstructed views across the city.

Arziani ended his call and came to the balcony to shake hands. 'Sorry,' he said. 'There were a couple of break-ins in Vake last night. Including the Justice Minister's apartment—he's not too pleased.'

'I'm sure he's not. Do you need to handle it?'

'I already did. Take a seat,' Arziani said, gesturing towards a table and chairs.

Jaqeli came through with a cafetiere of coffee, mugs and sugar and placed them on the table, smiling at Arziani as he helped take them from the tray.

Donadze waited until she had returned through the balcony door. 'Irina told me she's moving in.'

'Yes, but we're not telling many people about it for now.'

'Makes sense. It's a commitment for you both though, isn't it?'

'Maybe, we'll see.'

'Is that what you want?'

'Yes, I think so—we haven't really discussed it. Anyway, enough of that. How did your visit to the prison go? You wouldn't have expected poor Otar to leave us so soon.'

'No, and it's a pity he has.'

'Really? I wouldn't have thought he'd be your favourite person.'

'He wasn't, but he might have known who was behind the murders. We won't get that out of him now.'

Arziani frowned. 'Am I missing something, Ramaz?'

'What?'

'Basilia has been in prison for, what, four or five months? He's had no direct contact with the outside world.

If he had information on Kazbegi Avenue then someone gave it to him. All you have to do is find that person and ask him what he knows.'

Donadze pushed the plunger on the cafetiere. 'That's pretty smart, Misha,' he said.

Arziani grinned. 'Not really, you would have got there soon enough.'

Jaqeli returned with a large, circular tray containing fruit juice and plates of cold meat, cheese and bread. 'I hope you're hungry,' she said.

'Always,' Arziani said, returning her smile.

Donadze felt his phone buzz in his pocket. 'Thanks, Irina,' he said, reading the message. 'We'll have to be quick. It's Colonel Meskhi.' He held up his phone to let her read the screen.

She passed a plate to Donadze. 'Okay, ten minutes, then,' she said.

NINE

Colonel Meskhi was dressed—as always—in a dark suit, shirt and tie, no concession being made to weekend working. He looked up from the document on his desk. 'Lieutenant, Detective. Sit down,' he said. 'I was about to have coffee—join me.'

'Thank you, sir,' Donadze said.

'Thank you, Colonel. May I pour?' Jaqeli suggested.

'No, Detective. I'm quite capable.'

Meskhi poured from the flask with care, giving it a gentle shake to dislodge the last drips from its spout. Jaqeli declined sugar and passed the bowl to Donadze. He splashed six cubes into his mug while Meskhi frowned his disapproval.

'What are the latest developments in your investigation, Lieutenant?' Meskhi asked, closing his eyes.

Donadze paused to gather his thoughts. 'We're looking at Vano Chedia, sir. We found an offshore account in his wife's name with thirty thousand dollars in it. We haven't asked her about it yet and she may not even know it exists. But we think Chedia may have had some involvement in the robbery and the thirty thousand dollars was his payment. If that's the case, then he was probably killed because he was seen as a weak link, a loose end to tidy up.'

'Do you intend speaking to Mrs Chedia about the account?'

'Yes, Colonel. Quite soon. We found the details in a safety deposit box rented by Chedia. We'd hoped to keep the discovery to ourselves but it seems our investigation created some kind of trail which Christoph Maier became aware of.'

Meskhi opened his eyes. 'I'd already heard about the money and the offshore account.'

'May I ask how, Colonel?'

'Let's come back to that. Do you have a theory on why Sophia Brachuli was killed?'

'Nothing firm, sir. It's possible her killers didn't see her murder as particularly incremental. Kill Chedia and you may as well kill Sophia too. After all, she may have seen something which we could have found useful—so why take that risk?'

Meskhi looked unconvinced. '*May* have seen something which *could* have been useful? I think you can do better than that, Lieutenant.' He paused. 'What else do you have?'

Donadze took a moment to refocus. 'You heard Otar Basilia was murdered in his cell last night?'

'Of course.'

'I spoke to him only two days previously.'

'Coincidence?'

'I doubt it. The bank was on his territory, robbing it was a challenge to his authority. He was looking for the people responsible.'

'And his curiosity got him killed?'

'We think that's possible.'

'Very well.' Meskhi took a sip from his mug and nodded his approval. He put the mug down. 'I spoke to an old friend yesterday,' he said. 'Christoph Maier. That's how I learned about the thirty thousand dollars. But that's not why Mr Maier contacted me. He's unhappy with you, Lieutenant.'

Donadze sat straighter in his chair. 'I'm sorry to hear that, Colonel.'

'Yes, he only wanted to offer his support but you rudely ignored him. He instructed his executive assistant, a certain…'

'Emzar Kesaria.'

'Yes, Emzar Kesaria. He instructed Kesaria to act as his intermediary—but you aggressively declined that offer as well.'

'I don't think I was rude or aggressive, Colonel. Just not prepared to divulge confidential information to civilians.'

'You recall us discussing the oddities of this case, Lieutenant?'

'Yes, sir.'

'And given these oddities, don't you think it advisable to have a friend *inside* the Bank?'

'Do you mean *your* friend, Colonel?'

'Watch your tone, Donadze,' Meskhi said evenly. He paused a moment, waiting for Donadze to nod his contrition. 'I *am* referring to Mr Maier. I've told him we will accept his generous offer.'

'You want me to divulge confidential material to the Bank?'

'No.' Meskhi paused. 'For your information, Lieutenant; I have never truly liked Christoph Maier and I certainly don't trust him. He, however, does not have to know that. Work with Kesaria and see what you can learn from him. Don't tell *him* anything of significance. I've already informed Maier that you are a difficult man to deal with and he'll expect you to exhibit a certain attitude. Do you understand?'

'I think so, sir.'

'Good. And for the purposes of this exercise, consider yourself formally reprimanded. Now, if you've finished your coffee, you may get back to work.'

'Sir,' Donadze and Jaqeli replied in tandem, standing to leave.

Jaqeli waited until they were walking back to the elevator. 'Did you follow all of that?'

'Just about.'

His phoned buzzed the arrival of a text from Tamuna, *Lela staying for few days call me T xxx*

'Everything okay?' Jaqeli asked.

'I don't think so. Let's get back to the car.'

Music was playing softly as Donadze opened his apartment door and walked into the living room. Tamuna and Lela were on the couch, his mother on the armchair facing them.

Lela was feeding Eka from a bottle and she looked up and gave him a tentative smile. 'I'm sorry about this, Ramaz,' she said.

Donadze shook his head. 'There's nothing to be sorry about.'

'You knew, didn't you? I could tell by the way you spoke to Niko at the restaurant.'

'It's my job to notice things. Are you okay, did he hurt you?'

Lela glanced at Donadze's mother, embarrassed to be talking in front of her, he thought.

'Give me the baby, Lela. She can have the bottle in her room,' his mother said.

Lela smiled gratefully, kissed Eka on her forehead then stood and passed the baby to the older woman. '*Madloba.*'

'You don't have to talk about it if you'd rather not,' Donadze said.

'No, it's okay. I want to.' She paused. 'Yes, he hurt me. It was at the restaurant.' She unbuttoned the cuff of her shirt and pulled up the sleeve to reveal a large, purple bruise. 'It doesn't look that much, does it?' She pulled the sleeve down and buttoned the cuff.

'It does to me. Was that the first time?'

'Yes, but I knew it was something he'd wanted to do for a while. Something in the way he looked at me. But he'd held back—until then.'

'And this was at the table?'

Lela nodded. 'It was after you and Tamuna had left. He said there was something about Tamuna he didn't like and no car dealer wants policemen poking around. He told me I wasn't to see either of you again,' she said, her voice catching.

Donadze watched as tears welled in her eyes. She pulled a tissue from its box as Tamuna slid across the couch to give her a comforting hug. 'We *really* don't have to talk about this now, Lela,' she said.

'No, it's good to be able to speak about it, at last.'

'What led to him hitting you?' Donadze asked.

'He didn't hit me as such, not then anyway. I told him *no*, Tamuna's my best friend and he couldn't stop me seeing her. And that's when he took my arm and squeezed it—hard. You've seen him, he goes to the gym a lot—he's strong.' She paused again. 'The funny thing is—while he was leaning across the table squeezing my arm, hurting me—there were other people in the restaurant: customers and waiters. He was looking at me and smiling, almost daring me to cry out. And I didn't—like it would have been shameful for *me* to let other people see what *he* was doing.'

'You said he didn't hit you *then*?'

'No, it was later, when we went back to his apartment. "Come here," he said. He was smiling and I thought he wanted to make up, to explain. But no. I went to him and he punched me—in the stomach. Just once, but very hard. I fell over, couldn't breathe. I thought I was going to be sick.' She placed her hands subconsciously across her abdomen. 'He left me then, went through to the lounge. But he came back a few minutes later, helped me up, held me, told me—'

'Told you he was sorry? Promised it wouldn't happen again? Maybe that he was under a lot of pressure at work? Business in trouble, perhaps? Implied you had provoked him somehow, but that didn't excuse what he'd done? Told you he loved you? Maybe suggested you get married, have children, that—'

'Ramaz!' Tamuna snapped.

No one spoke for a long moment. 'How did you know?' Lela said, eventually.

'I told you, it's my job...'

'I'm tired, I should go to bed...'

'You understand none of this is your fault, don't you, Lela?'

She stared at Donadze but didn't answer.

'Ramaz is right, Lela,' Tamuna said. 'You're not responsible for Niko's behaviour. You did the right thing coming away with me.'

'Tell me you know it's not your fault,' Donadze said.

She raised her head. 'I *do* know it's not my fault...'

'Good. You're safe here. He's not going to hurt you again—I promise you that.'

Misha Arziani was calling. 'Hey, Ramaz. Are you home?'

Donadze reached for his coffee. He was sitting on his balcony and it had cooled in the evening air. 'Yes, what's happening?'

'I'm with Soso—we're at Gldani Prison, just about to go in. The prison director thinks he's found the men who killed Basilia. We're going to take them to the station. See what they can tell us.'

'Do we know them?'

'Phillip Lataria and Zviad Tatishvili,' Chichua said, his voice faint over the phone. 'Probably before your time. Both are more than ten years into thirty year sentences. Lataria went down for abduction, rape and murder—a young girl going home after a party.'

'He's being modest, Ramaz,' Arziani said. 'It was Soso who took him down.'

'I was on the team but, yes, I had the pleasure of making the arrest.'

'Well, I'm sure he'll be pleased to see you again, Soso. How about Tatishvili?'

'Another killer—he doesn't like gay men. Murdered two that we know of but probably more.'

'How did the director find them.'

'They'd obviously been in a fight—against each other they said. But their wing was searched and clothing found—covered in blood of course. We won't have a problem with evidence.'

'No. But we need them to tell us who ordered the hit.'

'Do you want to sit in on the interviews?'

'Yes, if that's okay.'

'First thing tomorrow morning, then.'

'Okay, thanks.'

Donadze ended the call and checked the time on his phone—nine ten. Tamuna and Lela were tired and had already gone to bed and his mother rarely stayed up after nine. He decided to wait another thirty minutes and slid the balcony door open then crossed to the kitchen to refresh his coffee.

It took only fifteen minutes before he heard a car crunching across the surface parking area. He stood and looked over the balcony rails; a large SUV pulled to a stop and its engine shut down. The car's courtesy lights came on and a man got out and walked to the entrance. Donadze crossed the apartment and eased the bolts on the front door, stepping through and pulling the door closed behind him.

A few seconds passed before he heard footsteps on the stairs.

The footsteps grew louder as the man climbed to the fourth level. He flinched when he saw Donadze standing by his apartment door.

'Hello, Niko. What are you doing here?' Donadze said.

'I want to speak to Lela, get her out here,' Shaveis growled, closing in on Donadze, his breath and body alcohol-sour, his eyes red and puffy.

Donadze raised his hands to stop him getting closer. 'That's not going to happen, Niko.'

Shaveis pressed against his outstretched hands; taller, bigger, stronger. 'You're such a runt, Donadze. You wouldn't have the guts to stand there without your badge and gun.'

'I don't have my badge or gun now, Niko,' Donadze said, his voice low and even. 'You need to leave.'

'Lela!' Shaveis shouted at the closed door. 'Come home. We'll talk about this. You don't need these people. Lela!'

Lights came on in the apartment and the door opened. 'This isn't doing any good, Niko,' Tamuna said. 'Lela isn't going anywhere with you. Please go home.'

'You bitch! Don't you think I know it was you who talked her into leaving me? What's wrong with you—are you jealous? Was it because you had to settle for *him*?' he hissed, jabbing Donadze with his finger.

'Last warning, Niko,' Donadze said, pressing Shaveis back by his shoulders.

The swinging punch was telegraphed and slow and Donadze released the pressure on Shaveis' shoulders, allowing the bigger man's momentum to carry him forward, then brought his elbow up sharply to connect with his chin.

Shaveis staggered, stunned but conscious and Donadze closed in, cupping the back of his head with both hands, jerking it down ready to finish the fight with a knee to his face.

'Ramaz!' he heard Lela shout. The red mist lifted and he let Shaveis go, watching as he fell to his knees, swaying, his eyes closed, his mouth open.

Lela crossed to Shaveis and knelt beside him. She put her arms around his wide shoulders. 'It's over, Niko,' she said. 'Go home, don't look for me again.'

TEN

Sleep hadn't come easily to Donadze and the face that stared back at him from the shower room mirror was pale, puffy and drawn. He pushed the plug into the sink and turned on the hot water tap, leaning against the porcelain for support as steam rose and the glass misted. He shut off the tap, tested the temperature of the water and splashed it over his face and head, massaging his skin and scalp, trying to pump oxygen to his brain and flush away his fatigue.

The atmosphere in the apartment was subdued and cool after his fight with Niko Shaveis. Donadze had helped him to his feet and into the elevator and watched from the balcony as he'd eased himself into his car and driven off. Lela had thanked him but was upset to see the man she'd loved—and who she thought had loved her—on his knees and broken. Only his mother had been supportive, patting his arm and whispering, 'You did the right thing, *Ramazi*.'

Tamuna had accused him of setting a trap. He'd explained there had been no trap, only that he'd anticipated

Shaveis' next move. He knew a confrontation had been inevitable and was convinced it'd been right for him to be there to protect Lela and, by association, his own family. He didn't regret his actions; he'd seen and experienced too much violence in his life but held to his conviction that—whilst always ugly—force sometimes had to be met with more force. And if force *was* necessary, it should be decisive. In ten thousand years mankind might evolve beyond the need for violence—but Donadze lived in the here and now.

He pushed these thoughts to the back of his mind and bolted down half a mug of scalding coffee, resisting his mother's pleas to eat something before leaving the apartment to drive to Mtatsminda Station

Misha Arziani was also looking tired but cheerful as Donadze walked into the detectives' bureau. 'Hey, Misha. Long night?'

'Yes, picking up Lataria and Tatishvili wasn't as straight-forward as we'd thought. All sorts of transfer-of-custody forms to sign and an escort required to see them off the premises.'

'Did they say much on the way over?'

'What do you think?'

'I'd guess they'd have nothing to say without their lawyers being present.'

'And you'd be right. They've both been through the system too many times, they know the score.' He glanced at the wall clock. 'Their lawyers are coming in now. We'll be speaking to Tatishvili at nine and Lataria after that. One thing though, Ramaz; Captain Rapava wants to conduct the interviews himself. But don't worry, I'll sit out, you can take my spot.'

Donadze looked up to see Rapava staring at them from his office. 'That's okay, Misha. You brought them in, I'll watch through the mirror.'

'Okay, if you're sure. I doubt we'll get much from them, anyway. We don't have a lot to offer and they've both still got nearly twenty years' prison-time to serve. So what's another fifteen or twenty on top of that, right?'

'They won't last that long. Killing someone like Otar Basilia has consequences. They've already got targets on their backs.'

'Put there by Basilia's gang. Yes, but they'll be dead if they do talk; snitches usually have a short life expectancy.'

'Right, but that could be your way in, Misha. If they stay in Gldani, they're dead. It's just a matter of time. But we could speak to the judge, let him know we've had their cooperation and request they get a transfer out of Gldani, maybe to another city. Kutaisi would be a good option for them.'

'That's a great idea, Ramaz.'

'You'd have got there soon enough,' Donadze said.

Arziani laughed. 'Do you want to take it to Rapava?'

'No. He's more likely to agree if it comes from you.'

'What's up with you two, Ramaz? You used to get along okay. Has something happened?'

Donadze hesitated. 'It's probably just a personality thing. We'll work it out. Do we know who's representing Lataria and Tatishvili?'

Arziani mentioned two well know lawyers from the same firm.

'Expensive. That should tell us something.'

'Yes, someone's looking after them.' Arziani glanced at

the commander's office. 'I'll see what Captain Rapava thinks of your idea.'

'Okay, but don't tell him it was my idea…'

Arziani shook his head. 'Are you sure there's nothing between you?' he said, standing to walk to Rapava's office.

Donadze took out his phone. He had a voice mail from Emzar Kesaria. '*Lieutenant Donadze*,' he said, his tone obsequious. '*It's Emzar from First National Bank. I'm so glad you agreed to accept Herr Maier's offer of help with your investigation. I'm sure you'll find us a useful resource. Could we please meet to discuss? Please call me back. Thanks again.*'

'He wants to see you,' Misha Arziani said, nodding towards Captain George Rapava's office.

Donadze looked up, Rapava was staring at him through his window. 'Okay,' he said.

'Moving Lataria and Tatishvili out of Gldani—he guessed that came from you.'

'Did he agree to it?'

'He didn't say.'

'Okay, Misha. I hope this hasn't caused you any trouble.'

'I don't think it has, but you need to sort this thing out. It's not good for anyone.'

'I know, you're right. I'll see what he wants.'

Donadze stood and walked to Rapava's office. 'You wanted to see me, Captain.'

'Shut the door, Ramaz.'

Rapava waited until Donadze had sat down. 'Two

things I want to discuss: Lataria and Tatishvili and then I want to discuss you and me.'

Donadze straightened in his chair. 'Yes, okay...'

'Now, about Lataria and Tatishvili. I like your idea. It might work, there's not much else we can offer to secure their cooperation. But how about doing it this way: we offer the deal to both of them, but only the first to agree gets it. The other one goes back to Gldani. And the information must be good—if not, the deal's off. Do you think that would be a better approach?'

'Yes, Captain, I do.'

'Because it might focus their minds, encourage one to grab the offer before the other one can?'

'Yes, it's dog eat dog in their world.'

'Okay then, that's what we'll do. I'll tell Misha to set it up.' He leaned back in his chair. 'So that brings us to you and me. Do you agree that—between us—we've just come up with a sound plan to deal with Lataria and Tatishvili?'

Donadze guessed where their conversation was heading. 'Yes, I do agree, Captain,' he said.

'Good. And do you also agree it would have been more efficient if you'd brought your idea to me directly instead of using Misha as your intermediary?'

'Yes, I do.'

'Okay. So do you want to tell me why you didn't do just that?' Rapava said, his voice rising. 'And then explain to me why our professional relationship broke down after your visit to Levan Gloveli in Shindisi.'

Donadze realised he was in dangerous territory and now was the time for a careful response. 'I know about you, Captain,' he said.

'You know about me? What does that mean?'

'I know you're a sexual predator. Women aren't safe around you.'

'Ah, there it is.' Rapava paused a moment. 'You're telling your commanding officer that he's a sexual predator. And that came from Gloveli, I presume?'

Donadze shook his head, declining to answer.

'So, Ramaz,' Rapava said eventually. 'It appears I have an issue to manage. I know how people feel about you at this station, some would probably prefer you as station commander. But I was appointed and you and Misha are my deputies. I don't have a problem with Misha but I do have a problem with you. If you were in my position, what would you do?'

'You'll do what you have to do, Captain.'

'You're right, I will. Get back to work, Donadze.'

Neither Phillip Lataria nor Zviad Tatishvili took the deal. Arziani spoke to both men in their cells and, following his script, had tried to convince them that killing Otar Basilia had consequences. He told them that even if Basilia's gang couldn't get to him, whoever ordered the hit might decide to tie-up all loose ends. And if they could get to a crime boss like Basilia, they could certainly get to them. Either way, they wouldn't survive long in Gldani and their best option was to cooperate with the police in return for transfer to a prison outside Tbilisi.

It was a strong argument but Arziani couldn't convince them. Neither man would admit any involvement in

Basilia's murder and both were confident that their expensive lawyers would bring them acquittals when they went to trial. But the real problem was neither believed a transfer out of Gldani Prison to Kutaisi would be safe in the long term—and Donadze knew their assessment was probably correct.

The formal interviews hadn't gone any better. Donadze and Jaqeli had watched from their side of the one-way glass as each man had given virtually the same rehearsed answers to the questions put by Rapava and Arziani. None of their tried-and-tested interrogation techniques had worked and the lawyers had guided their clients effectively. Arziani had played good cop to Rapava's bad cop and Donadze thought they'd worked well together—but the problem was Lataria and Tatishvili had seen it all before.

His thoughts drifted to his confrontation with George Rapava. He realised he had fallen into a trap; Rapava had manipulated him into admitting collaboration was a more effective way of working and then demanded to know why he wouldn't work that way with him. That suggested a lack of professionalism on Donadze's part. It was a clever approach; no one could suggest Rapava's actions were unreasonable. But Donadze knew their relationship was irretrievably broken, that he'd been manoeuvred into accusing a superior officer of being a sexual predator—an act of gross insubordination. But it wasn't the first time he'd been insubordinate and he didn't regret his words.

Arziani was winding up Lataria's interview and Donadze signalled to Jaqeli he was going to make a call. He needed air and carried his phone into the warm, bright sunlight at the station entrance.

Emzar Kesaria answered almost immediately, '*Gamarjoba*, Lieutenant, you got my message?'

'Yes.'

'Wonderful. Well, I really hope we can help you with your investigation. Have there been any new developments?'

'That's not something to discuss over the phone. We'll meet you tomorrow morning at eleven.'

'Tomorrow at eleven? Just let me just check my schedule.' Donadze heard a keyboard clicking. 'Sorry, Ramaz, I'm tied up at that time—would sometime after twelve work for you?'

'No, it has to be eleven.'

'Ah, I see. Well, eleven it is, then. Should I come to Mtatsminda Station?'

'No, Detective Jaqeli and I will come to you. We'll see you tomorrow,' he said, ending the call.

ELEVEN

'How could you say that to him?' Jaqeli demanded.

'Is it true?'

'Yes, it's true. Lots of things are true. But it's not down to you to fix them all.'

'Isn't that our job?'

'No it's not. But even if it is, you don't have to blow yourself up in the process.'

'I don't think—'

'And who were you doing it for, anyway? It had better not have been for me.'

'No, it wasn't for you. Not directly anyway.'

'Oh, Ramaz, you're completely hopeless,' she said slumping in her seat.

Donadze eased his car around the first of the many hairpin bends on the steeply rising road to Shindisi. He'd felt the need to get out of Tbilisi and decided to visit Levan Gloveli. Jaqeli had waited until they'd cleared the city streets before quizzing him on his row with George Rapava.

'And that's why we're going to Shindisi...' Jaqeli said after several minutes of silence.

'What do you mean?'

'It's a pattern, Ramaz. You get yourself into trouble and you go to Levan for advice. For forgiveness, almost.'

'Gloveli was my commanding officer. He's in no position to forgive me or anyone else. But he's the best policeman I know and I respect his opinion.'

'He's more than that though, isn't he?'

Donadze didn't respond for a long moment. 'Maybe,' he said.

'Ramaz, may I ask you something—as a friend?'

He glanced at her. 'Okay,' he said, at last.

'After your sister died in Abkhazia...'

'After she was raped and murdered, you mean?' Donadze snapped. He took a deep breath. 'Sorry.'

'It's okay. After your sister was murdered, were you given the chance to talk to anyone about it?'

'A shrink, you mean? No, Irina, of course not. Ana was one of thirty thousand. That's why it was called genocide. She was nothing special as far as the rest of the country was concerned. And neither was I.'

'I'm sorry, Ramaz. I don't mean to upset you.'

'You're not. It was a long time ago. I don't think about it that much now.'

'Well maybe you should.' She paused. 'If I were to put you in contact with someone, would you talk to him?'

'A shrink? No, I've lived with this for a long time, Irina. I don't need a psychiatrist, now.'

'He's a counselling psychologist, a friend of mine. We were at university together. He could help you come to terms with what happened to Ana.'

'What if I don't want to come to terms with it?'

'Maybe you should think what Ana would have wanted for you. She was your sister, she loved you. She wouldn't have wanted you to carry this burden around forever.'

'No, she wouldn't.' He paused a moment, unused to talking about himself and feeling uncomfortable doing so now. 'Don't you think I know it's not healthy—in lots of different ways? But without this *burden*, how do I help people like Ana, like Sophia, like Vano Chedia?'

'You're not the only detective in Georgia, Ramaz—there are others who can help. But what about Tamuna, Eka and your mother? They need you too.'

Donadze dropped his speed to negotiate the last of the hairpins before they arrived in Shindisi. 'I know they do,' he said.

They continued their journey in silence and within a few minutes arrived at Gloveli's house. Donadze stopped the car's engine, applied the brake and returned both his hands to the steering wheel, staring through his front window at nothing. He unbuckled his seat belt and opened his door. 'Okay,' he said. 'Let me think about it.'

'Ramaz, Irina, it's good to see you,' Gloveli said, holding his front door open.

Jaqeli kissed him on his cheek. 'How are you, Levan?'

'I'm old, Irina, very old,' he said, walking stiffly behind them into his small living room.

'Veronika's not here, Major?' Donadze asked.

'No, she's with Lasha. Wedding planning, probably.'

'She must be worried about her mother and sister.'

'Of course she is. It looks like Putin's not leaving Ukraine any time soon.'

'What are your contacts saying?' Gloveli had served in the KGB when Georgia was a Soviet republic and had maintained his networks ever since.

'They're not stupid, no one believes this is a *special military operation*. Some have family in Ukraine. They know it's not good, but they have to keep their heads down—just like everyone else in Russia.' He threw up his hands. 'Enough of that, let's have some wine.'

Gloveli made a token protest but allowed Jaqeli to organise food while Donadze lifted glasses and selected a plastic bottle from the collection on the stone floor. They seated themselves around the small table and Gloveli poured the wine. He lifted his own glass, held it to the light then placed it under his nose. Satisfied, he raised the glass high. 'To the heroes,' he toasted. '*Gaumarjos*.'

'*Gaumarjos*,' Donadze repeated the salutation while Jaqeli, as was customary for women, left her glass on the table.

Gloveli took a generous sip of his wine. 'Okay, Ramaz, what's wrong?' he asked.

'Nothing's wrong, Major. We just want to get your thoughts on the Kazbegi Avenue murders.'

'Tell him, Ramaz,' Jaqeli said.

'No, that's not why we're here.'

'Okay, but since you are here, why don't you tell me what's wrong.'

Donadze recounted his argument with George Rapava

while Gloveli listened, rubbing his arthritic knee to aid his concentration.

'It's my fault,' Gloveli said when Donadze had finished. 'I shouldn't have told you about him, I should have realised how you'd react.'

'No, it had nothing to do with you, Major. I would have heard about him eventually.'

'What can Ramaz do now?' Jaqeli asked.

'Did anyone else overhear this conversation?'

'No, we were in his office, the door was closed.'

'So, it's your word against his.'

'I'm not going to lie, Major.'

'Why not? He doesn't deserve your honesty—he's a rapist.'

'That depends on how you define *consent*, doesn't it?' Donadze said, quoting the old policeman.

'It's a pity your mouth doesn't work as well as your memory, Donadze.' He thought for a moment. 'You're not going to apologise, I presume?'

'Would you?'

'No, probably not.' He lifted the bottle and topped up their glasses. 'What you said to Rapava was gross insubordination. It could be bad for you…'

'*Could* be bad for me?'

'It *will* be bad for you. Unless you can prove that it's true—that he really is a sexual predator.'

'I'm not going to be able to do that. It's only hearsay.'

Gloveli held his glass to his lips and tipped the contents into his mouth. 'Well, Ramaz,' he said. 'You won't lie, you won't apologise and you can't substantiate your allegation. What does that tell you?'

'That I'm in trouble?'

Gloveli examined his glass, frowning to see it was empty. 'I'd say so,' he said.

'I'm sorry, Ramaz, I'm in your way,' Lela said.

'No, you're not. How are you?'

She gave him the smile he remembered. 'Good, actually. Better than I've felt for some time. Positive.'

'Well, why wouldn't you be?'

'You're right, but it took you and Tamuna to get me there...'

'I didn't do anything.'

'Yes, you did. How about you, Ramaz? How are *you* doing?'

'I'm fine. Some issues at work, but okay. Where's Tamuna?'

'Her clinic ran late but she should be back soon. Your mother's taken Eka for a walk and some fresh air.'

Donadze looked at his watch. 'They might get air but it won't be fresh. Not at this time of day.'

Lela laughed. 'That's true.' She pointed to a carrier bag. 'I'm making dinner. Help me—you can tell me about your issues at work.'

'I'll help you with dinner but I've not got much to say about work.'

'Well, let's see. It'll be nice to talk about something other than myself for a change.' She pointed to a paper bag. 'Tomatoes for the salad,' she said.

Donadze rummaged in a unit and found a colander.

He poured the tomatoes into it and washed them under running water.

'So, your issues: professional or personal?' she said, turning the oven on.

'It's not a big deal, Lela. Do you want onions with the salad?'

'Yes, but don't change the subject. Professional or personal?'

Donadze put the chopping board on the bunker and selected a knife from its rack. 'You're not going to let up, are you?'

'No, it's not in my nature.'

'I can tell. Well, it's personal. I may have spoken out of turn to my boss.'

'Speaking out of turn doesn't sound that serious.'

Donadze finished chopping the tomatoes and used his knife to push them into a bowl. 'It was a bit more than that,' he admitted. He opened the fridge and retrieved a cucumber and two onions. 'Parsley and coriander?'

'Yes.' She opened a pack of diced pork. 'Could you chop onions for the *shashlik*? So what did you say?'

Donadze put his knife down. 'I told him he's a sexual predator and women aren't safe around him.'

'Ah…' She opened a drawer. 'Do you know where Tamuna keeps her skewers?'

He opened another drawer and counted out four. 'Is that enough?'

'Should be. So is he? A predator, I mean?'

'Yes, he is.'

She pushed pork cubes onto the skewers. 'Can you finish these off after you've made the salad? Don't put them in the oven yet, they won't need long.' She washed her hands, dried them then went into the carrier bag to remove the *khachapuri*. 'Do you want wine with your meal?'

Donadze's eyes were stinging as he cut the onions. 'Definitely.'

'Five minutes will be enough for that,' she said, placing the *khachapuri* on a baking tray. She opened the fridge and took out a bottle of *Tsinandali*. 'Is this okay?'

'Better than okay.'

'Tell me, Ramaz. Your boss: was he doing something illegal?'

'Probably.'

'And you're a policeman…'

Donadze shook his head. 'It's not that simple.'

'Well, maybe it should be. Sometimes you just have to do what's right and accept the consequences.'

'Yes, and that's probably what's going to happen.' He arranged the *shashlik* on a tray. 'Thanks, Lela.'

'No problem.' She looked over their food preparations. 'Nearly forgot,' she said. 'Would you slice the cheese?'

TWELVE

There were only a few cars dotted around the Dream Casino's parking area, most belonging to its staff, Donadze thought. The Dream never closed but it was only nine in the morning and most of the services it offered were in greatest demand after dark.

It had been several months since Donadze and Jaqeli had arrested Otar Basilia on these premises. The crime boss had blustered and threatened but had eventually been tried, sentenced and incarcerated in Gldani Prison where—four days previously—he'd been stabbed to death in his cell.

Donadze and Jaqeli walked past banks of slot machines to the central stairway where they were intercepted by a familiar face.

'Lieutenant, Detective, welcome back,' Tengo Sakhokia, the Dream's security manager blustered, looking anything but welcoming.

'We've come to see your boss,' Donadze said.

'My boss? I'm afraid things have been a little fluid since

Mr Basilia left… Let me see if I can find someone to help you.'

Donadze reached to stop Sakhokia speaking into his radio. 'Thanks, Tengo, but that won't be necessary. We're going to Otar's office—come with us.'

'I don't think—'

'Come with us, Tengo.'

Sakhokia followed a few paces behind as Donadze and Jaqeli continued up the stairway. They reached the office where the head of the Kaldani crime family controlled its various legal and illegal enterprises. Donadze swung the door open.

A man in his early thirties was sitting behind his desk, an open laptop in front of him. 'Lieutenant Donadze and Detective Jaqeli,' he said with a pleasant smile. 'I thought I'd be seeing you.'

Donadze nodded his greeting. 'Shalva Khapava,' he said. 'I didn't expect to find *you* here.'

Khapava closed the laptop's lid and stood, gesturing for Donadze and Jaqeli to enter. He was slim and good looking with dark hair gelled into what looked like a careless style, but probably wasn't. He had full eyebrows, three days' stubble and was casually dressed in slim-fit trousers and a polo shirt. He noticed Sakhokia standing by the doorway looking uncertain what to say or do. 'We'll be fine, Tengo,' he said with a friendly nod. 'You can go.'

Khapava watched the security manager turn and leave. He waited until Donadze and Jaqeli had sat down before taking his own seat. He shook his head. 'One of Otar's people.'

'South Ossetian?'

'Yes, his family were displaced in 2008,' Khapava said, referring to the war with Russia. He placed his hand over his desk phone. 'Water, coffee?' he offered.

Jaqeli shook her head.

'How did you do it?' Donadze asked.

'Do what?'

'Take over the organisation from Basilia. There must have been others higher up the food chain than you.'

Khapava laughed good naturedly. 'Food chain, that's good—but I know what you mean. Yes, there were individuals higher in the *food chain*, but Otar chose me as his successor. Most of our people respect that decision.'

'Most of your people?'

Khapava shrugged. 'One or two may be disappointed, I imagine. Ambitious people. Some may have preferred an Ossetian.' He glanced at his watch. 'Could we discuss the reason you're here?'

'You said you were expecting us…'

'Yes. Can we speak freely or should I bring my attorney in?'

'I think we can speak freely.'

Khapava nodded. 'You want to discuss the Kazbegi bank robbery.'

'And the two people murdered—yes, that's why we're here.'

'I thought so. And I may be able to help.'

'Even though Basilia couldn't—or wouldn't?'

Khapava took a moment to respond. 'There's something you need to understand, Lieutenant. Otar Basilia was like a father to me—a father I loved and respected.' He looked at Donadze and Jaqeli in turn. 'But Otar was an emotional man and emotions can cloud our judgement and cause us to make bad decisions.'

'And that's what Basilia did?'

'Otar's organisation had *interests* in Kazbegi Avenue. He was *unhappy* someone chose to rob that bank. He was *affronted.* He believed the robbery was a test of his resolve, his ability to defend his interests from within Gldani Prison. But his anger coloured his judgement.'

'You don't think he was being tested?'

Khapava shrugged. 'No, I don't. That's what I meant by his judgement being off—he was looking in the wrong place.'

'Why do you say that?'

'There's too much about this robbery that doesn't feel right. The cost-benefits just don't make sense. Or do you think I'm wrong?'

'No,' Donadze said. 'I don't think you're wrong. So, if Basilia was looking in the wrong place, where's the right place to look?'

'Means, motive and opportunity; that's what the police look for, isn't it? The means and opportunity are clear—I think you need to look at motive again.'

'Is that what you've done?'

'It's what I'm doing.'

'I asked Basilia if he would help us find the men responsible. He wasn't prepared to do that—are you?'

'Yes, I am.' Khapava smiled. 'We were discussing food chains a moment ago. I told you most of our people respect Otar's decision to appoint me as his successor. But respect must be earned *and* retained. If Otar died because he was looking for the people behind the robbery, then this organisation—my organisation—expects me to find them.'

'And if you do?'

'They'll get the justice they deserve.' Khapava smiled. 'So, Lieutenant Donadze, on that basis, do you still want my help?'

Donadze held Khapava's gaze. 'Yes,' he said, eventually. 'We do.'

The First National Bank's head office was situated in the old German neighbourhood of Marjanishvili. The Bank had purchased, renovated and modernised one of the area's grand old buildings on Marjanishvili Square to provide a home reflecting its status on the national and international financial stage and to afford an efficient platform for its staff working in the digital age.

'Do *you* bank with First National?' Jaqeli asked.

'Doesn't everyone?'

She shrugged. 'Eighty percent of us, apparently.'

Donadze looked at her inquisitively.

'Research,' she said.

There was a parking space a few metres from the Bank's entrance.

'Okay?' Jaqeli said, opening her door.

'Just a minute.' Donadze turned to look at her. 'Colonel Meskhi told me to report to his office. I've to go there later this afternoon.'

Jaqeli slumped back in her seat. 'Because of what you said to George Rapava?'

'I think so.'

'What do you think's going to happen?'

'A disciplinary hearing, probably. Suspension, demotion—I really don't know.'

'Do you think you'll be taken off *this* case?'

'Yes, that's likely.' He opened his door. 'But it hasn't happened yet—let's speak to Kesaria.'

Donadze walked to the Bank's entrance and held the oversized door by its brass handle for Jaqeli to enter. An attractive young woman was sitting behind the reception desk. She smiled a professional welcome as they approached.

Jaqeli showed her ID. 'We have an appointment with Emzar Kesaria.'

'Of course.' The receptionist lifted a handset and pressed a button on her desk phone, carefully avoiding damage to her perfectly manicured nails. She spoke a few words then replaced the handset, smiling sweetly. 'Please take a seat, Mr Kesaria will be down shortly.'

Donadze looked at his watch. 'Thank you, we'll wait here.'

The receptionist appeared momentarily uncertain, her authority threatened. 'Of course, if that's what you prefer.'

A few minutes passed before Kesaria arrived, moving quickly down the ornate stairway and crossing to the reception area. He nodded to the young woman and held out his hand to Donadze. 'Lieutenant, Detective, thank you so much for coming to see us.'

'*Us*?' Donadze asked.

'Yes, Mr Maier will join us today. Will that be a problem?'

'No problem.' Donadze made a show of checking his watch again.

'Sorry, I know you're busy people. Please come with me.'

If the building renovations had extended to installing an elevator, Kesaria didn't use it. He led Donadze and Jaqeli up two long flights and along a short corridor to a door bearing the nameplate, *Christoph Maier, CEO.* He opened the door and went in, holding it for Jaqeli and Donadze to follow. A middle aged woman was sitting behind her desk, guarding Maier's inner sanctum. She appraised the three intruders over her tortoiseshell glasses.

'Can Mr Maier see us now, Nina?' Kesaria asked, offering her his best smile.

The smile wasn't returned. Without replying, she picked up her phone and waited until it was answered. She spoke a few words then hung up. 'You can go through now,' she said with undisguised distaste.

'The friendly face of banking,' Donadze said, quoting a First National Bank's advertising slogan just loud enough for her to hear.

Maier had removed his suit jacket but still looked expensive, Donadze thought. He stood to greet them from behind his executive's desk and blessed them with his easy smile. 'Lieutenant, Detective, so good to see you again,' he said in accented Georgian, crossing his office to shake their hands. He turned to Kesaria. 'Where are we meeting Emzar?'

'I thought here, in your office, would be suitable, sir. But we can move to a conference room if you prefer.'

'No, here is fine. Please take a seat, Detectives,' he said, gesturing towards a round table located in front of an ornate window. 'Have you been offered coffee?'

Donadze declined, fearing what Nina might add to their cups.

They took their seats and Maier got down to business. 'So, Lieutenant, Detective, what more can you tell us about your investigation?'

'Let's discuss how this relationship will work first,' Donadze said.

'Relationship?'

'You suggested Mr Kesaria will act as an interface between your bank and the police. What exactly does that mean?'

Maier looked surprised. 'Why, it means Emzar will help with your investigation in whatever way he can. And *you*, in return, will help *me* to manage any issues which may affect our—that is to say—the Bank's reputation. I think we're on the same side here, Lieutenant.'

Donadze and Jaqeli had discussed tactics ahead of the meeting. They had concluded that Kesaria and Maier probably had one or more sources of information and already knew everything about the case that they were prepared to tell them.

'Good,' Donadze said. 'So here's what we've learned so far.' He summarised their investigation to date including the discovery of thirty thousand dollars in Eliso Chedia's name and their belief that Otar Basilia hadn't been responsible for the robbery or murders.

Maier's bored expression confirmed none of that information was new to him.

'So, this Otar Basilia—I saw he was killed in his prison cell?' he said.

'That's correct.'

'Shortly after you visited him. Coincidence?'

'Probably,' Donadze lied.

Maier nodded, unconvinced. 'Why do I feel you're holding something back, Lieutenant?'

'It may just be your suspicious nature, Herr Maier.'

Maier smiled. 'No, I don't think it's that,' he said, choosing to take Donadze's observation at face value. 'Tell me, Lieutenant, how much do you know about my bank?'

'You're the biggest in Georgia, other than that—nothing.'

'Well, you're right, we *are* the biggest in Georgia. But our stock is traded on the London exchange because we're also big internationally. We're trusted by our investors, we manage very large financial transactions, we facilitate inward investment and we are a major employer—all of that makes us important to Georgia. We should be important to you, Lieutenant.'

'All victims of crime are important to me, Herr Maier.'

Maier shook his head. 'Disappointing,' he said. 'Well, if that's all we have to discuss, Emzar will show you out.'

'You said Mr Kesaria will help us in whatever way he can.'

Maier closed his eyes momentarily, allowing his exasperation to show. 'Yes, and he will.'

'Good, then we'll need access to your records.'

'What records? From our Kazbegi Avenue branch?'

'And other branches if necessary. Possibly records from this office.'

'That's ridiculous, why would you need these?'

'Something strange was going on at Kazbegi Avenue and it may be that similar things are going on at your other branches. And possibly here. Maybe even in London—because apparently, you're also big internationally. We need to look at all your records.'

'Well, Lieutenant, that won't be happening,' Maier said, attempting and failing to resurrect his smile. 'Not without a court order.' He crossed to his desk and sat down. 'Make sure our visitors don't get lost on their way out, Emzar,' he said, reaching for his keyboard.

'Did you really want to see Maier's bank records?' Jaqeli asked. 'Or were you just trying to antagonise him?'

Donadze shrugged. 'Maybe a bit of both.' He checked the time—twelve fifteen. 'Colonel Meskhi wants to see me at three. Let's head back to the station for a couple of hours.'

'I'll leave you to go on your own. I've got something to take care of.'

Donadze looked at her expectantly.

'Good luck with Colonel Meskhi,' she said, opening her door.

He watched Jaqeli walk towards Marjanishvili Street, her hand outstretched to hail a taxi. He started his engine and drove to Mtatsminda Station.

George Rapava was huddled with his smoking buddies at the station entrance, a fresh supply of cigarette butts littering the concrete walkway. Their conversation stopped as Donadze approached.

'Lieutenant,' Rapava said, a smile playing on his lips.

'Captain,' Donadze replied evenly.

The Desk Sergeant was smirking at him.

'Someone else looking after your desk today, Archil?' Donadze asked.

'I gave Sergeant Nakania permission to take a break,

Lieutenant,' Rapava said, still smiling. 'Is that a problem?'

'No problem, Captain.' He walked through the group, forcing them to shuffle out of his way, their heads down and avoiding eye contact.

He was pleased to see a friendly face in the detectives' bureau. 'Hey, Misha,' he said.

'Are you okay, Ramaz?'

'Just about. You know what's happening, then?'

'Some of it. Rapava's been telling everyone you're up on a disciplinary.'

'It looks that way. I'm seeing Meskhi at three.'

'He said it was insubordination…'

'I think so.'

'But why, Ramaz? What did you say to him?'

'Something he didn't want to hear. But you're best staying out of it, Misha.'

'Okay…' Arziani said reluctantly. 'Can I get you a coffee, at least?'

'Thanks. Plenty of sugar. I think I'm going to need the energy.'

Donadze sat at his desk, attempting to review and update his case notes but conscious of the scrutiny of station personnel drifting in and out of the detectives' bureau. *Dead man walking*, he thought. At one point Rapava ambled past, shaking his head in mock sympathy as he made his way to his office.

Time passed too slowly and Donadze abruptly stood and walked out the station. He drove quickly and arrived at the Ministry of Internal Affairs forty minutes ahead of his designated time. He shut down his engine and strode to the building's entrance. Four people were waiting at the reception for security passes but he went to the front of the queue, presented his ID and told the sceptical receptionist that he'd been summoned by Colonel Meskhi on urgent business. Clipping his pass to his jacket pocket, he took the elevator to the fourth level and walked to the door bearing Meskhi's name and rank. He steadied himself with three deep breaths, knocked on the door and pushed it open.

Meskhi was at his conference table, Jaqeli sitting opposite him. 'Come in, Donadze,' he said. 'We were just talking about you.'

THIRTEEN

'What's going on, Irina?'

'I said *come in*, Lieutenant,' Meskhi repeated. 'Don't make me say it again.'

'Sir.' Donadze stepped into the office and took a seat beside Jaqeli.

'Do you know why I called you here?'

'Yes, sir.'

'Tell me.'

'Captain Rapava believes I have been insubordinate.'

'And have you?'

Donadze hesitated. 'Yes. I accused him of something for which I have no evidence.'

'You accused him of sexual misconduct.'

'It's worse than misconduct, Colonel.'

'Indeed. And you stand by your allegation?'

'Yes, sir. I do.'

'Even though, as you admit, you have no evidence?'

'My information comes from trusted sources.'

Meskhi looked at him expectantly.

'I'd rather not say, sir.'

'You don't have to. One of your sources is Major Levan Gloveli.' He paused. 'Your other source is Detective Jaqeli.'

Donadze turned to look at her. She returned his look, her face impassive.

Meskhi sat back and appraised him. 'You should have handled this better,' he said.

'I'm sorry, sir. I don't understand.'

'Don't you? It's simple enough. Captain Gloveli called me this morning and told me he was the source of your information. He assured me your accusations are well founded. And a short while ago Detective Jaqeli called and insisted on seeing me. She accused Captain Rapava of inappropriate behaviour towards her and other female personnel at Mtatsminda Station.'

Donadze turned to Jaqeli. 'You shouldn't have—'

'Kindly address your comments to me, Lieutenant,' Meskhi said. He waited until he had regained Donadze's attention. 'Detective Jaqeli's actions were entirely appropriate. My question is: why didn't you do something similar?'

'Sir?'

'You were provided with incriminating information from a trusted source. Why didn't you bring it to me yourself?'

Donadze hesitated. 'I'm not sure, Colonel...'

'Was it because you thought I wouldn't take appropriate action?'

'No, it wasn't that.'

'So you acted on impulse. And not for the first time.'

He closed his eyes as if to think, his fingers drumming the table.

Donadze turned to Jaqeli again. She met his gaze, her mouth tight.

'Very well,' Meskhi said. 'The behaviour described by Major Gloveli and Detective Jaqeli is entirely unacceptable. It is however *my* responsibility to ensure a safe working environment for all my people. Culture is set at the top and if you did not feel confident about reporting your concerns, then that's something I need to address.' He paused for a moment. 'I take responsibility for your actions, Lieutenant—you have nothing to answer for on this occasion.'

'Thank you, sir, but I don't think that's entirely fair to—'

'Fair to me? This isn't a debating society, Lieutenant. I think I've made my position clear.' He looked at Donadze and Jaqeli in turn. 'The allegations made against Captain Rapava will be properly investigated. Procedure requires his temporary suspension from duty and that will require me to make changes to my reporting lines.' He nodded as though coming to a decision. 'Lieutenant, you will report directly to me until further notice.'

'Yes, sir. And Detective Jaqeli?'

'Thank you, Lieutenant, I hadn't forgotten Jaqeli.' He turned to her. 'Detective, thank you for bringing this matter to my attention,' he said. 'I realise it must have been quite difficult for you. You will continue working with Lieutenant Donadze on your current assignment. Is that clear?'

'Sir,' Jaqeli said.

'Is there anything else we need to discuss?'

'No, sir,' Donadze said.

'In that case, you're both dismissed.'

'I wish you hadn't done that, Irina,' Donadze said.

Jaqeli slammed her door closed. 'Why don't you just say *thank you*, Ramaz?' She clipped in her seat belt. 'Or better still, say nothing at all.'

Donadze looked at her. 'Have I done something wrong?'

She turned in her seat to face him. 'Have you done something wrong? Yes, of course you have. Do you think I wanted to speak to Meskhi? Of course I didn't, but you left me no choice. I told you I could handle Rapava. I told you I don't need your protection. And I *really* didn't want Misha to become involved.'

'He won't be. He asked why Meskhi wanted to see me and I advised him to stay out of it.'

'Okay, and what do I tell him when he hears Rapava has been suspended?'

'Tell him the truth.'

'Like when I told you the truth. How well did that work out?'

'Misha's not like me, Irina.'

'No, he's not. But he's a man just the same. I know how he'll react.'

'Do you want me to speak to him?'

She turned away. 'No, of course I don't,' she said, softly.

'You should ask for a new partner.'

'Yes, I should.' She paused a moment. 'But I won't.'

Donadze ran his hands around his steering wheel, thinking. He came to a decision. 'That shrink you mentioned. Maybe I do need to see him.'

'He's a counselling psychologist. Yes, you should see him, but don't do it for me. Take a few days to think about it, discuss it with Tamuna—then let me know.'

He nodded. 'Okay…'

She tapped the dashboard clock. 'You said you wanted to visit Eliso Chedia…'

'Don't you want to talk to Misha first?'

'No, we'll talk this evening.'

'Irina, I'm—'

'Don't. It's over. Let's talk to Eliso…'

'Okay.' He took a breath. 'She said she works in a florist shop near the cemetery. See if you can find it on your phone.'

'She might be at home.'

'I know, but let's try the florist first.'

Donadze started the engine and eased his car into the city traffic. Jaqeli identified a florist near the entrance to Kukia Cemetery and he drove to it, their conversation stilted and uncomfortable on the thirty minute journey.

He pulled up outside the shop and saw Eliso serving a customer inside. 'She's here,' he said.

'Good.' She gave him a tight smile. 'Don't look so glum, Ramaz—I told you it's over.'

They got out of the car but stayed outside the shop until the customer bustled out carrying a small arrangement of white flowers wrapped in clear cellophane. She held the door open for them and they went in. The shop was well stocked with a variety of cut flowers and Donadze drew cool, fragrant air deep into his lungs.

'*Gamarjoba*, Eliso,' Jaqeli said.

She was wearing blue jeans and trainers, her hair held in a loose pony tail. She looked like she was beginning to get her life back in order, Donadze thought, although he recognised the hoodie she was wearing under her florist's apron—her dead husband's.

She wrapped her arms around herself, looking wary. '*Gamarjoba*.'

'The shop seems quiet. Do you think you could close for ten minutes to let us talk in private?'

She looked confused for a moment then crossed to the door and locked it, turning a sign to read *closed*. She returned to face the detectives, her arms wrapped around herself once more. 'I'll have to reopen soon,' she said.

'You're back at work,' Donadze stated.

'Yes, I didn't have much choice—not without Vano's salary.'

'Hasn't the Bank helped?'

'No, nothing.'

'What will you do now, Eliso?' Jaqeli asked.

She shrugged. 'I can't stay in Tbilisi.'

'Why not?'

'Why not? Because I can't afford to. Not after the baby's born. I'll have to go back to Kakheti and live with my parents. Vano and I wanted to bring up our children in the city—but what choice do I have now?' She brushed a tear aside. 'I really do have to reopen soon. Why are you here?'

'Sit down for a minute, Eliso,' Donadze said, taking her arm and manoeuvring her to an upright wooden chair. He knelt in front of her. 'Did Vano ever talk to you about money?' he asked.

'What do you mean? We talked about money all the time. Neither of us earned much, paying the bills wasn't easy and with a baby coming along…'

'Did he ever talk to you about bank accounts?'

'Bank accounts? No, not really, just how we had to keep them out the red, how we had to pay off our credit card on time. What's this about?'

'How about foreign bank accounts?'

'I really don't know what you're talking about, Lieutenant. Have I done something wrong?'

'Do you know where Belize is, Eliso?'

'The country Belize? Roughly, I think. Why are you asking me about Belize?'

Donadze put his hand on her arm. 'This is important, Eliso,' he said, locking his eyes on hers. 'Did Vano ever mention an account with The United Bank of Belize?'

She stared at him. 'He had an account in Belize?'

'No, Eliso, you do.'

'I don't.'

'You do. It has thirty thousand dollars in it.'

'Thirty thousand dollars—no! It's got nothing to do with me.'

'Someone opened the account in your name.'

'Vano?'

'Possibly.'

'Whose money is it?'

'We don't know yet.' He stood, noticing his knee was damp from spilled water. A customer was trying to open the door. 'Thanks, Eliso. We'll be in touch.'

Donadze dropped Jaqeli at her apartment block. He watched for a moment as she walked to the building's entrance without turning or waving goodbye.

Misha Arziani had called while they'd been driving from Eliso Chedia's home. He'd told them George Rapava was suspended and he'd been given temporary command of the station. But he was frustrated that—although rumours were circulating—no one would say what had triggered the suspension. Jaqeli had kept her tone light but Donadze had caught her accusing glance as she'd told Arziani she would explain later that evening—it wasn't quite over between them, he'd realised.

It had been a difficult day and Donadze felt weary as he opened his apartment door. He heard laughter from the living room. Lela was on the floor playing with Eka, his mother and Tamuna watching the little girl with obvious adoration.

'Hey, Ramaz,' Lela said, smiling at him. 'I've been trying to persuade Tamuna to take you out.'

'Out where?'

'Anywhere. What was that old town restaurant you used to like?'

'The King David. We still like it, just haven't managed to get to it for a while.'

'Right, that's settled then. Take your daughter a minute,' she said, passing Eka to him and retrieving her phone from the breakfast bar.

Donadze threw an inquisitive glance at Tamuna as he jostled the little girl in his arms.

'Lela's found an apartment. She's moving out tomorrow and wants to treat us to a meal.'

'Do you *want* to go out?' Donadze said, his tone suggesting that he really didn't.

'It's been a while—we should.'

Lela returned a moment later. 'They remembered you, Ramaz—you must be a big tipper!' she said. 'Eight p.m. Your favourite table's reserved.'

'I didn't know we had one.'

'Ignore him, Lela. We do have a favourite table at the King David,' Tamuna said. She turned to Donadze's mother. 'Will you be okay putting Eka down?'

'We'll be fine,' she said, reaching to take the baby from Donadze.

'I'll be okay like this, won't I?' he asked.

The three women appraised him.

'There's a clean shirt in the wardrobe, Ramaz,' Tamuna said.

'You've got a mark on your trouser leg,' Lela added, pointing to the location on her own leg.

'You've got time for a shower, *Ramazi*,' his mother whispered, intending and failing to be discreet.

'So not okay, then,' he said, female laughter following him to the bedroom.

The tourist season hadn't started yet and the King David Restaurant was quiet. It had been several months since their last visit but they were given a warm welcome and shown to the table Donadze had denied being their favourite.

Tamuna looked around the ancient, vaulted cellar, once storage for merchants trading on the River Kura. 'I'd almost forgotten how lovely it is here,' she said.

Donadze gazed at his wife as she spoke. The candlelight cast her face in shadow and accentuated the dark smudges that had appeared under her eyes in recent months. He knew she was tired; tired from working at the clinic and from tending to their baby. But beautiful, he thought.

'What?' she smiled at him.

He lifted her hand from the table and kissed it. 'Nothing,' he said. 'I'm just glad I persuaded you to come out with me tonight.'

FOURTEEN

Donadze gave Jaqeli five minutes warning before arriving outside her apartment. She and Misha Arziani were waiting for him as he pulled up. Arziani nodded a greeting, his usual friendly smile not on display. Jaqeli gave him a perfunctory goodbye kiss before getting into the car and pulling the door shut.

Donadze drove off, watching in his rear-view mirror as Arziani turned to walk back to his apartment, his hands plunged deep into his jacket pockets.

'He didn't take it well?' Donadze asked.

She shook her head. 'I don't want to talk about it.'

Donadze nodded and they drove in silence for a few minutes.

'Where are we going?' she asked eventually.

'Kazbegi Avenue. I want to see what's happening at the bank.'

'Okay.'

Nana Pachulia was unlocking the door as Donadze

parked beneath a shade-providing tree. She offered them a tight smile then returned inside, letting the door close behind her.

He turned to Jaqeli. 'Are you okay?'

'Yes, I'm fine.'

The detectives got out of the car and walked up the short flight of steps to the bank's entrance. The security guard they had seen on their last visit had been withdrawn. Looking through the glass window, they could see Nana Pachulia back behind her teller's desk, counting notes into a drawer.

A man approached them at the door. '*Gamarjoba.* Are you here to see Koba?'

'Yes,' Donadze said. 'You're Vano Chedia's replacement?'

The man nodded. 'Let me tell Koba you're here,' he said, stepping to the manager's office.

'Lieutenant,' Donadze heard Nana say softly.

He turned and crossed to her desk. 'How are you, Nana?'

'I'm okay,' she said. She turned to make sure no one was watching then pushed a slip of paper towards him. 'Call me tonight,' she mouthed.

Donadze put his hand over the paper and transferred it to his pocket in one swift motion. 'Well, don't worry, Nana. We're going to catch these men,' he said in a voice loud enough to carry to the far end of the building.

The teller returned. 'Koba said you've to go through,' he said, gesturing towards the manager's office.

Brachuli stood as Donadze and Jaqeli entered. He was dressed for business but his face was pale and waxy, his eyes shadowed and haunted. He shook hands with the detectives and invited them to sit.

'How have you been, Koba?' Jaqeli asked, her voice low and empathetic.

Brachuli shrugged. 'Second day back at work. It's like I've never been away. Nothing's changed but everything's changed.'

'How's Zaal?'

'Thank God he's got his Aunt Amelia. It's not like I've been much help…'

'You've been there, Koba. That's what he needs right now.'

'It's his mother he needs…'

Donadze allowed Brachuli time to compose himself. 'Are you still living with Amelia?'

'For now.'

'And London?' he asked.

'London's not happening, Amelia withdrew her application.'

'That's good, isn't it?' Jaqeli said.

'Not for her, it's not.' He straightened in his chair. 'How may I help you, Detectives?'

'We're here to update you on our investigation,' Donadze said. 'And to see if there's anything you need from us.'

'I take it you've not found Sophia's killer yet?'

'No, but she and Vano remain our top priority. We're making progress: eliminating suspects, examining motives. We're also receiving support from your bank. Christoph Maier, your CEO wants to help. Do you know him?'

Brachuli appeared to think for a moment. 'No, we've never met.'

'Well, he's appointed his executive assistant, Emzar

Kesaria, to act as liaison between the bank and the police.'

'Yes, Kesaria called me yesterday. He said there's a question mark against Vano.'

'What did he say?'

'Something about an unexplained sum of money in an offshore account.'

'Well, that's a line of inquiry we're pursuing but we've not reached any conclusion yet. Better to keep it to yourself for now.'

Brachuli shrugged and checked his watch. 'I appreciate you coming to see me, Detectives but if you've got nothing more…'

Donadze stood. 'Of course, sir. Thank you for your time, we'll be in touch.'

Donadze drove east along Kazbegi Avenue, one hand on the wheel as he fumbled for the slip of paper Nana Pachulia had given to him. He found it and passed it to Jaqeli.

'What does it say?' he asked.

'Just a phone number. Hers I presume. What do you think she wants to talk to you about?'

'I don't know. Maybe she's had a change of heart about helping us. I'll phone later this evening.'

'What did you make of Brachuli?'

'He's still suffering, isn't he? Probably back at work too soon.'

'Yes, that's probably it…'

Donadze glanced at her. 'What?'

'I was surprised when he made that comment about

Vano Chedia and the Belize bank account. I thought he would have been more supportive—they were colleagues after all.'

'Yes, but a colleague who may have been responsible for his wife's murder.'

'That's a bit of a leap, isn't it?'

'It is for us and it should be for him as well, but don't forget where he got his information from…'

'Emzar Kesaria. Maybe we're sharing too much with him.'

'We're only telling him—and Maier—what they already know. It's worth it to see if they let anything slip from their side.'

'I suppose.' Jaqeli paused for a moment. 'And London's off the table now…'

'Yes. Strange, you'd think Brachuli would be pleased but he sounded angry, if anything.'

'Disappointed for Amelia, do you think?'

'Maybe that's it. But we never really got a good understanding of why he wanted Zaal to go with her.'

'He said for better opportunities.'

'That's what he said…'

Donadze turned onto Kandelaki Street and pulled up outside his apartment.

'Did you forget something?' Jaqeli asked.

'No. I need coffee and you and I need to talk.'

Jaqeli groaned. 'Do we really?'

'Yes, I think we do.'

Tamuna was working at the clinic and his mother was out with Eka.

'We really don't have to do this, Ramaz,' Jaqeli said as

he carried a tray with coffee, mugs and biscuits onto the balcony. 'I told you, we're good.'

He poured coffee into their mugs. 'But you and Misha aren't good, are you?'

'We're good enough. Anyway, I'm not sure that's got anything to do with you.'

'It does if you hold me responsible—and you do, don't you?'

'Well yes. I told you I could handle Rapava.'

'I know you told me that, and I believed you. But what about the women who *couldn't* handle him—his other victims?'

'I don't know, Ramaz. Is that what this is for you; keeping every female in Tbilisi safe from George Rapava?'

'You remember Tamuna's friend, Lela?'

'Yes, she works with Tamuna at the Medifirst Clinic.'

'We were talking a couple of days ago. I told her about Rapava and the accusations I'd made against him. She told *me* that sometimes we just have to do what's right and accept the consequences.'

'But it's not just the consequences for *you*, Ramaz. It's for everyone else as well. You go through life leaving a trail of destruction behind you.'

'Okay, sometimes I do. But if you take yourself out of the equation, do you think what I did with Rapava was wrong?'

Jaqeli took a long moment before answering. 'It's the way you went about it...'

'Yes, and I know that caused you problems—but did I do the right thing?'

Jaqeli gave a mirthless laugh and shook her head. 'Yes,'

she conceded eventually. 'Rapava *is* a threat, someone had to do something about him. Maybe it should have been me.'

Donadze took a drink from his mug. 'Maybe it should have been,' he agreed. 'Can we talk about Misha for a minute?'

'Why not?' she said, defeated.

'I can guess how he reacted when he found out about Rapava and you?'

'Because you would have reacted the same way?'

'No. I would have done something stupid, acted without thinking, made matters worse. I told you, Misha's not like me.'

'He is and he isn't.'

'You're a psychologist, Irina. You understand how men think and act.'

'Yes, but that's the trouble. Where women are concerned, you don't think—you're driven by testosterone.'

'Okay, but if that's the way we are...'

'No, I don't accept that. You've got brains, you don't have to act like cavemen. That's something you choose to do.'

Donadze topped up their mugs, thinking. 'Yes,' he conceded. 'You're right. I hadn't thought about it that way.'

Jaqeli laughed with real humour this time. 'So, that round goes to me then. Should we call it a draw?'

'Okay,' he said. 'A draw sounds about right to me.'

'Nana, it's Lieutenant Donadze. I'm outside...'

'I wanted you to call.'

'I know, and that's okay, we can still talk over the phone if you'd prefer. I just thought it would be better to meet face to face.'

She hesitated a moment. 'Where?'

'Leave your apartment and walk towards Pekini Avenue. I'll catch up with you—just friends taking an evening stroll.'

She hesitated again. 'Give me ten minutes. I'll have to tell my parents something…'

'No problem, take as long as you need.'

'I don't mean to be rude, Lieutenant but please stay back until we're on Pekini Avenue. I'd rather our neighbours didn't see us together.'

'I understand, see you soon,' he said, ending the call.

It was nearly twenty minutes before Donadze saw Nana leave her apartment block. He crossed the road and followed her to the junction with Pekini Avenue.

'Hey, Nana,' he spoke softly, trying not to startle her.

She jumped regardless. 'Lieutenant,' she said.

'Better if you call me *Ramaz*.'

The lights from a passing car lit up her pretty smile. 'Okay, *Ramaz*.'

As he fell in beside her, Donadze was reminded of how Nana's slight frame and pixie-like features made her look more like a young teenager than the twenty two year old woman she was. She'd changed out of her work clothes into a long skirt and a blouse buttoned up to her neck, but the silver chain he'd noticed previously was still around her neck, its cross lying close to her heart.

'Let's walk,' he said.

'I can't be long…'

'That's okay, we won't be. What did you want to talk to me about?'

She waited until a young couple had passed, self-obsessed and barely glancing in their direction. 'You told me that Vano might have been involved in the robbery. Do you still believe that?'

'We just don't know at this stage, it's possible. That's one of the reasons we asked for your help, we'd like to rule him out if we're able.' Donadze glanced at her as they walked, thinking again of how young and vulnerable she looked and conscious that he was trying to manipulate her into helping him. 'We need to know what's been going on at your bank.'

'And you can't get your information any other way?'

'We could try. We've been speaking to your boss, Christoph Maier. He said he would help but his priority is to protect the Bank's interests.'

'Yes, that sounds about right.'

'You've met him?'

'I saw him talking to you after the robbery. But he'd visited a couple of months before then, spoke to everyone at the branch after we'd closed for the day.'

'Everyone? Including Koba?'

'Of course, he's our manager. Why would you ask that?'

'No real reason,' Donadze said, remembering Koba Brachuli had told him he'd never met Christoph Maier. He changed the subject. 'You still haven't told me what you want to talk about.'

She paused. 'I've thought about it and I may be able to help you…'

'Okay, that's good.'

'You said you're looking for anything out of the ordinary or strange.'

'Yes, and you're obviously in a much better position to recognise something like that.'

'If there's anything left to recognise...'

'What do you mean?'

Several young girls were tottering towards them wearing short skirts and high heels and Nana moved to one side of the pavement to let them pass, a wave of excited chatter and a cloud of perfume trailing in their wake.

'You remember Mr Berishvili?' Nana said as they resumed walking.

'Yes, I spoke to him at your branch. He was covering for Koba.'

'He might have been doing a bit more than that. It's subtle but things changed while he was with us: paperwork missing; files deleted; money moved; accounts closed; new accounts opened…'

Donadze stopped walking and turned to look at Nana. 'What do you think he was doing?'

'I don't know.'

'It sounds to me like he was cleaning up, removing evidence.'

She shook her head. 'I don't know what he was doing. It may have been legitimate…'

'Do *you* think it was legitimate?'

Nana hesitated before answering. 'No,' she said. 'I don't think so.'

FIFTEEN

Donadze's phone buzzed on his bedside cabinet. He woke, groaned and willed his eyes open. He took a second then slid his legs out from under the duvet and lifted the phone, the caller ID withheld.

Tamuna was stirring and he shook his head to throw off the last vestiges of sleep then stood and carried the phone to the living room.

'Who's this?' he demanded.

'*Gamarjoba*, Ramaz,' a man responded, his voice muffled.

'Who are you and what do you want?'

'The Kazbegi Avenue bank heist—I've got something you'll want to hear.'

'Do I know you?'

'Do you want to hear what I've got or not?'

'Go ahead.'

The man laughed. 'It's not that easy, Donadze. I'm not giving it to you over the phone.'

'Why not, what difference does it make?'

'I don't know, maybe I want to hear you thank me in person.'

'No, that's not going—'

'Okay, never mind, I'll give it to someone else, maybe Misha Arziani or—'

'No. I'll meet you.'

'Thought so. There's a car wash on the Embankment, do you know it?'

'No,' Donadze lied.

'You'll find it. It's two fifteen now. Be there at two fifty.'

'It'll take me longer than that.'

'I thought you didn't know where it was? Listen, Donadze, I'm doing you a favour so don't fuck with me. Leave your car and walk—it's thirty minutes from your apartment. You'd better get going because I won't wait.'

'I'll be there.'

'Good. And make sure it's only you. Anyone else turns up and you'll never hear from me again,' the man said, ending the call.

Donadze looked at his phone for a moment then returned to the bedroom to scoop up the clothes he'd discarded the night before.

'You're not going out, are you?' Tamuna said from the bed, groggy with sleep.

He leaned over to kiss her. 'I won't be long.'

He carried his clothes out of the bedroom and quickly dressed, pulling on his shoes and collecting his pistol. He hurried out of the apartment, wanting to arrive ahead of the time specified by the caller. He thought about taking his car from the underground car park but realised it might be recognised. He pressed the elevator call button but decided not to wait for it. As he ran down the stairs, he used an app on his phone to call a taxi. The arrival time indicated eight minutes but it came in five. He told the driver to take Gotua Street, a narrow road running parallel to President Heydar Aliyev Embankment on the right bank of the River Kura. He stopped the taxi at a medical facility behind the car wash and checked his watch—he'd arrived nearly fifteen minutes early. He took out his phone, pinned his location and sent it to Jaqeli along with the message, *Call you in 1 hour.*

Donadze waited until the taxi had driven off before taking his pistol from its holster, sliding off the safety and cocking the hammer, the weapon now ready to fire. He'd checked his maps app on the short taxi ride and had identified a narrow lane connecting Gotua Street to the Embankment. He crossed to the unlit lane and stood stock-still, pistol held loosely by his side, allowing his eyes to adjust to the dim light and listening for movement or people talking. Seeing and hearing nothing of concern, he moved silently into the lane.

The car wash had huge capacity, with cars being washed manually or by machines located in multiple bays. It was closed overnight but the forecourt and office were protected by floodlights set on poles. He approached the premises from the rear and took cover behind the office.

He could see a car parked in a shaded area of the forecourt. The driver was smoking a cigarette, its tip glowing red as he inhaled, his smoke being exhaled through the open window in a long, soothing stream. He typed the car's plate number into his phone and sent it to Jaqeli.

Donadze checked his watch again—he had seven or eight minutes remaining. He continued to observe the car and its driver, listening for sound or movement in the area but hearing nothing other than road noise from vehicles speeding along the Embankment.

He returned his pistol to its holster—hammer cocked and safety on—and took a deep breath to steady his nerves. Stepping out from behind the office, he moved through shadows to approach the car from the rear.

The driver must have seen movement in his mirror. He startled then, indecisive for a moment, flicked his cigarette to the ground, its smouldering tip flaring red and sputtering off the broken asphalt.

'Who are you?' Donadze said, stooping to get a better look at the man.

The driver was wearing a balaclava, his identity hidden and Donadze knew he was in trouble. He took a step backwards, reaching for his pistol. He heard a rush of feet behind him and saw the driver throwing his door open. He didn't have time to clear and raise his pistol and he stepped forward and kicked the car door, using his weight and momentum to slam it shut. The driver screamed as his fingers were crushed between the door and pillar. Donadze was spinning to face the running men when he felt a blow behind his ear. Stunned and with his vision blurred, the men were on him, punching, kicking and pulling him to the ground. He knew he couldn't get to his feet and instinctively curled into a foetal position, his hands and arms covering his head as blows rained in until, at some point, a foot connected with the back of his head and he felt nothing more.

It took Donadze a moment to realise he wasn't wakening in his bed, that Tamuna wasn't beside him, that he was lying with his face pressed onto a hard, unforgiving surface. His hearing was the first sense to return; the rumble of fast-moving traffic on a nearby road. He managed to open one eye and saw black, broken asphalt and weeds stretching to his near horizon. His ears were ringing and someone was speaking to him as if under water. He tried to move his head and vomited, the pain from his chest excruciating, an acid sting in his nostrils. His memory of the fight began to return.

'Don't move, Ramaz,' a female voice, clearer now.

'Irina?'

'Yes, don't move, there's an ambulance coming. You're okay, just stay still for now.'

A man said something he couldn't understand.

Donadze spat vomit from his mouth, everything seemed to be moving slowly, a sharp pain in his chest as he breathed.

'Ramaz,' the man insisted. 'Do you know where you are?'

'Misha?' Donadze's head was clearing and pain was flooding his body. 'How…'

'You sent Irina your location—remember?'

'What were you thinking, Ramaz. Why didn't you call me?'

'Help me up…'

'No, stay there. The ambulance will be here soon,' Arziani said.

'Tamuna…'

He heard Arziani and Jaqeli conferring.

Jaqeli took his hand. 'Ramaz, listen to me. Misha will stay with you until the ambulance arrives. I'm going to your apartment to speak to Tamuna. Don't worry, she'll be okay. So will you.'

Pain was building and Donadze felt himself drifting out of consciousness.

'Stay awake, Ramaz,' Arziani commanded.

He forced his eyes open. 'When did you get here?'

'Don't worry about that for now. We'll talk in the hospital.'

'When?'

'You sent Irina your location. Said you'd call her in an hour. But she guessed you were doing something… rash. We got here as soon as we could.'

'Did you see them?'

'Yes, it looked like three men. They were pulling away as we arrived. I called it in but they could be anywhere by now.'

'You got the plate number I sent?'

'Yes, what was the model of the car?'

'BMW saloon, 3 series.'

'Switched then, the plate you saw came from a Toyota. What about the men who attacked you?'

'One had his face covered, didn't see the others…'

'Do you have any idea who they are?'

Donadze heard a siren. 'Is that the ambulance?'

'Yes, it'll be here soon. You know you've been lucky, don't you, Ramaz?'

'Lucky?'

'These men could have killed you, but they didn't—do you know who they are?' he asked again.

The ambulance pulled into the forecourt, its emergency lights flashing.

Donadze didn't answer and Arziani stood.

'What have we here?' one of the paramedics asked.

'This is Detective Lieutenant Ramaz Donadze,' Arziani said. 'He's been assaulted. Unconscious for maybe two minutes. Seems to be having trouble breathing, maybe a rib injury.'

Arziani stepped back as the paramedics got to work.

'What did you say?' one asked, stooping to hear Donadze speak.

'Maybe I do know who they are,' he said.

Gloveli peered into Donadze's hospital room. 'Can I come in?'

'Yes, of course,' Tamuna said. She stood and gave him a long, tight hug. 'Thanks for coming, Levan.'

He nodded and crossed stiffly to the bed.

'What brings you to the city, Major?' Donadze asked.

'I like to visit Gomorrah now and again—it reminds me why I left.' He took Donadze's hand and held it for a moment. 'What have you been up to now?'

Donadze forced a smile. 'It looks like I upset someone.'

'I hope you don't think this is funny, Ramaz,' Tamuna said, her eyes flashing. She placed a second chair by the bed and Gloveli lowered himself onto it.

The old policeman winced as he stretched his legs along

the vinyl floor. 'No, it's certainly not funny. How are you feeling?'

'I'm okay.'

'Well, you don't look okay.' He smiled at Tamuna. 'When did *you* get here?'

'I don't know, I think it was about five.'

'Well that's long enough. Why don't you get yourself something to eat? Rest for a while. I'll stay here till you get back.'

'I don't know. These men, Levan, do you think they could come back?'

'No, this is over now. He's safe, I promise you.'

'Levan's right, Tamuna. I'll be okay, why don't you get some rest.'

She looked uncertain. 'Okay, I know you two want to talk. I'll go now and speak to your doctor.' She looked at the wall clock. 'I'll be back in a couple of hours.'

'Take as long as you need, I'm not going anywhere,' Gloveli said. He waited until she'd left the room. 'How do you really feel?'

Donadze let out a long sigh. 'Like I've been hit by a train.'

'How's your breathing?'

'It hurts all the time.'

'Yes, bruised ribs will do that. Lucky for you they're not broken. You know you've got to keep taking deep breaths to help keep your lungs clear, don't you?'

'Yes, that's what Tamuna said.'

'Well she should know.' Gloveli leaned across the bed and lowered his voice. 'Don't worry, I'll take care of this,' he said.

'What do you mean?'

'You're a police officer, you've been ambushed and put in hospital. We need to find the men responsible.'

'And then what?'

'Better you don't know.'

'No, that's not what I want, Major.'

'Why not, they sent you a message, didn't they? You need to send them one back.'

'I don't think anyone sent me a message—I think I was being punished.'

'That doesn't make sense. If this was to do with your investigation then the chances are you got too close to something or somebody and you're being told to back off. There's no point in *punishing* you just for doing your job. Even the scum you come across would understand that.'

'Exactly, this has got nothing to do with the investigation or the *scum* we come across. As I said, it seems like I upset someone…'

'So if it's not your investigation…' Gloveli sat back in his chair, thinking. 'George Rapava…' he said at last.

Donadze's head sunk deeper into his pillow. He was exhausted and needed pain relief. 'Yes, George Rapava,' he said.

SIXTEEN

'How long are you being kept in?' Jaqeli asked.

Donadze's lips were cracked and swollen. 'The doctor said overnight, maybe two nights…'

'What did you say?'

'I said I might as well be home as in here.'

'Did Tamuna agree?'

'No.'

'I'm not surprised. Listen, Ramaz, I don't think you realise how upset she is. No woman wants to be woken in the middle of the night and told her husband's in hospital—condition unknown. How would you feel if it was the other way around?'

Donadze shook his head then closed his eyes as a wave of nausea hit him. 'I don't even want to think about it.'

'So you shouldn't make it any worse for her.'

'I suppose it's only one night.'

'Or two. If nothing else, you'll sleep well—no baby to wake you.' Jaqeli reached out to touch his battered face.

'Did Rapava really do that to you?'

'I think so. It's probably not the worst thing he's done.'

'But he wasn't there himself?'

'No, I would have recognised him. He knew that, couldn't take the chance.'

'Other cops?'

'That would be my guess.'

'From our station.'

'I don't know, maybe.'

'What are we going to do about it?'

'What we always do—find enough evidence to bring a prosecution.'

'Are you sure that's what you're going to do, Lieutenant?' Colonel Meskhi said from the doorway. 'Your friend, Major Gloveli had other ideas.'

Jaqeli stood. 'Sir,' she said as Meskhi crossed to the bed.

He looked down on Donadze. 'I spoke to your doctor. He said your injuries are largely superficial—other than bruising around your ribs. He was a little concerned about your concussion, however.'

'Yes, sir. But I was only out for about a minute.'

Meskhi looked at Jaqeli.

'A short time, Colonel. But at least two minutes,' she said.

'That's long enough—you can't take chances with brain trauma.' Meskhi raised a rare smile. 'But I'm sure you'll make a full recovery, Lieutenant.'

'Thank you, sir.'

'I'll leave you and Jaqeli to talk. Let me know if there's anything—'

Pain shot across Donadze's chest as he tried to sit up.

'Lie back, Lieutenant,' Meskhi said. 'What's on your mind?'

Donadze took a moment to catch his breath, 'The bank investigation.'

'Couldn't that wait? I'd rather you rested.'

'It could, sir, but—with respect—it shouldn't.'

Meskhi tugged his tightly creased trousers over his knees and lowered his tall frame onto the bedside chair. 'What's on your mind, Donadze?' he asked again.

'The First National Bank. We spoke to one of the tellers at Kazbegi Avenue branch. Her name's Nana Pachulia. She told me a stand-in manager called Berishvili has been behaving in ways which look suspicious.'

Donadze paused to gauge Meskhi's reaction. His eyes were closed.

'I'm listening, Lieutenant,' he said.

Donadze spoke slowly, fighting the pain in his chest. 'Berishvili was covering for Koba Brachuli after his wife was killed. But he was also doing some kind of clean-up. Nana noticed changes: paperwork being removed, files deleted. I asked if there could be a legitimate reason for him doing that—she didn't think there was. The bank was being sanitised.'

Meskhi opened his eyes and smiled. '*Sanitised*—that's rather a dramatic term, don't you think? But if the bank was being *sanitised*, what do you propose doing about it?'

'Get a warrant. Send in our financial investigators. Find out where the bank's money comes from, how it's being moved, where it goes to.'

'The entire First National Bank or just the Kazbegi Avenue branch?'

'We follow the money trail: head office; other

branches; their international operations.'

'No, that's far too wide. We'd never persuade a judge to issue a warrant based on a single employee believing something is amiss.'

'Then just Kazbegi Avenue to begin with.'

'*Just* Kazbegi Avenue. I'm sure you've heard Christoph Maier talk about the importance he places on his bank's reputation. What effect do you think a police investigation would have on that?'

'I can't worry about that, Colonel.'

'I know *you* can't.' Meskhi stood and straightened his trousers. 'I'll think about it.'

'Thank you, sir.'

'Get well, Donadze.' Meskhi looked down on the bed. 'And as for George Rapava—you'll leave him to me. Is that understood?'

'Who did this to you, *Ramazi*?' Donadze's mother asked, placing her warm, paper-dry hand on his forehead.

He had dreaded his mother coming, knowing how he must look to her but realising she would never have stayed away. 'I don't know, *Deda*. But we'll find them, won't we Soso?'

Chichua had picked his mother up from their apartment and brought her to the hospital. 'Yes, definitely,' he said.

Donadze took her hand in his. The harsh lighting had turned her face grey, her eyes shadowed, the lines around her mouth deep, her skin slack. He thought she looked old and exhausted. 'There's no need to worry, *Deda*. I'll be out tomorrow—there's not that much wrong with me.'

She looked doubtful. 'Are you in pain?'

'No, not much.'

She let out a long, deep sigh and eased herself onto the bedside chair.

'I'll leave you to talk, Mrs. Donadze,' Chichua said. 'I'll come and get you in about an hour if that's okay?'

She smiled at Chichua. 'Thank you, Soso. That's very kind of you.'

Chichua left the room, hitching his trousers as high on his waist as his swollen belly would allow.

'You're lucky to have such lovely friends, *Ramazi*,' his mother said.

'Yes, I am…'

She reached across to squeeze his hand. 'Is this worth it?'

'I think so, *Deda*.'

'I know *why* you think that. It's because of what happened to Ana,' she said, her voice faltering. 'But you have your own family now. You can't keep putting yourself at risk like this.'

'No, it wasn't for Ana. Not this time anyway. And I didn't think I was putting myself at risk. I thought I was going to be given information—I had to go.'

'Yes, but on your own?'

'That's not unusual.'

She smiled and squeezed his hand again. 'I didn't come here to nag you.'

'You're not. I had a similar conversation with Irina. She thinks I should see a psychologist.'

'A psychologist? Why?'

'To help me come to terms with what happened to Ana.'

His mother took a moment before answering. 'Are you going to see him?'

'Do *you* think I should?'

'No. How could you possibly *come to terms* with something like that? It was just *wrong* and should never have happened.' A red glow flushed her grey cheeks. 'I'm sorry, *Ramazi*. Irina gave you good advice—tell her you'll go.'

'No. I've already decided—I'm not going to see him.'

'Don't listen to me, you should go…'

'No, *Deda*. You're right. I don't want to come to terms with what happened to Ana, or to our family—and I don't think I should.' He let go of his mother's hand. 'How's Eka?' he asked, steering the conversation onto her favourite topic.

She smiled, happy to change the subject. 'She's lovely. You and Tamuna are so lucky.'

Donadze was tired and content to lie back and listen while his mother talked.

Time passed quickly and Chichua returned to the room. 'Are you ready to go home, Mrs Donadze?' he asked.

'Yes, thank you, Soso,' she said, picking her bag off the floor and standing.

Chichua was fidgeting by the bed. 'Everything okay, Soso?' Donadze asked.

'I don't know.' He patted his jacket pocket. 'I just had a call from Colonel Meskhi. He wants to see me tomorrow—eight o'clock at the station.'

'What does he want?'

'He didn't say. Do you think it's about you, Ramaz?'

Donadze thought for a moment. 'I think it could be,' he said.

Donadze had slept badly despite taking his painkillers. Tamuna had arrived as soon as hospital visiting rules allowed and told him he wouldn't be leaving hospital unless discharged by his doctor. Donadze hadn't argued but had already decided he was leaving that morning, regardless of what the doctor might think. He was out of bed, dressed and sitting on a chair—bored and impatient—when the doctor eventually arrived.

'Does this mean you're not enjoying our hospitality?' he asked, lifting Donadze's case notes from the rail at the foot of his bed.

'I'm enjoying it well enough, Doctor, but you've got people who need the bed more than me.'

'My patients normally let *me* decide that, Lieutenant.' He wrote something on the notes and returned them to the rail. 'I would have preferred to have kept you here another night—but that appears not to be an option?'

'It certainly wouldn't be a good option for me.'

The doctor gave a dubious grunt. 'So, what are your plans—if you insist on leaving us today?'

'He'll come home with me, Doctor,' Tamuna said. 'I've taken time off work to keep an eye on him and I'll assess his condition again tomorrow. He won't go back to work unless I think he's fit enough.'

Donadze had made the doctor aware that Tamuna was an orthopaedic surgeon.

'Well, you're in good hands then, Lieutenant.'

'I know, that's why I married her.'

The doctor gave the same dubious grunt and turned to Tamuna. 'You know what to watch for with minor brain trauma. The rest will take care of itself, given time.'

They had to wait for an orderly to arrive with a wheelchair to escort them off the premises. Misha Arziani was in the car park and stood by the door of his Mercedes as Donadze manoeuvred himself into the passenger's seat, trying not to wince as pain shot across his injured chest.

Arziani drove them home, moderating his customary driving style in consideration for his injured passenger. Tamuna fussed as Donadze extracted himself from the car and hovered as he crossed stiffly to the elevator, his face streaming sweat from the effort.

His mother was standing by the open apartment door. She looked at her son and shook her head sadly. 'Soso's here,' she said in a soft voice.

Chichua was in the living room. 'You're looking better, Ramaz,' he said, rising from the soft, low chair with some difficulty.

'Better than what?' Donadze said, declining Tamuna's help to sit. 'Have you seen Colonel Meskhi?'

'Yes, that's why I'm here.' He glanced towards Donadze's mother.

'I think Soso and Ramaz want to discuss police work, Tamuna,' she said. 'Shall we take Eka for a walk?'

'You don't have to leave,' Donadze said without conviction.

'Yes, we do,' his mother replied. She smiled at Arziani and Chichua. 'Thank you, Misha, Soso. Please help yourself to coffee, I doubt *Ramazi* is up to making it.'

Donadze waited until he heard the door closing. 'What did Meskhi want, Soso?'

'As I thought—it was about you. I'm glad we're on the same side because I wouldn't want him as an enemy.'

'What do you mean?'

'I wondered why he came to the station instead of getting me to go to his office. But it wasn't just me he wanted to see. He called everyone into the incident room—detectives, uniforms, admin—told them what had happened to you, how it had been a cowardly ambush—three against one. He said he knew police officers were behind it and that he had appointed me to find them. He said an attack on a fellow officer represented the worst kind of police corruption and finding the cops responsible was his highest priority. He *assured* everyone they *would* be found and warned them what would happen if they didn't cooperate with my investigation.'

'Wow,' Arziani said.

'Yes, I've never seen anything like it.'

'How can he be certain it was cops.'

'Process of elimination, he told me. He asked the right people and believed the answers they gave him.'

'Did he tell you who he thinks is behind it?'

'He didn't have to—I told *him*; if cops were responsible, it has to be George Rapava.'

'Did you know Rapava before he was appointed to Mtatsminda Station?'

'I've been around a long time, Ramaz. I know everyone.'

'And this is something he would do?'

'Yes, I think so.'

'Why did Colonel Meskhi pick you, Soso?' Arziani asked.

'As I said, I've been around a long time—I know everyone.'

'You realise this could be difficult for you, Soso,' Donadze said. 'A cop investigating other cops. Do you want me to speak to Meskhi, ask him to find someone else?'

'Meskhi gave me the option, I wasn't ordered to do it. No, these guys crossed a line, Ramaz—I want to do this.'

SEVENTEEN

Jaqeli picked up after a couple of rings. 'Aren't you meant to be resting?' she asked.

'I am, a phone call won't kill me.'

'How are you feeling, Ramaz?'

'I'm okay. I told Tamuna I'll go back to work tomorrow.'

'What did she say?'

Tamuna was feeding Eka in her high chair. He looked at her and winked. 'She didn't argue too much, surprisingly.'

'Well, don't rush back if you're not ready but it would be good if you do come in—there's a lot going on.'

'I know. Were you in the station when Meskhi came in?'

'Yes. It's hard to tell with him but I think he's furious about what happened to you. He's got everyone in the station terrified. Even me, and I'm completely innocent!'

Donadze laughed and felt an immediate stabbing pain

in his chest. 'I feel sorry for Soso,' he said after the pain had subsided.

'You shouldn't. No one I've spoken to is holding it against him. They know what happened to you was wrong.'

'How is he running his investigation?'

'He reckons he knows who could have been involved. Rapava made allies—dinosaurs like himself—everywhere he worked. Soso knows who they are. He's making a list and he's going to interview them—it'll just take one to crack and give up the others.'

'That doesn't look good for George then…'

'Or his crew. Listen, Ramaz, I'm glad you called. I'm just back from Kazbegi Avenue.'

'Okay…'

'I would have run this by you first but I didn't think I should bother you while you're recuperating.'

'That's okay. What was it?'

'I decided to speak to Koba Brachuli again. I visited the bank and told him I was there to give him an update. But I really wanted to test him on a couple of points, given that we think there's something going on at his branch.'

'That sounds like a good move. And probably better that I wasn't there, he might have felt we were harassing him otherwise.' He paused. 'So what points did you test him on?'

'Well, I asked him how Zaal was coping and if going to London was still an option. It still seems strange to me that he'd send his son away.'

'And to me. Is it still an option?'

'It's none of my business, apparently.'

'Exactly what he told me when I asked. What else?'

'I asked about his stand in—Berishvili. I tried to keep

it light; asked if he was happy that the bank had been run properly during his absence. But I really wanted to check his reaction. If Nana Pachulia noticed Berishvili was involved in some kind of a clean-up then Brachuli should have noticed as well. And if he did—why was he going along with it?'

'Let me guess; no issues whatsoever?'

'Pretty much. He said Berishvili is an experienced manager who routinely covers his and other branches. Everything was how it should be.'

'Was Nana Pachulia there?'

'Yes, behind her desk keeping her head down. I didn't speak to her.'

'Good. Did Brachuli ask where I was?'

'He did and I told him the truth. He made the right noises but didn't seem surprised—I think he already knew.'

'It's possible. The First National Bank—and Christoph Maier in particular—seem to be well informed. Maybe Maier heard what happened to me and passed it on to Brachuli. I'm not sure that tells us much, other than who's in and who's out the loop. What was your overall impression, Irina? Did Brachuli seem nervous, maybe acting like he had something to hide?'

'My overall impression is that Koba Brachuli is not a happy man—and not just because he lost his wife. And yes, I do think he's keeping something from us.'

'Well, let's see if we can figure out what that is.' He hesitated. 'One more thing, Irina. I've thought about what you said and I do appreciate your advice. But the psychologist: I'm not going to see him.'

He heard Jaqeli sigh. 'Why am I not surprised?'

Donadze was up and moving around the apartment—stiff and sore—before his alarm sounded. He swallowed painkillers with a glass of water and stood in front of the mirror to appraise his injuries: the bruising on his chest and legs had spread; a laceration above his right cheek had scabbed over but wasn't infected and the area around his right eye had darkened to multiple shades of purple and black. He held his nose between his thumb and forefinger and wiggled it from side to side. It had been broken and badly reset during Army service and he was relieved that no further damage had been inflicted during the assault.

He took a shower, struggling to bend and turn to dry himself and to get dressed, but refusing any assistance from Tamuna.

'You're looking better, *Ramazi*,' his mother said as he came out the bedroom.

She was spooning Eka baby food and Donadze—supporting his chest with his arm—leaned over to kiss the little girl. 'Yes, I'm feeling much better, *Deda*.'

She smiled in relief. 'Have something to eat.'

Donadze took it as a good sign that he was hungry. He eased himself onto a stool and ate some of the food his mother placed in front of him.

He finished his coffee and stood. The painkillers had kicked in and he felt a surge of optimism and an urgent need to get back to his investigation. He said goodbye to his family and took the elevator to ground level. He'd promised Tamuna he wouldn't drive and called a taxi to take him to Mtatsminda Station.

He got out of the taxi and walked to the entrance. The smoking fraternity was once again huddled in front of the doors, gratefully inhaling carcinogens deep into their lungs but noticeably more subdued without their leader—George Rapava.

They nodded their greetings as Donadze approached. 'Welcome back, Lieutenant,' Desk Sergeant Archil Nakania said, without conviction.

Donadze looked through the glass doors. A civilian was waiting in Reception for Nakania to finish his smoke. 'Thanks, Archil,' he said, extending his hand.

Nakania hesitated then took the outstretched hand. Donadze squeezed lightly and observed the Sergeant wince. He pulled him close, progressively increasing pressure on his hand until he felt the bones crush.

'Something wrong, Archil?' Donadze asked with mock concern.

Nakania used his free hand to push against Donadze's shoulder as he struggled to break free.

Donadze squeezed harder still and Nakania fell to his knees. 'Stop,' he gasped.

'What are you doing, Lieutenant?' a uniformed officer demanded.

Donadze released the Sergeant's hand and stood over him as he swayed drunkenly on his knees, cradling his injured fingers with his good hand.

'On your feet, Archil,' Donadze said. 'Soso Chichua wants to speak to you.'

Chichua entered the detectives' bureau, wiping his sweaty face with an off-white handkerchief as he approached Donadze's desk. He lifted a chair, placed it by the desk and lowered himself onto it with a deep sigh.

'Are you okay, Soso,' Jaqeli asked.

'I'm fine. Not sure about the rest of the station though. It's not every day their desk sergeant is accused of assaulting a senior officer.'

'No, it's not. What's he saying?' Donadze asked.

'That he doesn't know what's going on. That he wants to know why you—Lieutenant Donadze—assaulted him without provocation.'

'Without provocation? Did you ask how his hand got injured?'

'Yes, he tripped at home and hurt it trying to break his fall.'

'Do you believe him?'

'Of course not. How did you know it was Nakania, anyway?'

'I didn't—not until this morning.' Donadze sniffed the air. 'I think it was his cigarettes. He'd been smoking at the car wash and I remembered the smell when he tried to get out of his car.'

'When you crushed his hand with the door you mean?'

'He must have still been feeling a little delicate this morning.'

'Not delicate enough for my liking.'

Donadze shrugged. 'Don't take it personally, Soso. Play by the rules—he's not worth anything more than that.'

Chichua laughed. 'Just like you did, Ramaz?' He shook his head. 'Turkish cigarettes are distinctive I suppose—but plenty of men in Georgia smoke them. What if you'd got it wrong? It'd have been assault in front of witnesses.'

'What would you have done, Soso?'

'Something similar,' Chichua admitted.

'Was Nakania on your list of suspects?' Jaqeli asked.

'No, but he should have been because I knew he was thick with George Rapava. Maybe not so much now though.'

'You could have a way-in with him, Soso,' Jaqeli said. 'Nakania didn't get the chance to actually assault Ramaz, so maybe you could offer him a lesser charge—providing he gives up the others.'

'Yes, but that's not my decision, Irina. Colonel Meskhi told me to call him if there were any developments—I've done that and he's going to be here soon. We'll be interviewing him together, you could watch if you want.'

Donadze thought for a moment. 'I don't think I want to do that. Nakania's already put himself in a bad place, there's no need for me to gloat.'

Chichua heaved himself to his feet and hitched his trousers. 'Well, as you say, Ramaz, *he* put himself in that place. You shouldn't feel sorry for him now.'

'I know and I don't.' He stood and patted Chichua's arm. 'Thanks, Soso. Good luck with the interview.'

Chichua nodded and walked out the bureau.

'He's not as tough as he likes people to think,' Jaqeli said.

Donadze remembered how upset Chichua had been on finding Sophia Brachuli's body in her apartment. 'I know, it's not just a job for him.'

His phone rang—Colonel Meskhi.

'*Gamarjoba*, sir.'

'You're back at work, Donadze?'

'Yes, sir. I was—'

'Good. I'm approving your recommendation to investigate possible financial irregularities at First National Bank—their Kazbegi Avenue branch specifically.'

'That's very good—'

'We have a meeting with Christoph Maier at three. Be ready to leave at two thirty.'

'No, we shouldn't do that, Colonel. It'll give Maier a chance to cover his—'

'I'm not debating this with you, Donadze. I'll be finished with Sergeant Nakania by two thirty—be ready to leave then.'

'Yes, sir,' Donadze said, but Meskhi had already hung up.

'You're looking quite pale, Lieutenant. Are you sure you're fit to be at work?'

'I've just taken more pain killers, sir. They've not kicked in yet but I'm feeling fine.'

'Very well. Let's go, I'll brief you on Sergeant Nakania in the car.'

Donadze struggled to keep pace as Meskhi strode out of the station. A black SUV was waiting for them, its grill lights flashing red and blue. The uniformed driver jumped out of the car and held the door open for Meskhi while Donadze eased himself in, wincing as he reached to pull the heavy door closed. The driver returned to his place behind the wheel and looked in his rear view mirror. Meskhi nodded and the car moved quickly into the traffic.

'Did your interview go well, sir?' Donadze asked.

'Confirming that four of my officers conspired to assault another officer is not something I would consider as *going well.*'

Meskhi sighed and took out his phone, frowning as he read and responded to texts and emails while Donadze—awkward and self-conscious—sat in silence as the car bullied its way through the congested streets.

Meskhi appeared to have caught up after about ten minutes and returned his phone to his pocket. 'Sergeant Nakania…' he said at last.

'Did he admit to being involved, sir?'

Meskhi shrugged. 'It didn't take much. He tried to justify himself on the grounds that you betrayed some kind of police brotherhood *omerta* when you made allegations against George Rapava. Utter nonsense of course, especially as *he* was happy enough to give up Rapava and the others.'

'Who were they?'

Meskhi named a sergeant and a detective from different police stations. 'Do you know them?' he asked.

'No, I don't think so.'

'Both close to Rapava I believe. I'll be talking to them soon.'

'And then what, Colonel?'

'They'll be dismissed and brought up on criminal charges.'

'Prison will be difficult for them.'

Meskhi shrugged. 'They should have thought about that before assaulting you.'

Donadze let a moment pass. 'Will you be appointing a new station commander, Colonel?'

'Are you asking me for the job?'

'No sir, but I would recommend Misha Arziani—this is the second time he's stood in as commander.'

'You have more seniority than Lieutenant Arziani, don't you?'

'Yes, but I think Misha is more suited to a command role than me.'

'*Misha* is? I'll bear that in mind but I'm in no rush to appoint anyone—especially as I seem to have got it wrong with Rapava.'

The car turned onto Galaktioni Bridge to cross the River Kura, the Bank's head office a few minutes away.

'Christoph Maier, sir? What are you going to tell him?'

Meskhi was looking out his window at the Biltmore Hotel, the huge blue-glass tower looming over the river, a metaphor for careless city planning. He shook his head. 'What an eyesore,' he said.

'Yes, Colonel. But Christoph Maier—what will you tell him?'

Meskhi looked surprised by the question. 'This is your case, Donadze. It was your recommendation to investigate the Bank. What *you* tell Christoph Maier is entirely up to you.'

EIGHTEEN

The car stopped in front of First National Bank's oversized doors. The driver glanced in his mirror and Meskhi shook his head, declining his assistance to get out. He stepped onto the wide pavement and waited for Donadze to join him. 'One hour,' he said and the driver nodded and drew away.

'Have you been here before, Colonel?' Donadze asked.

'No.'

'This way then.'

Emzar Kesaria was talking to the receptionist Donadze had met previously. She said something and Kesaria turned, switched on his smile and crossed to greet them.

'Colonel Meskhi?' he queried, offering his hand while Donadze introduced the two.

Kesaria looked at Donadze's battered face and grimaced. 'You've been in an accident, Lieutenant?'

'Something like that,' he said, suspecting Kesaria already knew how he'd received his injuries.

'Well, I hope you'll recover soon.'

Donadze smiled but didn't reply.

'Mr Maier is waiting for us. No need for security passes today, I'll be with you at all times. This way, please.'

They crossed to the stairway and Kesaria stopped and turned to Donadze. 'Our meeting room is on the next level. Will the stairs be a problem for you, Lieutenant?'

Donadze knew that climbing the stairs would be agony but he forced a smile and said, 'No problem at all.'

He gritted his teeth and followed Kesaria and Meskhi up the stairway. They walked a short distance to a door marked *Meeting Room 1* and Kesaria fixed his smile and opened it.

Christoph Maier was at the top end of a large oval conference table. Lekso Berishvili, the stand-in branch manager sat on his left and a woman who Donadze didn't recognise, was on his right.

'Colonel Meskhi, sir,' Kesaria said.

'And Lieutenant Donadze…' Maier added, scrutinising his injuries with obvious distaste and declining to stand or offer his hand. 'Take a seat, gentlemen.'

Meskhi stood in the doorway for a moment then crossed the room, straightening the creases in his trousers as he sat opposite Maier. '*Guten Tag,* Christoph,' he said.

Maier smiled and nodded. '*Gamarjoba* Gabi. Welcome to First National Bank.'

Donadze sat beside Meskhi. He nodded to the branch manager and looked to the woman on Maier's right.

'Gentlemen,' Kesaria said, hovering at the head of the table. 'This is Inga Palagi, our chief legal officer. Lieutenant, I think you've already met Lekso Berishvili, our branch manager.'

'Sit down, Emzar,' Maier said.

Kesaria appeared to consider which side of the table to choose then eventually took a seat beside the lawyer.

'What can I do for you, Gabi?' Maier said.

'Thanks for seeing us, Christoph. Lieutenant Donadze is leading our investigation and he will advise you how we intend proceeding.'

Maier raised his eyebrows and turned his attention to Donadze. 'Lieutenant?'

Donadze coughed self-consciously. 'Herr Maier, a short time ago you committed your bank to support our inquiries. In that spirit, we require your active participation in the financial investigation of your Kazbegi Avenue branch.'

Maier sat back and smiled. 'If I recall, Lieutenant, you suggested your investigation would cover all our branches, this office and even our UK operations?'

'We only need to look at Kazbegi Avenue—for now.'

Maier's mouth turned down. 'For now?'

Palagi spoke for the first time. 'I presume you've secured a court order?'

Meskhi took an envelope from his jacket pocket and slid it across the desk. She extracted a document, scanned it and nodded.

Maier frowned. 'Tell me, Lieutenant, what exactly do you expect to find at Kazbegi Avenue?'

'We don't know, maybe nothing if Mr Berishvili has done his job properly.'

Berishvili sat up in his seat. 'What do you mean by—'

'Thank you, Lekso,' Maier interrupted him. 'I'm sure Lieutenant Donadze isn't alleging any improper behaviour on your part.'

'Of course not,' Donadze said, smiling at the branch manager.

'We're not alleging anything, Christoph,' Meskhi said in an even tone. 'But the characteristics of this robbery and the murders are unusual and we feel it may be helpful to take a closer look at your branch.'

Maier turned to Kesaria. 'Well, Emzar it appears that Lieutenant Donadze has legal authority to send his investigators into Kazbegi Avenue. How may we best support him?'

Kesaria appeared to think for a moment. 'This will be quite disruptive for staff, sir. Especially for Koba Brachuli. We should appoint someone from outside the branch to support him.'

'You?'

'No, I'm not familiar enough with the operation there. Lekso would be the obvious choice.'

Maier turned to Meskhi. 'Reputation, Gabi. It's everything for my bank. Any accusation of impropriety—albeit a false accusation—could be very damaging. I trust your investigation will *not* be conducted in full media glare.' He looked at Donadze. 'Tempting though such publicity may be.'

Meskhi smiled. 'You're not accused of anything, Christoph. And any media interest won't be initiated by us.'

Maier let his eyes linger on Donadze. 'I hope so.' He appeared to come to a decision. 'Very well, the First National Bank fully supports this investigation. Lekso, you will liaise with Lieutenant Donadze and assist him in whatever way he requires.' He looked around the room. 'Is there anything else?'

Meskhi leaned across the table to shake Maier's hand. 'Thanks for your support, Christoph.'

Maier nodded. 'Emzar, see these gentlemen out.'

Donadze waited until Meskhi's car had driven off before reaching for his pain killers, swallowing two of the tablets dry. It was more than an hour until the dose was due but his ribs were aching and he was exhausted from the meeting with Christoph Maier. He checked his watch—it was just after four and he resolved to return home early to rest.

He walked along Marjanishvili Square and took a seat in the patio of the first coffee shop he came to. His drinks arrived quickly and he took a gulp of his water. He added six sugars to his coffee before taking a tentative sip—it was as strong as he'd hoped and cool enough to drink. He took out his phone and called Jaqeli.

'How did it go?' she asked.

'It was okay. Although Christoph Maier seemed a bit more relaxed than I would have liked.'

'You expected him to resist the investigation?'

'He couldn't—not with a court order in place. But I'd hoped he would have been more worried about it. "*Reputation, Gabi. It's everything for my bank,*"' Donadze said, impersonating the banker's Viennese accent.

'Why do you think he's not worried?'

'Possibly because there's nothing left for us to find.'

'No, I don't believe that. You can't just remove or delete stuff without leaving a trail. If something's not right, our finance people will find it.'

'I hope you're right. We've been assigned Tina Ninua—the woman who helped you investigate Vano Chedia's affairs.'

'Tina seemed pretty good to me, I'm sure she'll do a good job for us.'

'She'll do what she can but she may find it difficult. When it comes to finance, the First National Bank can afford the best. If I were a financial expert I'd be working for the Bank, not the police.'

'No you wouldn't. Have more faith, Ramaz—Tina's good.' Jaqeli paused. 'So what's the plan?'

'Tina's coming to Mtatsminda tomorrow at eight. We'll brief her then go to the bank after that.'

'Do we need to do anything before then?'

'Yes, I was thinking about Nana Pachulia. We don't want anyone at the bank to suspect she's helping us. Could you speak to her this evening? Tell her we'll be at the branch tomorrow but ask her to act naturally. We'll do the same. I don't want anyone else to know about her—not even Tina.'

'Do you think she's at risk?'

Donadze hesitated. 'No, but I made a mistake. I was trying to unsettle Berishvili and I let slip that we knew he'd been cleaning up the branch.'

'And Nana was one of the few people who could have told us that…'

'Yes, it was stupid of me. Meskhi smoothed things over but I should have been more careful.'

Jaqeli didn't reply and Donadze took her silence as agreement that he had been careless—or stupid.

'It's done, Irina. I can't change things now.'

Jaqeli hesitated. 'Ramaz, do you think you're ready to

be back at work? The painkillers you're taking—do you think they could have affected your judgement?'

He bit back a terse response. 'It's possible,' he conceded, eventually. 'I'll see you tomorrow, Irina.'

Donadze ordered a taxi, left enough money on the table to cover a tip then stood and walked to the pavement edge. He looked up and down the road then took a few more stiff steps to the nearest storm drain. He took the painkillers from his pocket, unscrewed the lid and poured the contents of the bottle into the drain. He put the empty bottle back in his pocket and stood for a moment—thinking about Nana Pachulia—then stepped back from the pavement edge to wait for his taxi.

Donadze had barely slept but felt more alert having not taken painkillers. He resolved that, regardless of the pain and his stiff, bruised flesh, his life would return to normal that morning. He drove himself to Mtatsminda Station and parked. There were no smokers at the entrance and a smartly dressed young cop, his sergeant's chevrons proudly displayed on his upper arms, was on duty at the desk.

'Promotion, Dato?' Donadze asked.

The young officer smiled and patted his stripes. 'Only confirmed yesterday, Lieutenant.'

'Very well deserved, Sergeant,' Donadze said, thinking the station already looked and felt more professional under Misha Arziani's stewardship.

He walked to the detectives' bureau.

Arziani was talking on his phone in the station

commander's office. He raised his hand in greeting, put the phone down and crossed to Donadze's desk.

'Hey, Misha,' Donadze said. 'That office suits you.'

Arziani laughed. 'Thanks. I heard you're bringing Tina Ninua in this morning.'

'That's right. You used to go out together, didn't you?'

Arziani shrugged. 'It was a while ago.'

'Is that going to be awkward?'

'No, it'll be fine. Listen Ramaz, I don't have to say this, but you'll keep me up to speed on the bank investigation, won't you? I know you report directly to Colonel Meskhi but I think I need to be in the loop as well.'

'Of course you do, but Irina knows everything I know—just ask her.'

'No point, she wouldn't speak to me unless you okayed it. She's only respecting the chain of command of course.'

'But you're our boss, Misha. You're at the top end of the chain.'

Arziani grimaced. 'Yes, but it'd still be better if you told her it was okay.'

Donadze knew that Arziani was ambitious and wanted his temporary promotion to be made permanent. That would be more likely if he could demonstrate he was on top of all police business at Mtatsminda Station. 'No problem, Misha. I'll tell her it's okay to discuss the case with you,' he said.

His phone rang—the Desk Sergeant advising him that Tina Ninua had arrived. He promised Arziani an update later in the day and left to meet her.

She stood as Donadze approached.

'Tina?' he said. 'I'm Ramaz Donadze.'

She was about thirty, slim and pretty, her highlighted brown hair cut shoulder length. She had dressed in a dark-blue trouser suit with flat business-like shoes and was holding an expensive looking briefcase. Donadze thought she'd look more at home in a board room than a police station.

She was too polite to ask about his battered face and smiled, holding out her hand. 'Lieutenant,' she said.

Jaqeli was waiting for them in the incident room. 'Nice to see you again, Tina,' she said.

'How much do you know about this investigation?' Donadze asked.

'A little. I helped Irina dig out some information on a First National employee a few days ago—Vano Chedia. Nothing much there as I recall other than finding money deposited in an offshore account. I know we're going to look at the branch where Chedia was killed.'

'Yes. There's a lot about this robbery which doesn't seem to make sense.' He glanced at Jaqeli. 'And we think someone from First National has gone into Kazbegi Avenue branch to hide, remove or destroy evidence. We need your help to understand what's been going on there.'

Tina had sensed his caution. 'When you say you *think* someone has tampered with evidence…'

He didn't want to compromise Nana Pachulia further. 'We received information to suggest that,' he said. 'It's better we don't say any more for the moment.'

Tina nodded. 'I understand. Well, what is it you want me to do?'

'Follow your usual methods. Check as much as you can. If evidence *has* been tampered with, what was the Bank trying to hide? Try to establish if other parts of First National are involved. If so, help us build the justification for looking there.'

'How long will you need, Tina?' Jaqeli asked.

She shrugged. 'It depends on what I find. How deep I have to go. Probably three to five days and another day to pull my report together.'

Donadze looked at his watch. 'Okay,' he said. 'We'd better get going.'

NINETEEN

The Kazbegi avenue branch of the First National Bank did not open for business that morning. A sign on the door stated it was closed for *technical reasons* and apologised to customers for the inconvenience caused.

Nana Pachulia was hovering by the entrance as they arrived. She let them in and locked the door behind them. The blinds on the windows and door were drawn shut and the premises felt closed-in and oppressive.

'Your face, Lieutenant...' she said.

Donadze touched the wound above his cheek. 'It's nothing.'

She shook her head, unconvinced. 'Mr Berishvili is waiting for you.'

Donadze glanced at the manager's office. The door was closed. 'Isn't Koba coming in today?' he asked.

'I don't know, please ask Mr Berishvili.'

He turned to Tina and Jaqeli. 'Wait here.'

He crossed to the office, knocked on the door and pushed it open. Berishvili was at his desk reading a document, a gold fountain pen in his hand. He smiled at Donadze, made a notation on the document and put the pen on his desk. '*Gamarjoba*, Lieutenant.' He looked at his wall clock. 'Didn't we say nine?'

'I thought you were here to support Brachuli, not to substitute for him.'

'Mr Maier told him to stay home. He was worried your investigation would be too stressful.'

'That was considerate of Herr Maier.'

'He's a considerate man.' Berishvili looked at his wall clock again. 'Are you ready to start?'

'We'll need somewhere to work.'

'Like a conference room you mean? Sorry, there's nothing like that here.' Berishvili sighed. 'You can use this office. I don't suppose I'll get any work done today anyway.'

'We'll also need some help with your records. The young woman who let us in—Nana?'

'Nana Pachulia—yes.'

'Does she know your systems well enough?'

'Nana!' Berishvili shouted without warning.

She appeared at the door a moment later, a fawn caught in headlights.

'I want you to work with Lieutenant Donadze today,' he said. 'He wants you to help send Mr Brachuli to jail.'

'Sir?' Nana said, startled.

Berishvili shook his head. 'Just do what the Lieutenant tells you.' He picked up his pen. 'Give me ten minutes.'

Donadze left the office, shutting the door behind him. He walked with Nana to the tellers' desks.

'He knows,' she whispered.

'No, he doesn't. Just be yourself, everything will be okay.'

Tina had placed her open briefcase on top of a filing cabinet and was sifting through documents.

'Tina, this is Nana,' Donadze said. 'She'll help you find anything you need.'

'Hey, Nana,' Tina said, offering her hand. 'That'll be useful.' She glanced at Donadze and he realised she'd guessed the source of his information.

He shook his head in warning and she nodded in reply.

Donadze looked at the closed office door. 'I'm not sure how cooperative Berishvili will be…'

'It doesn't matter,' Tina said. 'The outcome will be the same, it might just take a little longer…'

'I'm going to leave you with Irina, I'll check in with you later today.'

'Where are you going, Ramaz?' Jaqeli asked.

'To speak to Koba Brachuli—Christoph Maier doesn't strike me as the considerate type.'

The apartment block on Abashidze Street was sparkling in the midday sun as Donadze parked near its gated entrance and crossed to the lobby. He took the elevator to the fifth level and walked to Amelia Nanava's door. He rang the bell and waited. There was muffled noise inside but no one came to the door. He rang the bell more insistently and heard locks turning and bolts sliding back.

Koba Brachuli opened the door. He was wearing

tracksuit trousers and a T-shirt printed with a faded Rolling Stones logo. His feet were bare. He looked at Donadze through red, puffy eyes and coughed to clear his throat. 'Okay,' he croaked and leaned against the door while Donadze walked past him into the lounge.

The blinds on the floor-to-ceiling windows were closed, the room dark and dismal. The television was booming, its screen's high resolution and the clarity of the sound somehow accentuating the mediocrity of the production Brachuli was watching.

Donadze traced the room's acrid stench to a plate balanced on the arm of an easy chair, a collection of cigarette butts ground onto its patterned glaze.

Brachuli shuffled into the lounge and fell heavily onto the chair, knocking his makeshift ashtray to the floor. 'What do you want?' he said, his tongue thick.

Donadze turned the television off. He wondered if Brachuli had been drinking and glanced around the room looking for an open bottle or glass but saw nothing.

'You're not looking so good, Koba,' he said.

'Are you married, Lieutenant?'

'Yes.'

'What's your wife's name?'

Donadze hesitated. 'Tamuna,' he said.

'Does she love you?'

'I hope so.' He nodded to himself. 'Yes, she does.'

'You're a lucky man then. I loved my wife, she loved me…'

'I'm sure she did. Where's Zaal?'

'Amelia took him to school.' He reached into his pocket to retrieve his cigarettes. He fumbled one from the packet and lit it with a shaky hand.

'You didn't go to work today?'

'Do I look like t*he friendly face of banking?* he asked, laughing at his own joke. He stopped abruptly and his mouth turned down. 'No, Berishvili told me to stay home.'

'Berishvili told you?'

'Yes, Berishvili.'

Donadze paused. 'He thought it'd be too stressful for you?'

Brachuli laughed. 'Yes, I'm sure that was the reason.'

'You know why we're at your branch, don't you?'

'Of course I do.'

'What do you think we'll find there?'

Brachuli shook his head but didn't answer.

'You could help us, Koba. It'd be easier for you—easier for Zaal and Amelia—if you did.'

'No,' he said. 'It wouldn't.'

'It's only a matter of time.'

'I know.' He noticed the cigarette smouldering between his fingers, the ash teetering and ready to drop onto his lap. He looked for the plate and seemed surprised to find it lying on the floor. It hadn't broken and he picked it up and ground the half-smoked cigarette onto it with more venom than either deserved. 'Sometimes you're given no choice, Lieutenant,' he said. 'I hope that never happens to you.'

'Let me help you, Koba.'

'You can't.' Brachuli stood. 'Are we done?'

Donadze also stood and put his hand on Brachuli's shoulder. 'It doesn't have to be like this.'

Brachuli turned his head and stared at Donadze's hand until he took it away. 'I'll show you out,' he said.

Donadze returned to his car. Spring had given way to summer and he closed his eyes to absorb the warm rays streaming through the glass.

He had been shocked by Koba Brachuli's appearance and demeanour. Brachuli had seemed to accept the police investigation would uncover wrong doings at his branch, but what had he meant when he'd said, 'Sometimes you're given no choice'?

Donadze was tired, his body stiff and sore. The car was comfortable and warm. He felt himself sinking into delicious, restful sleep and told himself, *why not?* His head jerked forward a moment later. He willed his eyes open, cranked down his window, took two deep breaths and started his engine. He took a moment to recover his senses then joined the traffic rumbling along Abashidze Street.

He still felt groggy as he parked on Kazbegi Avenue. The bank's doors remained locked and he knocked on the glass to attract attention. A moment passed and Nana Pachulia drew back the slats on a window blind and peered out. She nodded, closed the slats and let him in.

Lekso Berishvili was perched on an uncomfortable looking chair in the waiting area, his laptop on his knees, a second chair enlisted as a makeshift desk. He looked up as Donadze approached, shook his head and returned to his laptop.

'Having fun, Lekso?' Donadze asked as he walked to the manager's office.

The door was closed and he knocked and went in. Tina Ninua was behind the desk, folders organised into short stacks in front of her. Jaqeli was sitting to her side, phone in her hand and looking bored.

'Found anything?' Donadze asked.

'Still looking,' Jaqeli said. She brought her finger to her lips.

Donadze nodded, the office might be bugged. 'How's Berishvili been?'

Jaqeli rolled her eyes. 'He's been cooperative, probably a bit upset that we've disrupted his day.'

'That's understandable.' He winked. 'It was good of him to give up his office. Do you need me to stay?'

Jaqeli looked at Tina. 'No, why don't we get back together at the station? Is five okay?'

Donadze nodded. 'Keep digging.'

Berishvili stood as Donadze crossed towards him. 'Mr Maier wants to know what's happening.'

'He called you?'

'Emzar Kesaria called me. What will I tell him?'

'Tell him our investigation is ongoing.'

Berishvili shook his head derisively. 'Is that the best you can do?'

'It is for now. See you tomorrow, Lekso,' Donadze said, walking to the door.

Donadze realised he'd been neglecting his family. He worried they would get used to his prolonged absences and that he'd become progressively less important in their lives. He hoped his anxiety was largely a reflection of his own insecurity but he resolved to keep his meeting with Tina

Ninua and Irina Jaqeli brief and to return home as soon as possible afterwards.

Jaqeli seemed to sense his urgency but Tina loved her job and loved talking about it even more. She insisted on explaining her investigatory processes which—Donadze surmised—involved nothing more than data collection and analysis.

She explained that she was in data collection phase but would eventually be able to track the movement of nearly all monies going in and out of the Kazbegi Avenue branch.

He asked if she'd come to any tentative conclusions and she conceded there appeared to be an unusually large number of cash and non-cash transactions for a branch of that size. But she refused to speculate if that indicated evidence of money laundering or other illicit activities.

Misha Arziani took up more of their time by dropping in to say hello to Tina. She gave him a hug and they exchanged pleasantries for a while. Arziani clearly felt awkward in the company of both his former and current girlfriends and Donadze noticed him glancing at Jaqeli, trying to gauge her mood while she unsuccessfully hid her amusement.

Arziani eventually asked for an update on their investigation and that gave Donadze an excuse to leave Tina and Jaqeli on their own while they went to the station commander's office.

'I'm glad that wasn't awkward for you,' Donadze said.

'What wasn't awkward?' Arziani asked, with studied lack of guile.

Donadze decided to let him off the hook. 'Don't

worry, Misha. Irina knows all about you and Tina and she's clearly not worried. Why would she be?'

'Tina told her?'

'They've been working together and had to talk about something—why not talk about you?'

'I should have mentioned it to her.'

'Yes, that would have been a good idea.'

Arziani looked relieved. He gave Donadze his characteristic, cheerful smile. 'Not often you get to give relationship advice, Ramaz.'

'No it's not, thanks for the opportunity.'

Arziani laughed and punched him on the shoulder. 'So, all good then.' He paused. 'Tell me about your investigation.'

Donadze summarised the case to date while Arziani jotted notes on a pad.

He glanced at the pad. 'So this bank manager—Koba Brachuli—admitted there's something off at his branch?'

'No, he wouldn't go that far. But he didn't deny it either.'

'That's strange, isn't it?'

'He knows we'll find something, he might just be beyond denying it any longer.'

Arziani nodded and closed the pad. 'Thanks, Ramaz. It feels like we're making progress.'

'Yes,' Donadze agreed. 'It feels that way to me as well.'

He excused himself and hurried home, arriving at his apartment as his mother was serving their meal.

She staggered as she straightened for his kiss, taking a moment to steady herself against a stool.

Donadze took her arm. 'Are you okay, *Deda*?' he asked.

'Of course I am.' She smiled. 'I just stood up too quickly, that's all.'

'Good timing, Ramaz,' Tamuna said, coming into the living room. 'Your daughter needs her nappy changed.'

Donadze looked at his mother uncertainly then crossed the room to kiss Tamuna. He held out his hands to take the baby. 'Okay, *chemo gogona,*' he said, blowing a raspberry on the little girl's belly. 'Let's get this done.'

His mother's food was delicious and comforting as always, and especially so when accompanied by two glasses of *Mukuzani*. He felt mellow and would have been content to stay home, to doze on his chair, to go to bed early and—if things worked out as he hoped—to make love to his wife.

He forced himself out of his lethargy. 'Let's go for a walk,' he said.

Tamuna looked at Donadze's mother, her question unspoken.

'Yes, that's okay,' she said. 'I'll put the baby to bed.'

They left the apartment and Tamuna took Donadze's arm as they joined couples and groups of young people strolling in the early summer's warmth.

'How are you feeling now?' Tamuna asked.

'Good. I'm a quick healer.'

'No one's that quick.'

'I am—I'll prove it you later,' he said, squeezing her arm.

'Big talk, Lieutenant Donadze.'

He heard his phone buzz.

Tamuna heard it as well. 'Take it, Ramaz,' she sighed.

Donadze drew her to the side of the pavement. 'Hey, Irina.'

'Sorry, Ramaz. I thought you'd want to know. Amelia Nanava just called. Koba's missing, she's worried that something's happened to him.'

'Why would she think that? It's not late, maybe he just went out for a walk or to buy cigarettes.'

'No, he's taken his car but left his phone and wallet. And his apartment keys. She thinks it's because he isn't coming back.'

'He didn't leave a note to say where he was going?'

'Nothing. She's worried, Ramaz.'

'Okay, put out an APB,' Donadze said. 'Koba Brachuli is a person of interest and we've to be notified if he's found.'

'Do you think he's on the run?'

Donadze's gut clenched. 'I hope so,' he said.

TWENTY

Donadze and Jaqeli arrived at the scene, pulling up on the narrow road behind a patrol car and two vans belonging to the forensic examiner and the Tbilisi fire department. Crime scene tape had been strung between trees and a uniformed officer was controlling access to the cut in the woods where Koba Brachuli's car had been found.

An elderly man walking his dog near Lake Lisi had found the body. He'd thought the figure reclined on the car seat was sleeping or sick until he'd read the warning signs taped to the windows—TOXIC KEEP CLEAR! As a retired water engineer, he'd recognised the rotten-egg stench and had called the police, warning them that the car's interior was probably full of poisonous hydrogen sulphide gas and that the occupant was almost certainly dead. The police had identified the car's owner as Koba Brachuli and Jaqeli had been notified as the APB required.

Natia Gagua was the duty forensic examiner. She was

in a huddle with two firemen. One was being helped to don protective coveralls and gloves. A self-contained breathing apparatus set was lying on the ground behind them.

Gagua saw Donadze approach and gave him a huge, toothy smile. 'Ramaz Donadze! My dream come true,' she gushed, clasping her hands to her heart and fluttering her eyelashes. Gagua was, by Donadze's estimation, the best examiner in her department but he knew she viewed him as an easy tease.

'Hey, Natia,' he said, frowning at the grinning firemen. 'When did you get here?'

Gagua sighed theatrically then got down to business. 'About ten minutes ago.' She nodded to Jaqeli. 'Irina,' she said, offering her binoculars. 'Recognise him?'

Jaqeli focused the binoculars on the car. 'Yes, that's Koba Brachuli, our missing person,' she said. 'Does it look like suicide to you?'

'That's how it looks,' Gagua said. 'Or that's how it's been made to look, possibly.'

'What's your plan?' Donadze asked.

'My plan is to retrieve the body. You've heard of chemical suicide?'

'Yes, you mix up chemicals in an enclosed space and the gas kills you.'

'That's right. It's a common method now. All you need are ordinary cleaning products. It's the way to go if you're that way inclined but the gas can be dangerous for responders. We need to make it safe.'

The fireman was pulling on his breathing apparatus. He opened a valve and pressed the mask to his face to test his air supply. 'Okay?' he asked.

'Yes,' Gagua said. 'Remember, try not to disturb the scene too much. Watch out for footprints. Try to open the front passenger door and if it's locked smash the glass—but use just enough force to break it. Don't walk round the car trying different doors. You'll probably see the chemicals he used on the seats or on the floor—leave them there. We just want the car ventilated with as little disruption as possible.' She gave the fireman a smile. 'Thanks, Giorgi.'

'No problem.' He held the mask to his face, tightened the straps and changed the demand valve setting so that air flowed into the mask. His colleague handed him an axe and he walked to the front of the car. The passenger door was unlocked and he was back in less than a minute.

'Did you see a note, Giorgi?' Donadze asked.

The fireman took off his mask and poured water from a bottle over his head and face. 'No, but I wasn't looking for one either.'

Donadze nodded. 'What now, Natia?'

Gagua looked at her watch. 'We'll give it thirty minutes then Giorgi will test for any residual gas and then…' She smiled at Donadze. 'It's business as usual.'

Donadze nodded. 'We'll have to notify Amelia… and Zaal.'

'Do you want me to go?' Jaqeli asked. 'You could stay here with Natia.'

'No, I'd like us to go together.' He turned to Gagua. 'When can you let us know what happened here?'

'I think suicide is a reasonable assumption for now. I'll check the scene and call you in a couple of hours with my preliminary findings if that's okay?'

Donadze held out his hand to take the binoculars. He

focused the powerful instrument on the body. Brachuli looked peaceful, his eyes closed as if sleeping and ready to be shaken awake. He remembered his conversations with the dead man, his initial strength after losing his wife transforming to despair, his love for his son. 'Why did you do it, Koba?' he mumbled. 'What was going on in your head?'

'Did you say something, Ramaz?' Jaqeli asked.

He shook his head and handed the binoculars back to Gagua. 'No,' he said. 'Let's go, we'd better let Amelia know what's happened.'

'Are you okay, Irina?' Donadze asked.

Jaqeli snapped out of her reverie. 'Yes, I was just thinking about Zaal.' She turned in the car seat to face him. 'Do you think we have some responsibility for this? Did we put Koba under too much pressure after he'd lost his wife?'

Donadze wanted to say, *no, it wasn't our fault* but he'd already had the same thoughts. He shook his head. 'At least Zaal still has his aunt…'

Jaqeli pressed the elevator call button. 'Does this ever get any easier, Ramaz?'

'No,' he said. 'Not for me...'

They took the elevator to Amelia Nanava's apartment. She opened the door almost immediately.

Zaal was right behind her, clinging to his aunt's leg as if she had power to make the bad things go away. 'No, I don't want him here,' he said, pointing a small finger at Donadze, his lower lip quivering.

Amelia lifted the little boy and he buried his face in her shoulder. She blinked mist from her eyes then turned and walked back into her apartment, leaving the door open behind her.

Donadze nodded to Jaqeli and they followed her into the lounge.

'You've found him then…' Amelia said in a small voice.

Jaqeli crossed the room and stroked the little boy's head. 'I heard you have a really cool bedroom, Zaal. Could you show it to me?'

He shook his head to throw off Jaqeli's hand and tightened his arms around his aunt's neck. 'No,' he said. 'I don't want to.'

Amelia nuzzled his neck. 'Please, *t'k'bilo.* Just for a minute. I'll be right here speaking to this police officer.' She put the boy down and knelt beside him. 'Just for a minute, okay?'

Jaqeli smiled and offered Zaal her hand. 'I'd really like to see your room,' she said brightly.

The boy looked accusingly at Donadze. 'I've got a new bike,' he said then walked off, ignoring Jaqeli's outstretched hand.

Donadze waited until they'd left. 'I'm sorry, Amelia,' he said.

She sank into a chair, shut her eyes for a long moment then swallowed hard. 'How?' she asked, her voice tight.

Donadze sat. 'We think Koba took his own life. He was found in his car near Lake Lisi—there wouldn't have been any pain.'

'Well, good for him,' Amelia said, colour rising to her cheeks. 'What about his son? What about me?'

'Yes, I know. I'm sorry.'

She shook her head and wiped away tears with the back of her hands. 'Poor Zaal, what can I tell him?'

Donadze knew she didn't expect an answer. He waited a moment. 'I didn't know Koba for long, but it seemed to me that he was holding up well. At first anyway.'

'Because he didn't break down in front of you? Is that what you mean, Lieutenant?' she snapped. 'That *really* doesn't mean he was holding up well.'

'Yes, I understand that. But he had Zaal to think about. What would make him take his own life now, had something changed for him recently?'

'No, nothing I was aware of.'

Donadze looked closely at the young woman. 'Did Koba mention that we're investigating suspected irregularities at his bank?'

She fixed Donadze with a fierce stare. 'How dare you?' she hissed.

'I'm sorry, Amelia. I hadn't meant to imply that Koba was involved in anything improper.'

'That's exactly what you did imply. You're suggesting that's the reason he killed himself, aren't you?'

'No, I'm not suggesting that. We just need to understand what could have been worrying him enough to take his own life.'

'I don't believe you. Why *would* you need to understand why Koba killed himself—unless you thought it was connected to your investigation? You and your friend are detectives, not grief counsellors—why would you care?'

'I'm sorry, Amelia, I know how difficult this is for you.'

'You know nothing of the kind, Lieutenant.'

Donadze nodded. 'Yes, you're right—how could I?' He watched as her anger dissolved into despair. 'What will you do now?'

Amelia shook her head. 'I don't know. Zaal will stay with me. I'll raise him as my own, be a mother and father to him. Maybe I'll get a transfer at work. London's probably gone now, but maybe Berlin or Brussels would be a good option. There's nothing to keep us in Georgia now…'

'That was awful,' Jaqeli said.

Donadze started his engine. 'Yes, it was.'

'The bank?'

He nodded and pulled onto Abashidze Street. He thought about Zaal, already devastated by his mother's death and now being told by his aunt—possibly at this very moment—that he'd also lost his father. He knew the boy would carry that pain forever.

Natia Gagua called him on their journey to Kazbegi Avenue. A note had been found in the car with a single hand written word: *Sorry.* There were no obvious signs of anyone else being present in or around the car at the time of Brachuli's death and she was classifying the event as probable suicide.

Jaqeli knocked on the bank's door to attract attention. Nana Pachulia pulled the blind to one side, nodded in acknowledgment and let them in.

Tina Ninua was standing behind a teller's desk, working with documents in the limited space available. She looked up and smiled. 'Everything okay, Ramaz?' she asked.

He shook his head. 'Not really. Why are you working out here?'

She shrugged. 'Mr Berishvili needed his office back.'

Donadze looked at the closed office door. 'I'll speak to him,' he said.

He crossed to Berishvili's office and pushed the door open. The banker was behind his desk. Its surface was clear apart from his open laptop. He made a show of looking at the wall clock. 'Glad you could make it, Lieutenant,' he said.

'Busy, Lekso?' Donadze asked, standing in the doorway.

'Always. What can I do for you?'

'You heard about Koba Brachuli?'

'Yes, your girl told me.'

'She's not my *girl.* What did Tina say?'

Berishvili smiled. 'That this branch needs a new manager.'

Donadze stepped into the office and kicked the door shut behind him. 'You think that's funny, Lekso?'

Berishvili got to his feet. 'What do you want, Donadze?' he demanded, his voice less certain.

Donadze took two steps closer to the desk. 'I spoke to Koba yesterday, a few hours before he died. He told me, "Sometimes you're given no choice." What do you think he meant by that?'

Berishvili threw his hands in the air. 'How would I know? Listen, Lieutenant, Koba was clearly distraught. His wife is dead and you were poking about in the branch he managed. I don't know what you expect to find here but maybe that's what was on his mind?'

Donadze closed the remaining distance to the desk without responding.

Berishvili took two steps back, his hands raised in surrender. 'What do you want, Lieutenant?'

Donadze stared at the banker for a long moment then reached down to close his laptop's lid. 'Thank you for your cooperation, sir,' he said. 'I'll tell Tina your office is free now.'

TWENTY-ONE

'There was definitely something off at that branch,' Tina Ninua said.

'There *was* something off?' Donadze asked.

'Yes, it's not happening now and someone's tried to cover it up, but there are always clues, footprints in the sand. It just takes a bit longer to find them—but I'm almost there.'

'Money laundering?'

Tina hesitated, reluctant to commit herself, he thought. 'Yes, almost certainly...'

'Tell Ramaz what you told me, Tina,' Jaqeli said.

'I don't know, I could be wrong…'

'Wrong about what?' Donadze asked.

She let out a long breath. 'You know how money laundering works, don't you?'

Donadze didn't want Tina to deliver a lengthy discourse on her favourite topic. 'Yes,' he said.

She looked at him expectantly.

'Okay,' he sighed. 'Criminals generate revenue from various illegal activities. That money's considered *dirty*. The onus is on the criminals to account for cash from all sources. But they obviously can't admit they were involved in anything illegal. So they *launder* the dirty money by mixing it with clean money from their legitimate or semi-legitimate businesses, like their casinos for example. Once laundered it can be spent or distributed freely.'

Tina nodded her approval of Donadze's summary. 'That's right—at a basic level at least,' she qualified. 'Did you know the term *money laundering* came from when Al Capone used his laundromats to disguise—'

'Yes, I think I'd heard that, Tina.'

'Sorry.' She got back on track. 'Now, it shouldn't be that easy for the criminals. Banks should recognise when unusually large or frequent transactions are made. And they're obliged by law to report any suspicions they have. But that doesn't always happen.'

'Would Koba Brachuli have recognised that type of transaction going through Kazbegi Avenue?'

'He was the manager, he must have.'

'But he didn't report anything.'

'Not as far as we know. Maybe he reported internally.'

'To his management?'

'Yes. But then they should have reported it to the police.'

'We know how keen Christoph Maier is to protect his bank's reputation. Being accused of association with money launderers wouldn't go down well on the markets.'

'No, but bigger banks than First National have been caught up in stuff like this—and they're still here.'

'Does any of this tell us why Sophia Brachuli and Vano Chedia were killed? Or Otar Basilia for that matter?'

'Tell Ramaz what you told me, Tina,' Jaqeli repeated.

Tina smiled. 'Yes, of course, sorry.' She turned to Donadze. 'When you brought me onto your investigation, I suspected I'd be looking for evidence of money laundering. But I thought it'd be stuff I've seen before: dirty money generated locally and washed through local, cash-rich businesses. Lots of cash coming in and lots going out. And I think that *has* been happening…'

'But?' Donadze said.

'But there's more to it than that. I think money's been moved internationally—in and out of Georgia.'

'Do you know which countries are involved?'

'Not yet. But there's something else to think about: scale and complexity. Kazbegi Avenue is a small branch with only a few people working there. There's a limit to how much money could be washed through it without attracting undue attention. But at the same time, it takes effort to move money across borders: setting up shell companies; disguising the source of your funds; buying protection from judges and paying-off the regulators, police and politicians. You couldn't justify that much effort for one small branch…'

'So to make the effort worthwhile?' Jaqeli prompted.

'You need more than one branch. This might be bigger than you think, Ramaz.'

Levan Gloveli's home was lying in early evening shadow as Donadze pulled up outside. The old policeman was drinking wine in his garden. 'I wasn't expecting you, Ramaz,' he said. 'Is everything okay?'

'Everything's good, Major.'

Gloveli appraised the younger man. 'You're looking better than last time I saw you. How are your ribs?'

Donadze ran his hand over his chest. 'Perfect, no pain at all now.'

'Well, I don't believe that. But it's good to see you, anyway. Sit down, I'll get you a glass.' He limped into the house, his arthritic gait seemingly more pronounced at this time of day.

Donadze took a seat at the small table, breathing the warm, clean air and absorbing the silence which was broken only by the buzz of insects flitting about the garden and the infrequent rumble of cars on the beat-up village streets.

Gloveli returned a moment later. 'Veronika's bringing another bottle.' He sat down heavily. 'I take it you weren't just passing?'

'No, I wasn't.'

'Kazbegi Avenue?'

'Yes.'

Donadze stood as Veronika Boyko came out of the house carrying a tray with wine, water, glasses and plates with nuts and cheese.

'*Gamarjoba*, Lieutenant,' she said, putting the tray on the table and kissing him on his cheek.

'*Gamarjoba*, Veronika. How are you?'

Donadze and the young woman briefly discussed her planned marriage and the ongoing war in her home country, Veronika concentrating on her newly learned Georgian language skills to affirm that Ukraine would ultimately, inevitably, be victorious over its Russian foe.

Gloveli's eyes followed her back into the house.

'You're going to miss her, Major.'

'Yes,' he admitted to Donadze for the first time. He raised his glass. 'Victory to Ukraine,' he toasted. '*Gaumarjos*!'

Donadze took a long sip of the cool wine and held it in his mouth for a moment, the sweet, fruity liquid tingling on his tongue. He swallowed and put the glass down. 'You remember we discussed Koba Brachuli?'

'The branch manager.'

'He's dead, killed himself yesterday.'

Gloveli swirled his wine and held the glass to the fading light. 'Yes, I'd heard that.'

'I'd spoken to him a few hours previously. He told me, "Sometimes you're given no choice." I should have realised what he was going to do, I might have stopped him.'

Gloveli shook his head. 'You couldn't, not if he was determined. Why do you think he did it?'

'We've been running an investigation at his branch. Tina, our investigator thinks the bank's been laundering money. And not just money from Tbilisi. She thinks it's been moved internationally, in and out of Georgia. It's something Brachuli must have known about. Maybe he thought he'd run out of options.'

'But we catch criminals every day, they don't usually kill themselves.'

'White collar crime—it's different.'

'Is it?' Gloveli paused. 'Does Tina know which countries the money was moved between?'

'Not yet. But there's something else. She doesn't know

this for sure, but she has a theory. The Kazbegi Avenue branch is too small to justify the effort required to move money across borders. She thinks there must be more than one branch involved.'

Gloveli lifted the wine bottle and filled their glasses. 'We always wondered about that robbery, didn't we? Why did these thieves—these professionals—pick on such a small branch? And why kill two people? But if more than one branch was involved then that raises the stakes, makes the killings easier to justify. Remind me how much cash was taken.'

'About four hundred thousand *lari*.'

'Right. That bank wasn't robbed for four hundred thousand *lari*. Not by these people.'

'I agree. But then why, if not for the money?'

'Maybe it was a diversion to stop you looking elsewhere.'

'At the other banks?'

'Possibly.'

'Why *possibly*?'

'You said Tina has a theory. A theory's not enough to build a case. You need to test it.'

'Yes, but I'll have to widen the court order to do that.'

'That's not going to be easy. You'll be up against vested interests, a lot of powerful people who could get hurt. You need to take it to Meskhi.'

'I know, and I'm going to. But it's still my investigation.'

'Meskhi might have other ideas.'

Donadze nodded his reluctant agreement. 'One other thing, Major. How do you think Otar Basilia fits into this?'

'Why was he killed you mean?'

'That's what I wondered. The robbery was on his territory. It wasn't sanctioned by him and he was trying to find who was behind it. We thought he'd got too close and that's why he was killed.'

'And you don't think that now?'

'I don't know. If the robbery was a diversion, maybe Basilia was as well.'

'That's why you need to keep an open mind. You'll talk to Meskhi tomorrow?'

'This evening, I think.'

There was little light remaining in the garden. Gloveli pulled himself to his feet and placed the wine bottle and glasses on the tray. 'In that case,' he said. 'It's time you went home.'

TWENTY-TWO

Donadze stood outside his apartment block waiting for Colonel Meskhi to arrive. Within a few minutes, a black SUV swooped in and braked by the pavement's edge, its flashing grill lights proclaiming the occupant was much too important to be delayed by other road users.

The driver lowered his tinted window and nodded in recognition but didn't get out of the car.

Donadze looked through the open window. Meskhi was in the back, his briefcase on his lap, a document in his hand. 'Get in, Lieutenant,' he said.

Donadze joined him, the car accelerating into traffic as he fumbled with his seat belt.

'How are you this morning?' Meskhi asked.

'Fully recovered, sir.'

Meskhi looked sceptical. 'If you say so.'

'We're going to your office, Colonel?'

'No, to the Ministry of Finance.'

He waited for Meskhi to elaborate. 'May I ask why?' he asked, eventually.

'To discuss your extended court order—there may be difficulties.'

'Sir?'

'Do you know Maka Lomaia, Deputy Minister of Finance?'

'No.'

'I know her quite well. I've been keeping her up to date with your investigation. I believe she has some concerns about your proposal to widen its remit.'

'Why, because it's First National we're investigating?'

'Her concerns are not unreasonable. First National Bank is the country's biggest financial institution and Mrs Lomaia is the Deputy Minister of Finance.'

'Isn't this a police matter, Colonel?'

'Of course it is.'

Donadze slumped into his seat. 'So we're not applying for a new court order?'

'That's not what I said, Lieutenant. Let's hear the Deputy Minister out.'

Meskhi returned to his paperwork while Donadze gazed out the car's tinted window as the sea of resentful traffic parted to allow the SUV unimpeded passage through the congested city streets.

The car slid to a smooth stop by steps leading to the tall, narrow Ministry building. A blue and gold EU flag fluttered hopefully at the entrance alongside the red and white, five-cross flag of Georgia as the country's European aspirations were judged by Commission overlords.

The driver stood by Meshki's door as he got out of the

car and began climbing the steps while Donadze scrambled to catch up. There were several people waiting at the reception but the police officers were taken to the front of the queue, provided with security passes and escorted to the elevators.

A young man met them as the elevator opened and they were led a short distance to double wooden doors, one bearing a nameplate indicating that the office belonged to Maka Lomaia, Deputy Minister of Finance. The young man knocked and opened the door. 'Colonel Meskhi and Lieutenant Donadze are here, Maka,' he said, standing to one side to allow them to enter.

Lomaia stood from behind her conference table and crossed the room. She was in her early fifties, slim and dressed in a dark blue business suit, her hair and makeup meticulous. She and Meskhi exchanged kisses and she offered her hand fleetingly to Donadze.

There were two other men in the Deputy Minister's office. Christoph Maier remained seated at the conference table while Emzar Kesaria hovered by Lomaia, waiting to offer his own greetings.

'Gentlemen, I think you know each other,' Lomaia said.

'Of course.' Meskhi smiled at Maier. 'I hadn't realised you would be joining us today, Christoph.'

Maier returned the smile. 'Why wouldn't I, Gabi? It's my bank we're discussing.'

'So it is.'

The young man was waiting to be dismissed. Lomaia turned to him. 'You didn't tell Colonel Meskhi that Mr Maier was attending our meeting today?'

He looked confused. 'No, but—'

'Never mind. I'll call you if I need anything.'

She waited until the door closed. 'I'm sorry,' she said. 'He hasn't been with me very long.' She offered the four men a bright smile. 'Well, we're all here now. Please sit down. I'm sure we can find a solution to our problem.'

Donadze glanced at Meskhi, expecting him to say he wasn't prepared to discuss police business in this setting.

Meskhi nodded. 'I'm sure we can,' he said, taking a seat and indicating to Donadze to join him.

Lomaia smiled again. 'Wonderful,' she said. 'Gabi, I think it would be useful if you could summarise your interest in Christoph's bank.'

'Of course. But Lieutenant Donadze is leading this investigation.' He sat back in his seat and steepled his fingers under his chin. 'Go ahead, Lieutenant.'

'Sir?'

'Go ahead. Start with the robbery at Kazbegi Avenue and the two murders.'

Donadze looked around the table. Lomaia was smiling at him expectantly while Maier tapped the table impatiently and Kesaria nodded encouragement. He took a breath and began summarising the case to date, giving as few details as possible, stressing the brutality of the murders and concluding that the financial investigation conducted by Tina Ninua indicated probable irregularities at Kazbegi Avenue, possibly extending to other branches and beyond.

'What kind of irregularities?' Lomaia asked.

'Money laundering, possibly more than that.'

Maier lost patience and threw his pen on the desk. 'Madam Deputy Minister, what Donadze isn't telling you is that his supposed *investigation* and the baseless accusations he has bandied around have already resulted in one of my managers taking his own life—leaving his young son orphaned. You must stop this madness now.'

'Must I?' She smiled at Meskhi. 'I think Gabi might have something to say about that.'

'Yes, I think I would, Maka,' Meskhi said. 'And to be clear, Christoph, we have not made any accusations as yet—baseless or not.'

'Thank you, Lieutenant, that was incredibly useful,' Lomaia said in a tone which Donadze took to be both insincere and patronising. 'I understand you wish to investigate other areas of Mr Maier's business and it was your intention to seek a court order to do so.'

'My intention is *still* to seek a court order to do so, Mrs Lomaia.'

Lomaia turned to Meskhi. 'I'm sure you understand the possible sensitivities that would create, Gabi. Assuming your application to the courts was successful of course.'

'Yes, Maka, I do. But I'm sure *you* realise the seriousness of Lieutenant Donadze's investigation. We obviously can't let business interests impede the course of justice.'

'Absolutely not! But there may be another way.' She paused. 'My responsibilities as Deputy Minister include audit of the country's financial institutions, including its banks. An audit of the First National Bank would uncover any irregularities, if indeed any such irregularities had occurred.'

Meskhi leaned forward in his seat. 'You're proposing an audit by your Ministry rather than a police investigation?'

'I believe the same outcome would be achieved. But a

court order wouldn't be required and Christoph wouldn't have to worry about the associated negative publicity. And if we had reason to suspect any criminal act *had* been committed, we would of course share all relevant information with you.'

Meskhi frowned as if thinking. 'Lieutenant?' he said after a moment.

'No, Colonel. This is a police matter. It must stay with us.'

Meskhi nodded. 'I can see Lieutenant Donadze's point, Maka. I don't think your proposal would work.'

Lomaia smiled. 'How about this then? Your investigator could join my audit team. She would have full access and would be able to brief you and Lieutenant Donadze first-hand.'

'Lieutenant?' Meskhi asked again.

'No, Colonel. Herr Maier's bank should not be given any special privileges.'

Meskhi shook his head. 'I don't agree, Lieutenant.' He turned to Lomaia. 'I believe your proposal would work, Maka.'

Lomaia smiled and turned to Maier. 'Christoph?'

'None of this is necessary,' he said.

'Well, I'm afraid Gabi thinks it is. And audits are routine for you after all, no one outside this room need know that there is anything different about this one.'

Maier fixed his gaze on Donadze. 'We'll see,' he said. He stood and leaned across the table to shake hands with Lomaia. 'Thank you, Madam Deputy Minister.' He nodded to Meskhi and walked to the door, followed by Emzar Kesaria who hurriedly shook hands with the others before rushing to catch up with his boss.

Meskhi also stood. 'Thanks for seeing us, Maka. Lieutenant Donadze will be in touch about audit protocols.'

Lomaia came around the table to shake hands with Donadze and to kiss Meskhi. 'Thank you, Gabi. I think we've found a pragmatic solution to our problem.'

Donadze followed Meskhi from the Deputy Minister's office to the elevator station and pressed the call button.

'You're not happy, Lieutenant?' Meskhi said.

'No, sir. This is a murder investigation. Maier or any other bank employee could be complicit. We should have retained control.'

The elevator doors opened and the police officers got in.

'Tell me, Lieutenant, given the gaps in our knowledge, how confident were you in obtaining a court order against the biggest bank in the country?'

'I don't know, but we should have at least tried.'

'Tried and failed. Let me tell you, the probability was not much better than zero. I understood that reality, as did Maka Lomaia. You should have understood it as well.' The elevator doors opened. 'I'm sure you can find your own way back,' Meskhi said.

Donadze called Jaqeli from his taxi and asked her and Tina Ninua to leave the bank and return to Mtatsminda Station.

'What's happening?' Jaqeli asked.

'There's been a change of plan. I'll explain when I see you.'

'Okay. Lekso Berishvili is still here. What do we tell him?'

'Christoph Maier knows what's happening—tell him to speak to his boss.'

The taxi dropped Donadze at the station. Arziani was in his office reading something on his computer screen.

'Having fun?' Donadze asked.

Arziani closed the laptop's lid. 'Would you believe me if I said I was?'

'Command not as exciting as you'd hoped?'

'A bit more bureaucracy, a bit less police work. I'll get used to it.'

Donadze suppressed a smile at Arziani's assumption that his promotion would be made permanent. 'Irina and Tina are returning from Kazbegi Avenue. Can we talk when they get here?'

'Something's happened?'

'In a way. I'll bring them here if that's okay.'

'Fine by me,' Arziani said, lifting the laptop's lid again.

Donadze decided to wait for Jaqeli and Tina at the station entrance. Arziani had made more changes there. The informal smoking station had been formally moved to the back of the building. The area had been tidied and visiting civilians didn't have to manoeuvre through huddles of intimidating police to enter the station.

He leaned against the wall and closed his eyes; warm rays on his face, the sun-baked bricks easing the tension in his shoulders and back. He thought about the meeting at the Ministry of Finance. It was clear to him that Meskhi and the Deputy Minister had colluded to substitute a police financial investigation with a Ministry audit. Meskhi had stated that there was little or no chance of the court granting a wider warrant. Donadze knew that assessment was correct.

He trusted Meskhi's judgement but was frustrated and angry that he'd lost direct control over an important line of inquiry. He was also worried about the Deputy Minister's motivation. Did she want the police investigation to be successfully concluded? Or was the audit her way of providing political cover for the Bank—the most important financial institution in the country?

Donadze heard two sets of heels on the concrete walkway and pushed himself off the wall.

'Hey, Ramaz,' Jaqeli smiled. 'Here we are, back as ordered.'

'Let's talk inside—Misha's waiting for us.'

'Exciting,' Tina said.

He turned and led the way to Arziani's office.

Arziani closed his laptop once more, stood and shuffled his feet, uncertain how to greet his former and current girlfriends.

'All right to talk now, Misha?' Donadze asked. He shot Jaqeli a warning glance—her amusement at Arziani's discomfort was too obvious.

'Yes, of course. It's a bit tight in here but sit down. Could you bring another chair, Ramaz.'

There was a brief exchange of pleasantries before Donadze provided a summary of his meeting at the Ministry. 'What do you think, Tina?' he asked.

She took a moment to consider. 'I'm not sure. I've not heard of that kind of approach before, but it could be okay I suppose. Would I be working under the lead auditor?'

'No, we'll make that clear. You're representing the police, you're not part of the audit team.'

'Okay. Well, something like this would normally be

scheduled months in advance. We can't wait that long, presumably?'

'No, we can't. I'll tell the Deputy Minister we want you to start tomorrow. Her team can catch up if necessary.'

'And you still have the existing court order, don't you, Ramaz?' Arziani said. 'Tina could work off that for a while if necessary.'

'That's right. If the Bank and the Ministry want to avoid adverse publicity, they know what to do.'

'Just be careful, Ramaz,' Arziani cautioned. 'We want to keep them onside, no need to be deliberately antagonistic.'

Donadze nodded. 'We won't be.' He looked at Tina. 'I'd like regular updates. You'll let me know right away if you spot something suspicious?'

Tina shrugged. 'Yes, of course.'

'So, it looks like Tina will be busy for a while, Ramaz,' Jaqeli said. 'What are we going to do?'

'We're going to the Dream Casino. Shalva Khapava called and asked to see me. I'm hoping he has something new to share.'

Arziani sighed. 'Proper police work...'

'You're in charge, Misha. It's up to you what you work on.'

Arziani patted his laptop and grinned. 'If only.' He looked at Donadze. 'Are we done?'

'I think so.'

The others began to rise.

'Tina...' Donadze said. He stood and put his hand on her arm. 'I'm sorry you've been put in this position. Let me know if it gets too difficult for you.'

She gave him a bright smile. 'Thanks, Ramaz, I'll be fine.'

TWENTY-THREE

Some primordial sense told the hyenas that lions—the police—were back in their den. Gamblers scooped their chips off the tables, heavily made-up, industrially perfumed young women deserted their prospective tricks and men with small, plastic baggies of white powder scurried for the exits.

Donadze paused inside the Dream Casino's gilt doors, scowling.

'You enjoy this, don't you?' Jaqeli said.

He fixed his gaze on a particularly nervous-looking punter, narrowing his eyes theatrically. 'You find your pleasures where you can,' he said, quoting from his favourite television crime drama. 'And look, here comes Tengo.'

Tengo Sakhokia, the casino's security manager approached, rubbing his hands together like an obsequious waiter. 'Detectives, it's good to see you again. You have a meeting with Mr Khapava?'

Donadze took a step forward. 'That's right, Tengo. But

maybe we should look around here first. It seems to me that—'

'Please let Mr Khapava know we're here,' Jaqeli said, ending Donadze's fun.

Sakhokia smiled at Jaqeli and spoke into his radio. He listened to the response and nodded. 'Mr Khapava will see you now. Let me show you up.'

'That's okay, Tengo,' Donadze said. 'We've been here before—remember?'

They took the stairs and crossed the corridor to Khapava's office.

The door was open. Khapava was at his desk signing documents being presented to him by a middle-aged woman. He looked up and signalled for the detectives to enter. He said something to the woman and she shuffled the documents into a folder, her lips pursed, her task interrupted. Khapava dismissed her with a movement of his head.

Donadze sat without waiting to be invited. 'You wanted to see us.'

Khapava smiled at Jaqeli and gestured towards the remaining free chair. 'Thanks for coming,' he said.

'What can we do for you, Shalva?'

Khapava's face hardened. 'Maybe you could drop the posturing, *Ramaz*? You're in *my* casino. *You* asked for *my* help—I'd appreciate you showing me some respect.'

Donadze hesitated a moment then nodded. 'Okay. What can we do for you, *Mr Khapava*?'

'It's what we can do for each other, Lieutenant. You asked me to help you find the men behind your bank robbery.'

Donadze straightened in his chair. 'It's not *my* bank

robbery,' he said, then added, 'You know who they are?'

'No. I know who the assassins are but I don't know who gave them their orders. That's what I still need to work out.'

'So who are the assassins?'

'I said this is about what we can do for each other. I know *who* these men are—I don't know *where* they are.'

'You don't have to. Give me their names and we'll find them.'

'It's not that simple. We talked about Otar choosing me as his successor. How his organisation—*my* organisation—expects me to find the people who had him killed.'

'And you think these men can tell you that.'

'They will if I ask them.'

'You'll *ask* them. Then what?'

'They'll tell me what I need to know.'

'And then you'll kill them.'

'No, they robbed that bank and shot two people. But they didn't kill Otar. I want whoever gave them their orders. Give me a day with these men—even one of them—then they're yours.'

'How would you get them to speak—torture?'

'No, I won't do that.'

'Then how?'

'I've offered you a deal, Lieutenant. Do you want it or not?'

Donadze looked at Jaqeli.

She shook her head, signalling, *no.*

'Yes,' he said. 'Give me their names.'

Khapava opened a drawer and removed two sheets of

paper. He slid them across the table. 'Andrey Belov and Oleg Galkin,' he said.

The papers were photocopies of Russian passports. The names didn't match the names Khapava had provided.

'Fakes?' Donadze asked.

'Yes. These were the passports Belov and Galkin were carrying when they came into Georgia.'

'From where?'

'From Russia through South Ossetia.'

'That's an illegal entry—there's no official border with South Ossetia.'

'Of course, they had to be assisted.'

'And that's how you came across them?'

'Otar's family was from South Ossetia. I still have interests there.'

'Why are you just telling us this now?'

Khapava shrugged. 'It took some time for my people to make the connection.'

'What do you know about them?'

'Professional hitmen, former FSB operatives.'

'Former? No current connection to the Kremlin?'

'No—they go where the money is now.'

Donadze lifted the papers again. 'They'll be back in Russia by now.'

'Possibly. But if they did return to Russia, it wasn't through South Ossetia. There's a good chance they're still here.'

'So why do you need the police? Why not just wait for them in South Ossetia and grab them there?'

'I could do that. But if these men are staying in Georgia, it's probably for a reason.'

'Another hit?'

Khapava nodded his agreement. 'It's what they do. Maybe on someone who's getting too close to the truth behind your robbery.'

'Someone like you, Shalva?'

'It could be,' Khapava agreed. 'Or it could even be someone like you, Ramaz.'

'So we just hand Belov and Galkin over to Khapava?' Jaqeli said. 'And hope he gives them back to us—unharmed?'

'That's what we agreed.'

'That's what *you* agreed.'

'Yes.'

'Would you really let Khapava have them?'

'No. And I don't believe he would return them to us either. They might just have been following orders but they robbed a bank on Kaldani family turf. Khapava couldn't let them walk after that.'

'So what was the point of your deal?'

'There is no deal. Khapava wants the Russians found and thinks his best chance of achieving that is if we're both looking for them. He's hoping we flush them out and he can grab them, maybe as they're escaping through South Ossetia. But there's a chance we'll get to them first.'

'How? Khapava has tentacles right across the city, people who would speak to him long before they'd speak to us.'

'Yes, but I've got an idea that might give us an edge.'

Jaqeli waited for him to elaborate.

'It's something I need to think about first,' he said.

Jaqeli shook her head. 'I don't know, Ramaz. Why go through that charade with Khapava if neither of you believes the other? A deal that's not a deal…'

'It seemed the right thing to do at the time. I was trying to keep him off balance, I think.'

'And he was doing the same to you. That's quite subtle, isn't it? Not the way Otar Basilia would have done it.'

'Otar would have turned the city upside down to find these men, beaten the information he wanted out of them, killed them and dumped them in a place they'd never be found. And he'd be sure that everyone knew what he'd done, that he'd sent a message he's not a man to mess with.'

'But look what happened to Otar.'

'Shalva Khapava is a different proposition,' Donadze agreed. 'Basilia chose his successor well—I'd say the Kaldani family is in good hands.'

'If it's good for them then it's bad for us.'

They drove in silence for several minutes, Donadze concentrating on finding a safe path through the early evening traffic.

Jaqeli turned to face him. 'So, if we don't believe Khapava will give up Belov and Galkin, what *can* we believe? We've only got his word that they're even responsible for the bank murders.'

'I don't think he was lying about that. Take another look at Belov's passport picture.'

She extracted the photocopy from its folder. 'What am I looking at?'

'His hair.'

She nodded her understanding. 'Zaal said the man who

shot his mother had red hair.'

Donadze reached over and tapped the picture. 'It's hardly conclusive but it does tend to support Khapava's version of events.'

They were approaching Jaqeli's apartment. 'Ramaz, if Belov and Galkin are still in Georgia, do *you* think it's because they have another job?'

'Another hit you mean. I think that's possible. They would have been safer going straight home to Russia.'

'And the other hit? Someone getting too close to the truth about the robbery as Khapava said?'

'Someone like him or me? It's not me. Killing me wouldn't stop the investigation. And if there's anything that'll provoke the police, it's an attack on one of their own. Things could only get worse for these guys.'

'So they could go after Khapava.'

'They could, but he knows that's a possibility.' He pulled up outside Jaqeli's apartment. 'I'll get the APB out this evening. Maybe we'll get lucky and a patrol car will spot them.'

TWENTY-FOUR

It was late when Donadze returned to his apartment. Only Tamuna was still up, the television turned low, the baby monitor balanced on the arm of her chair.

'How's everyone been?' he asked, peeling cling film off the dinner plate his mother had left for him.

'I need to speak to you about that. There's wine in the fridge, could you bring it over.'

Donadze placed the plate and two glasses on the table and retrieved the open bottle of *Tsinandali*. 'Is something wrong?' he asked.

Tamuna put a finger to her lips, advising him to lower his voice. 'I think your mother's struggling with Eka.'

'Why, what did she say?'

'She didn't say anything. And she's not likely to either. But she was exhausted when I returned home this evening.'

'Maybe she just didn't sleep well last night?'

'That's possible. But it's not the first time I've seen her like that. I talked to her about it and offered to get help.'

'Someone for Eka?'

'Yes, I said we could hire a nanny.'

'And she wasn't happy with that prospect?'

'No, she was quite upset.'

'I'm not surprised.' Donadze took a sip of his wine. 'It's the way she is, Tamuna. The way she's had to be ever since our family was forced out of Abkhazia. It's difficult to remember how bad it was back then. There wasn't work for anyone in Tbilisi, let alone for refugees like us. My father wasn't bringing money in. I was too young to help. She held the family together, managed to pay the rent, made sure there was food on the table. I don't know how she did it. She's proud, accepting help for Eka would be like admitting she can't look after her family anymore.'

Tamuna sighed. 'I know and I really didn't want to upset her. But she's pushing herself too hard.'

'Yes, but that's who she is.' He paused for a moment. 'Do you think Eka could be at risk?'

'No, not at all. It's only your mother I'm worried about.'

Donadze took another, more generous sip of his wine. 'She'll never be happy with a nanny. All we can do is try to take the pressure off her as best we can.' He lifted his plate in evidence. 'Like making my own meals, for example.'

Tamuna laughed. 'Do you think she'd even let you do that?'

'She wouldn't. Let's keep an eye on her—see if things get any worse.'

'I'll speak to her again in the morning. Tell her we won't look for a nanny.'

He drained his glass. 'Good, she'll be relieved.' He showed her the wine bottle.

'No, thanks. It's been a long day for me as well. I'm going to bed, don't stay up too late.' She kissed him and stood, leaving her unfinished wine on the table.

Donadze watched her cross the room. He flicked through a few channels, found nothing of interest and turned the television off. He added more wine to her glass and carried it and his food to the balcony, sinking into his wicker chair to enjoy the warm evening air and the relative quiet as traffic in the streets below thinned and calmed.

He held the wine to his nose and savoured its fruity aroma as condensation ran down the glass and dripped onto his shirt. He thought about his mother and how she'd aged since her heart attack over a year ago. He knew he relied on her more than he should but couldn't imagine life without her.

His thoughts drifted to the investigation and his conversation with Shalva Khapava. Finding FSB-trained killers wouldn't be easy for Khapava or the police. He'd told Jaqeli he had an idea on how to improve their chances but had wanted to think about it some more. He made up his mind.

Donadze checked his watch. It was almost eleven but he didn't think she'd mind a late call. He scrolled through his contacts until he found the name he was looking for.

Tatyana Rokva answered after a few rings. 'Ramaz, it's been a while.'

'Over a year. I need to speak to you.'

'Not a social call then.' She paused. 'And not over the phone. Do you remember where we met the first time?'

'Yes, but could we meet somewhere else this—'

'See you tomorrow, eight o'clock.'

The atmosphere in the apartment was strained as Donadze prepared to leave, his mother subdued, her eyes red and puffy. He looked at Tamuna and she shook her head—they would talk again after he'd left.

Donadze suspected he would be eating again soon and only nibbled at his breakfast. He gulped down coffee and kissed each family member in turn, his mother feeling small and brittle in his arms. He turned at the living room door and took a last, anxious look at the people he held most dear, then left the apartment.

He drove onto Kazbegi Avenue and called Jaqeli.

'Hey, Ramaz.'

He could hear music playing—she was still in her apartment. 'Have you heard from Tina yet?'

'No. But it's only seven fifteen.'

'Right. She's starting the bank audit this morning. I want to make sure she's okay. I don't want her intimidated by the Ministry or Maier's people.'

'She's not the type to be intimidated, Ramaz.'

'I know, but could you go along for the kick-off meeting? Help set out what we expect to get from it. You could ask Misha to go with you if you want.'

'So *I* don't feel intimidated, you mean? Don't worry, I think we'll be okay.'

'Yes, I'm sure you will.'

'Aren't you going to tell me what you're doing?'

Donadze hesitated, choosing his words carefully. 'There was a case I worked on a year or so ago. It got complicated and our Intelligence people became involved.

I'm meeting one of them this morning. I'm hoping she'll help us find the Russians.'

Jaqeli laughed. 'Ah, so that's your masterplan. You don't have to be so coy, Ramaz. Everyone knows about that case. It was even on television.'

'Yes, but no one from the Intelligence Service was on television—they like to keep a low profile.'

'Well, that makes sense, I suppose. Catch you later, 007.'

'Funny,' Donadze said and hung up.

East Point shopping mall was a fast drive along the Kakheti Highway. Donadze parked and walked to the McDonald's restaurant. He was twenty minutes early but Rokva had already arrived and was at a table in the far corner.

She was about to take a bite from her breakfast muffin when she saw him. She returned the food to its carton, wiped her fingers on a paper napkin and stood to kiss him. 'Hey, Ramaz, you're early.'

'So are you. No burger this morning?'

She pulled a face. 'It's a bit early, even for me.' She lifted her phone from the table. 'What do you want to eat? These muffins are good.'

'You're going to phone the waiter?'

She looked at him, checking to see if he was kidding. 'No, Ramaz. I have an app on my phone.'

'Just coffee, then. Black.'

Rokva took a moment with her phone then returned it to the table. 'I ordered you a muffin anyway. You don't mind me eating mine now?'

'Go ahead.'

She pushed her hair behind her ears and picked up her food, leaning over the carton in case its filling escaped confinement. 'How's Tamuna?' she asked.

'She's great.' Donadze asked if she still worked with Gia Pataraia, her partner when Donadze had first met her. They spent a few moments exchanging pleasantries but he realised he knew little of her personal life.

Rokva put her muffin down. 'What's on your mind, Ramaz?'

'I'm looking for two men—former FSB operatives turned freelance hitmen.'

'FSB. You're thinking we'd know something about them?'

'I'm hoping so.'

'Any interest for us?'

'Not specifically. We don't think they have any direct links to the Kremlin now—but they came into the country illegally through South Ossetia and we want them for two particularly nasty murders.'

'The First National Bank?'

'How did you—'

'Never mind.' She paused a moment. 'We like to keep track of all our FSB friends—current and former. Do you have names?'

Donadze removed a folded envelope from his jacket pocket and slid it across the table.

A waitress arrived a moment later with Donadze's food and coffee.

Rokva waited until she'd left. 'I'll see what I can do,' she said. She popped the last piece of muffin into her mouth, took a drink from her cardboard cup and stood, lifting the envelope. 'Enjoy your breakfast, Ramaz. I'll be in touch.'

Donadze watched Rokva stride out of the restaurant. He lifted the muffin she'd ordered for him, bit off a chunk, chewed it for a moment then—unimpressed—dropped the rest back into its carton. He picked up the coffee and carried it to his car. It was just after eight, the meeting with Rokva had been brief.

He took a sip of coffee, wondering what to do next. He considered crashing the Ministry of Finance's kick-off meeting. He was still angry that his financial investigation had been superseded by a Ministry audit and he wanted to put the audit team on notice that their approach had better be robust. But he'd asked Jaqeli to attend and he knew she'd achieve the same outcome without unnecessarily raising hackles.

He'd decided to return to Mtatsminda Station when Nana Pachulia called.

'*Gamarjoba*, Nana.'

There was no reply. 'Nana?'

'I wasn't sure about calling you,' she whispered.

'Why, what's wrong?'

'I've just been given a letter. I've to go to head office for a disciplinary hearing this afternoon. I'm really worried, Lieutenant, I can't afford to lose this job.'

'What does the letter say you've done?'

'Something about breaching confidentiality rules. It must be because I've been helping the police.'

'Read it to me.'

She read the letter from beginning to end. There was nothing specific about helping the police and it had been signed by Lekso Berishvili.

'You said you were *given* the letter?'

'Mr Berishvili came to our apartment this morning. My parents were so upset.'

'He hand delivered it to you?'

'Yes.'

'What did he say?'

'He didn't say much. But I think he was enjoying himself.'

'He threatened you?'

'Not in so many words, but you know how he is…'

'Yes, I do know. Don't worry, Nana, you're not losing your job. Had you planned to go into work this morning?'

'I was, but can't now. Not if I've been suspended.'

'Will Berishvili be there?'

'I think so.'

'Stay where you are, I'm coming to get you.'

'No, it's all right. I don't want to get into any more—'

'Stay there, Nana. I'll be with you in twenty minutes.'

Donadze ended the call, opened his door and poured his coffee onto the ground. He started his engine and accelerated out of the parking area and onto the Kakheti Highway. Traffic into the city was dense and he used his lights and siren, jumping lanes and forcing his way through the bedlam. He arrived outside Nana's apartment and called her from his car. 'I'm outside,' he said.

'There's really no need, Lieutenant…'

'I'm outside,' he repeated.

She appeared a few minutes later and he blipped his horn to attract her attention. He reached across to push the passenger door open and she got into the car. 'I wish I hadn't called you now,' she said.

'No, you did the right thing. Don't worry.'

They drove to Kazbegi Avenue in silence and Donadze parked outside the bank.

'Let's go, Nana,' he said, getting out the car and running up the short stairway to the bank's entrance.

The blinds were drawn and he hammered on the door with his fist, rattling its locks. He was about to hammer the door again when a blind was pulled aside. Berishvili smiled and let it close. The door opened and he stood in the doorway.

'What are you doing here, Nana? Didn't you read your letter? You're suspended and that means you can't come to work.'

'Yes, but—'

'I think there's been a misunderstanding,' Donadze interrupted.

'Really? I don't think so. I drafted the letter myself—it couldn't have been more clear.'

'No, it's you who doesn't understand, Lekso. Miss Pachulia is a material witness in a murder investigation and you attempted to intimidate her. That's obstruction of justice.' He showed Berishvili his handcuffs. 'Turn around—you're under arrest.'

TWENTY-FIVE

Donadze finished reading Lekso Berishvili his rights and called for a patrol car to take him into custody.

'Should I stay here, sir?' Nana Pachulia asked.

Berishvili's mouth turned down. 'Do what you want, why should I care?'

'I'd stay here for now, Nana,' Donadze said. 'Call your head office and tell them what's happened.'

'And make sure Mr Maier is informed,' Berishvili snapped. He smiled at Donadze. 'Enjoy yourself while you can—because this stupidity is going to cost you your job. Mr Maier will see to that.'

'Possibly. But just in case he doesn't, why don't you tell us what you know? We're going to find out anyway so it'd be better for you to tell us now. I'd be happy to have a word with the trial judge and tell him you've been cooperative.'

Berishvili laughed. 'You have no idea what you're up against.'

Donadze saw the patrol car draw up outside. 'Your taxi's here,' he said.

'Very funny, but it's you who's the joke, Donadze.'

'Maybe, but it's you who's under arrest.'

A uniformed officer opened the bank door. 'One to take in, Lieutenant?'

'Off you go, Lekso,' Donadze said. 'We'll speak soon.'

Donadze watched Berishvili being led away. He looked at Nana. 'Are you okay?'

She shook her head. 'You won't be able to make that charge stick, will you, Lieutenant?'

'No, but I'll make sure he doesn't bother you again.'

'What about my disciplinary hearing?'

'When you call your office, tell them you've been instructed by the police—by me—not to attend as doing so could compromise an ongoing investigation.'

'Are you sure?'

'Yes. Consider yourself so instructed.'

Donadze returned to his car and drove to Mtatsminda Station. Christoph Maier called as he was walking to the building.

'Herr Maier, I thought I'd be hearing from you.'

'*Gamarjoba*, Lieutenant,' Maier said. 'That was rather an extreme reaction, don't you think?'

'Not really, I don't like bullies.'

'No one does, but I don't think that's what this was about. You were upset that Colonel Meskhi agreed to the audit and you were looking for someone to take out your frustrations on. Someone to bully in fact.'

'Well that's certainly an interesting theory, Herr Maier. I'll be interviewing Berishvili soon. Are you sending your lawyer to represent him?'

Maier hesitated. 'Not at this time. Berishvili was acting under his own authority when he initiated disciplinary action against Miss Pachulia. Given there is a police investigation ongoing, I believe his actions were somewhat rash.'

'You're throwing him to the wolves?'

'No. But his interests and the interests of the Bank are not aligned at this time.'

'Tell me Herr Maier, how's the audit going?'

There was silence on the line while Maier considered his response. 'It's only just beginning of course but I suspect the audit will uncover a number of uncomfortable findings for my bank. I am, however, confident that only a limited number of bad actors were involved.'

'Is Berishvili one of these bad actors?'

'Let's see what the audit uncovers.'

'So you *are* throwing him to the wolves.'

'Not at all.'

'Make yourself a sheep and the wolf will eat you,' Donadze said, quoting Benjamin Franklin.

Donadze checked with the Desk Sergeant that Berishvili had been charged and was in a cell then went looking for Misha Arziani. He found him in his office, staring at his open laptop.

Arziani raised his hand in greeting. 'You've had a productive morning, Ramaz. Locking up the capitalist classes—Karl Marx would've been proud.'

Donadze showed him a clenched fist. 'Workers of the world unite…'

'Yes, but obstruction of justice?'

'I know, it's thin.'

'It's less than that. You're going to have to let him go.'

'I'm going to.' Donadze paused. 'Maier just called, he's not sending his lawyer for Berishvili.'

'Did he say why not?'

'He said their interests aren't *aligned*.'

'What did he mean by that?'

'He suggested that Berishvili acted rashly by initiating a disciplinary against Nana Pachulia. But Maier's not someone who cares about his staff and I don't believe that factored into his thinking. I suspect he knows the audit will uncover evidence of money laundering and he's lining up Berishvili to take the fall.'

'Could he do that?'

'I don't know. He'd probably like to. No one important would go to jail and the Bank would suffer minimal reputational damage. Which—as Maier told us—means everything for his bank. And probably for him as well.'

'Does Berishvili know he's not getting a lawyer?'

'No, he's not been in contact with anyone yet.'

'It'll be interesting to see his reaction when you tell him.'

'I'll be doing that soon. Something else occurred to me, Misha. We know the Deputy Minister doesn't want to see the Bank's reputation tarnished. This could be a good outcome for her as well.'

'You're not suggesting she's part of a conspiracy to set up Berishvili, are you?'

Donadze shrugged. 'Maybe it's a stretch…'

'Have you spoken to Colonel Meskhi about this?'

'No. I want to have a chat with Berishvili first.'

'Do you want me to sit in on the interview?'

'Yes. Let's talk to him now.'

Arziani called the Desk Sergeant and told him to take the banker to an interview room.

Berishvili was sitting very still when they arrived, his eyes closed as if meditating.

'Contemplating your future, Lekso?' Donadze said. He placed a mug on the table. 'Coffee.'

Berishvili opened his eyes and pointed a finger at Arziani. 'Who's he?'

'*He's* our station commander,' Donadze said.

'Am I supposed to be impressed?'

'We have a few questions to ask you, Lekso,' Arziani said.

'I'm in no rush. I'll speak to you when my lawyer arrives.'

Donadze looked surprised. 'You've called your lawyer?'

'Assuming that stupid girl did what she was told, a lawyer from the Bank will be here soon. I'll speak to you when he arrives.'

'Ah, I see. Well, I know that Nana *did* phone the Bank and Christoph Maier *does* know you're here. Unfortunately, Herr Maier is not sending a lawyer for you. His interests and yours aren't *aligned*, apparently. Do you know what he means by that?'

It took the banker a moment to generate a smile. 'Yes, I do and it makes perfect sense. I'll get my own lawyer.'

'I asked Maier if he was throwing you to the wolves.'

'I've no idea what you're talking about, Donadze.'

'I think you do. Why not get in front of this, Lekso?

Tell us everything you know: who's involved, how long it's been going on?'

Berishvili reached across the table to lift his coffee, took a drink and placed it back on the table. 'I've no idea what you're talking about, Donadze,' he repeated. He sat back in his chair. 'You've charged me with obstruction of justice. I'll take your questions on that—just as soon as my lawyer arrives.'

Donadze held the banker's stare for a moment then stood. 'No, that's okay, Lekso. You're free to go.'

Donadze arranged for Lekso Berishvili to be released from custody then sent a text to Jaqeli, *How's audit going?*

She answered almost immediately, *Good, decided to stay. See you at station.*

He had expected a more detailed response, specifically if any hard evidence of money laundering had been found. He typed, *Anything?* but deleted it without sending, hoping she would let him know if there was anything significant to pass on.

He returned to his desk and called Colonel Meskhi.

'Lieutenant,' Meskhi answered. 'One minute.' The line went quiet and Donadze imagined him stepping out of a meeting to take the call. He spoke again a moment later, 'Donadze?'

'The Kazbegi Avenue investigation, sir…'

'Yes, Lieutenant?'

'I had reason to arrest Lekso Berishvili this morning and—'

'You arrested Berishvili—on what charge?'

'Obstruction of justice. He's been released now but—'

'Then why charge him in the first place?'

'It's a little complicated, sir, but—'

'Never mind. What did you want to discuss?'

'Maier and Berishvili's relationship, Colonel. Maier wouldn't send the Bank's lawyer to represent Berishvili after he was arrested. That came as surprise to him. I think he feels let down, betrayed even. I asked him if Maier was throwing him to the wolves, setting him up to take the fall for the money laundering, the murders even. He put on a face but I could tell that possibility had landed.'

'That's interesting. It would certainly help if divisions were opening at the Bank.'

'Yes, I think Maier is preparing for the Bank to take a hit. But he wants to limit the damage. He told me he expects the audit to uncover—what he called—uncomfortable findings. But any issues, he said, will be limited to a small number of *bad actors*.'

'And you believe Berishvili is being set up as one of these bad actors?'

'I think that's possible, Colonel.'

'That's interesting,' Meskhi said again. 'Thanks for the update, Lieutenant, you seem to be making reasonable progress. Is there anything else?'

'Yes, sir.' Donadze hesitated, choosing his words carefully. 'Political interference, the role of the Ministry of Finance...'

'Specifically?'

'Specifically, we know the Deputy Minister believes the First National Bank is important to the country's economy.

She seems as keen as Christoph Maier to preserve its reputation. Also, part of her role is to regulate the banks; a major financial scandal would reflect badly on her and her ministry. I think she'd see the audit identifying something uncomfortable—rather than criminal—as a good result. Especially if it only involved a few *bad actors*.'

'Ah, I see. You suspect the Deputy Minister may be in cahoots with Christoph Maier to set up Lekso Berishvili? That seems rather fanciful to me, Lieutenant.'

'Is it though, sir? We know she was keen for us to drop our investigation in favour of her audit. It was a softer option for the Bank—and we agreed to it.'

'*We* didn't agree to it, Donadze—it was my decision.'

'Yes, sir.'

There was a long silence. 'Is there something you wish to ask me, Lieutenant?'

Donadze took a breath. 'How about you, sir. Would you see Berishvili taking the fall as a good result?'

There was an even longer silence before Meskhi spoke, his tone even. 'No, Donadze. I would consider that an extremely unsatisfactory outcome.' He paused. 'Do you believe that?'

Donadze hesitated before responding.

'I see,' Meskhi said. 'Well, Lieutenant, we'll discuss this another day. You may return to your investigation.'

'Sir,' Donadze said, but the line was already dead.

TWENTY-SIX

Donadze returned his phone to his pocket and played back the conversation with Colonel Meskhi in his head. He'd felt compelled to challenge Meskhi, some self-destructive trait in his own personality, he thought. But Meskhi was probably only managing the politics of their investigation, something he was incapable of doing himself. He thought his challenge had been unjustified, disrespectful and ultimately damaging to their professional relationship and to his own career.

But he couldn't turn back time. He checked his phone for further messages from Jaqeli. There were none and he logged onto his police account to distract himself in the world of administrative humdrum.

His phone buzzed after about an hour, caller ID withheld. *Lunch?*

It was two twenty and he was hungry. *No burgers!* he responded, guessing the text's origin.

He received a disappointed-face emoji back followed a moment later by, *Old Marriott 20 mins.*

It would take fifteen minutes to walk to the hotel and he retrieved his jacket from the back of his chair and hustled out of the station.

Sweat was beading on his forehead as he reached Rustaveli Avenue. He found the nearest tunnel and crossed under the wide tree-lined street, emerging a short distance from the Tbilisi Marriott Hotel, known as the *Old Marriott* to differentiate it from the Marriott Courtyard Hotel on Freedom Square. He nodded to the unsmiling doorman, his eyes on Donadze's back as he stepped into the lobby looking for the entrance to the lounge and bar.

Tatyana Rokva had taken a table by a tall window facing onto Rustaveli Avenue. She raised a hand to attract his attention and stood as he joined her, leaning in for a kiss. She was an attractive woman and he noticed several customers—men and woman—scrutinising them, surmising they were a couple and wondering, he thought, what she could possibly see in him.

He sat opposite Rokva, self-consciously pinching his crooked nose.

She smiled at him. 'You're not a gambler, are you, Ramaz?'

'Nothing against it,' he said. 'It just doesn't interest me. Why do you ask?'

She pinched her own nose. 'That's your tell. You do it when you're nervous.'

'Who said I'm nervous?'

She pinched her nose again. 'That did.' She smiled at him. 'Don't worry, not many people would notice. But I recommend you don't take up poker for a living.' She lifted a cafetiere and poured oily coffee into his cup. 'I've ordered sandwiches and pastries—I hope that's okay.'

Donadze glanced around the lounge. The other customers, having satisfied their curiosity, were focused on their food and drinks and their own companions. 'Have you found anything on Belov and Galkin?' he asked.

Rokva gave a small shake of her head as a waiter approached and placed two plates in front of them: one containing a selection of sandwiches cut into small, crustless squares, the other a selection of miniature, flaky pastries. He insisted on explaining what each was before wishing them *bon appetit* in improbable French and withdrawing.

Rokva looked disappointed. 'Not much to eat there,' she said.

'Go ahead, I'm not hungry,' he lied.

'You'd better have something.' She offered him the sandwich plate and he took one of the tiny squares and placed it on his own plate.

'Belov and Galkin?' he asked again.

She nodded to acknowledge his question, bit off half a sandwich and washed it down with a gulp of coffee. 'I've got a fast metabolism,' she felt compelled to explain, popping the other half into her mouth, her eyes closed. She took another sip of coffee. 'Andrey Belov and Oleg Galkin: who told you they're *former* FSB?'

'You mean they're still active?'

'Why not answer my question first, Ramaz?'

Donadze nodded. 'Have you heard of a gangster called Shalva Khapava?'

She shook her head. 'No.'

'The Kaldani crime family?'

'Of course.'

'Khapava told me. He's in charge now. Took over from

Otar Basilia after he was killed in prison. He thinks Belov or Galkin can tell him who ordered the hit on his old boss.'

'And that's something you're interested in?'

'These two are responsible for the bank murders—that's what I want them for. I don't care about Basilia.'

Rokva lifted another sandwich and scrutinised it before taking a bite. 'They're not too bad,' she said.

Donadze waited for her to continue.

'So, it seems your Russian friends aren't fully retired from the FSB,' she said at last.

'What does that mean?'

'It means they're freelance now, as you thought, but one of their clients is the Russian state. They've done work for Mr Putin recently.'

'Directly?'

'Hardly, the Tzar doesn't deal directly with his foot soldiers. But he does have friends with common interests.'

'Such as?'

'Such as getting their money out of Russia. Do you remember the *Russian Laundromat*?'

'Remind me.'

'You should read up on it. It was about ten years ago. Probably the biggest money laundering scheme ever. Up to eighty billion dollars moved from Russia through international banks, mostly in Moldova and Latvia.'

Donadze nodded his understanding. 'And with the West sanctioning Russia as punishment for Ukraine…'

'The *oligarchs* need to find new ways to shift their money.'

'Through Georgian banks?'

'Maybe. That's what your audit's supposed to tell you, isn't it?'

'I didn't say anything about an audit.'

Rokva smiled and turned her attention to the pastries. 'Andrey Belov's mother is living in Tbilisi,' she said.

'She's Georgian?'

'Yes. She married a Russian man, Belov's father, during Soviet times and they lived in Russia. That's where Belov was born. But she moved back to Georgia after her husband died and remarried.'

'Did Belov move with her?'

'No. He was grown by then and already making a name for himself in the FSB.'

'Does he love his mother?'

'She's probably the only person in the world he cares anything about. We know he tries to see her when he can.'

'He's staying with her now?'

Rokva laughed. 'Of course not.'

'But he's still in Georgia?'

'We think Belov and Galkin are both still in Georgia.'

'They've got another job? A hit?'

Rokva shrugged. 'It's what they do, Ramaz.'

'Who's the target?'

'You should have a better idea of that than us.'

'Are you watching the mother?'

'That would be a reasonable assumption.'

'And you're going to tell me who she is, where she lives?'

'No. My bosses are grateful that you've brought Galkin and Belov to our attention. But they feel we're better placed than the police to keep tabs on Belov's mother.'

'And if he tries to see her?'

'We'll deal with him.'

'What does that mean?'

Rokva picked up a pastry then returned it to its plate. 'These are Russians killing Georgians in our capital city, Ramaz. Why would you care what happens to them?'

Donadze left the Old Marriott with Rokva. She kissed him goodbye—with real affection or as cover, he wasn't sure which—and merged into the press of bodies bustling past the opera house, galleries, government buildings, churches, shops, restaurants and bars lining Rustaveli Avenue.

He checked his phone—still nothing from Jaqeli and he sent her a text, *When back?*

He was climbing the stairs out of the avenue's underpass when she replied, *Here now.*

See you in 15. He lengthened his stride to tackle the long ascent up Besik Street towards Mtatsminda Station.

Jaqeli was at her desk when he arrived.

'On your own?' he asked.

'Tina's gone home. I told her I'd brief you.'

'Is there much to brief?'

'Yes, I think so.' She flicked through her notebook. 'Emzar Kesaria was our host. He thanked us on behalf of Christoph Maier and assured us the Bank would take lessons from the audit's findings. He told us Maier expected...' She glanced at her notes. 'Some uncomfortable finding involving a small number of—'

'Bad actors? Sounds like they have a script. Maier told me much the same thing. Did you hear about Lekso Berishvili?'

'Yes, from Misha. He's one of the bad actors, I presume?'

Donadze nodded. 'You can see where this is heading, can't you, Irina? Any criminality Tina uncovers will be confined to a couple of junior managers: Lekso Berishvili and Koba Brachuli—a fall guy and a dead man.'

'Maybe, but I think whatever she does uncover will be more than just *uncomfortable.* We already know Kazbegi Avenue was money laundering and Tina's looking at the other branches Berishvili covered.'

'How long until she has something definitive?'

'A couple of days possibly. She has to follow audit processes—it's all very procedural.'

He shook his head. 'Yes, we should never have agreed to it.' He thought for a moment then drummed the table top with his fingers, smiling. 'But I think we *are* making progress.' He updated Jaqeli on his discussion with Tatyana Rokva.

Jaqeli leaned back in her chair, frowning. 'We should be able to find Belov's mother ourselves, why leave it to the GIS?'

'They're better at this kind of thing than us, probably because they don't have the same constraints.'

'I don't know, Ramaz. It feels a bit messy to me.'

'No. It's simple enough. Tina keeps working on the First National Bank and we find Galkin and Belov—preferably before anyone else is killed.'

We have guests, when will you be home?

Tamuna had attached a photo to her WhatsApp message. It had been taken in their apartment: Levan Gloveli standing by the breakfast bar, frowning; Donadze's mother beside him, her hand on his arm; Veronika Boyko holding Eka while Lasha, her fiancé stood slightly apart from the group, looking self-conscious even in the slightly out-of-focus picture.

Donadze glanced at the wall clock—five forty. He replied, *1 hour,* wondering why Gloveli and the others had travelled to Tbilisi.

Jaqeli was talking with Misha Arziani in his office and he gestured to show he was leaving. It was the worst time of day to be on the roads and he used the extended driving time to think over his investigation; searching for missed clues or potential new lines of inquiry while the chaos of rush hour driving raged around him.

He left his car in its parking slot and took the elevator to the fourth level. A buzz of animated conversation and the aroma of his mother's good cooking met him at the apartment door. He was hungry—he hadn't eaten since Tatyana Rokva had spared him a few scraps at the Marriott Hotel.

'This is a nice surprise, isn't it, *Ramazi*?' his mother said, pressed up unnecessarily close against Gloveli on their couch.

'It certainly is,' Donadze said. 'Who's looking after the village while you're here, Major?'

Gloveli got stiffly to his feet to greet him and, Donadze guessed, to escape his mother. 'I think Shindisi will manage without me for a few hours,' he said.

Tamuna pointed to two plastic bottles on the worktop.

'Levan's brought us some of his wine.'

His mother also got up. 'We'll be eating in about thirty minutes,' she said, smiling at Gloveli.

Donadze filled his glass and tore off a chunk of *lavash* bread, baked locally and still warm. '*Gaumarjos,*' he toasted and took a large sip of the wine.

He made small talk with Gloveli, doing his best to include Lasha in their conversation while his mother orchestrated the preparation of their meal

Several minutes passed before Gloveli laid his hand on Lasha's shoulder. 'I'm going to speak to Ramaz for a minute,' he said, nodding towards the balcony door.

Donadze picked up both their glasses and followed Gloveli onto the balcony. He closed the door behind them. 'Let me guess. You're asking permission to marry my mother?' he said with a straight face.

Gloveli laughed. 'I could do a lot worse. But no, it's not that.'

'So what is it then, Major?'

'I wanted you to know, I've signed my house over to Veronika. She and Lasha will need someplace to live when they're married and they've got no money of their own.'

Donadze paused, thinking Gloveli would say more. 'Well that's very generous, Levan. But why are you telling me?'

'You know I've got no family, Ramaz. You're the closest I have to a son, God help me. The house would have been yours when I'm gone. I just wanted to explain why I've given it to Veronika.'

Donadze took a sip of wine to disguise his emotions. He and Gloveli were close but it had never occurred to him that the old policeman thought of him as a son. 'That's fine,

Levan. Thanks for letting me know.'

Both men sipped their wine, too embarrassed to say more.

A few moments passed and Donadze's mother knocked on the glass door, raising both hands, fingers extended to tell them their meal would be ready in ten minutes, her eyes and smile on Gloveli.

'Are you sure you don't want to marry her?' Donadze asked.

TWENTY-SEVEN

Donadze was dressed and eating breakfast when Soso Chichua called.

'Are you watching the news, Lieutenant?'

'No, what's happening?'

'A car bomb on Barnov Street.'

'The Chinese Embassy?'

'That's what I'd thought as well. But no, not the Embassy and it's not terrorism either. It's been a hit, an assassination.'

'Who?' Donadze asked, although he'd already guessed the answer.

'That's why I called you, Ramaz. The car belonged to a manager at the First National Bank—Lekso Berishvili. You knew him, didn't you?'

'Yes,' Donadze said, noting Chichua's use of the past tense. 'I knew him. Are you there now?'

'Yes.'

'On my way, Soso.'

Donadze gulped his coffee and said goodbye to his family, calling Jaqeli whilst walking down the stairs. 'You've heard?'

'Yes, it's on the news. One dead, no other injuries.'

'Did they say who was killed?'

'No.'

'It's Berishvili.'

Jaqeli paused a moment. 'That's why Belov and Galkin stayed on in Georgia…'

'Yes. We should have realised Berishvili was their target.'

'I don't know, Ramaz. It wasn't really that obvious.'

'But it was though, Irina. Berishvili being set up to take the fall wasn't enough. Much safer to get rid of him as well. Add in Koba Brachuli and that's both of Maier's *bad actors* dead now.'

'Ramaz?'

'What?'

'Take a breath. This isn't our fault.'

He bit back a retort. 'I'm going there now,' he said.

'Okay, I'm on my way.'

Barnov Street had been closed off by barriers placed one hundred metres from both sides of the blast site. Donadze got out of his car and sniffed the air; the acrid fumes from burning plastic almost—but not quite—masking the nauseatingly sweet, barbecued-meat stench of charred flesh.

He showed his ID and ducked under the barrier, walking past the shops, businesses and apartment blocks lining both sides of the narrow street. Most business premises hadn't opened yet but several residents inadvisably hung out of their apartment windows, their phones pointing up the street, desperate to witness events and record them for the benefit of their friends and followers on social media. A woman shouted to Donadze as he passed, recognising him as police and demanding to be allowed out of her home.

He approached the blast site. Crime scene tape had been strung across the street, blocking off the parking area between two adjoining low-level apartment blocks where the shattered car still smouldered. It was a small SUV, the manufacturer's badge still attached to its twisted grill. The worst damage was to the rear. Paint had burned off the steelwork leaving it warped and blackened, the tyres blown out and melted. Fire had burned fiercely in the passenger compartment and a blackened form, barely recognisable as human, occupied what was left of the driver's seat.

Soso Chichua noticed Donadze and raised his hand in greeting.

Donadze lifted the police tape and crossed towards him. 'They're a bit late, aren't they, Soso?' he said, nodding towards a group of soldiers loading equipment onto a military vehicle marked *Bomb Disposal*.

Chichua smiled. 'Standard practice, Ramaz. In case there's a second bomb.' He gestured to the group and one of the soldiers broke off and walked over to them. 'This is my boss,' Chichua said. 'Lieutenant Ramaz Donadze.'

Donadze offered his hand. 'What can you tell us, Corporal?' he asked.

The soldier shrugged. 'Neat job, not too much peripheral damage. A *sticky bomb*, probably held in place by magnets. Plastic explosive, *Semtex* we think. About half a kilo placed under the tank to make sure the fuel ignited. It could have been detonated remotely but it looks like the device exploded when the car moved, so that probably means a tilt fuse.'

'Tilt fuse?' Chichua asked.

'Mercury in a tube. It flows through the tube when the vehicle moves, completes a circuit and blows the plastic.'

'Professional job?'

'Definitely.'

'Thanks,' Donadze said.

The soldier returned to his vehicle.

'You already know why Berishvili was killed, don't you, Ramaz,' Chichua said.

Donadze nodded. 'Yes, I do. I just can't prove it yet.'

'We'd like to speak to Mr Maier,' Jaqeli said, presenting her ID.

The receptionist smiled and moved her mouse, clicking buttons and scrutinising her screen. 'You didn't make an appointment,' she suggested.

'No, but it's important.'

'I'll check if he's available,' she said, reaching for her handset. 'I can see he already has—'

'Tell Herr Maier we need to speak to him now,' Donadze interrupted.

'I will do,' she said, her smile unwavering. 'Please take a seat, Detectives.'

'No, we'll wait here.'

'Of course. One minute,' she said, lifting the handset

to her ear and using a pencil to push buttons on her phone.

Donadze glanced at Jaqeli and she shook her head, reprimanding him for being abrupt. He nodded in return, acknowledging her rebuke.

The receptionist put the handset down. 'Mr Kesaria will be down shortly.'

'Thank you,' Jaqeli said.

'Yes, thank you,' Donadze added, noticing Jaqeli stifling her smile.

Emzar Kesaria appeared on the stairway a moment later. He waved and hurried to meet them, his hand already extended as he reached the reception area.

'Detectives, thank you for coming,' he said, as though Donadze and Jaqeli had been summoned. 'Such a terrible thing.'

'You're referring to Lekso Berishvili being killed?' Donadze asked.

'Of course, poor Lekso. Our security manager is briefing Mr Maier now. Perhaps you'd care to join us?'

'Yes, we'll do that.'

Kesaria led Donadze and Jaqeli up the stairway and along the corridor to Maier's office. Nina, his personal assistant was there, still guarding access to his inner sanctum. Her eyes were red and puffy beneath her glasses.

Kesaria pointed to Maier's door. 'Can I take these officers through, Nina?'

She managed a sad smile. 'Yes, of course, Emzar. Please go ahead.'

Kesaria knocked on the door and pushed it open. 'Lieutenant Donadze and Detective Jaqeli, sir,' he announced.

Maier was behind his desk. He declined to stand or acknowledge his visitors.

A squat, powerful-looking man in his early forties sat across from Maier. Kesaria introduced him as Lado Jojua, the Bank's security manager. He nodded to Jaqeli and shook Donadze's hand, his bone-crushing grip asserting his dominance, a classic alpha male, Donadze thought.

'So, Lieutenant,' Maier said at last. 'I take it you've come to apologise?'

Donadze took a moment to settle in his chair before answering. He looked at Maier and smiled. 'Apologise for what, Herr Maier?'

'For not keeping Berishvili safe, of course. Now we may never know who was responsible for infiltrating my bank.'

'You're suggesting that your bank was *infiltrated* and whoever did that had Lekso Berishvili killed?'

Maier looked to his security manager in exasperation. 'Well, Berishvili certainly didn't die from natural causes, did he, Lieutenant? How else would you explain it?'

'We like to keep an open mind, Herr Maier.'

Maier snorted in derision. 'Well, maybe Berishvili would still be alive if you'd done your job properly. If you'd been more *decisive* and less *open* in your thinking. Let me see if I can help you now.' He turned to his security manager. 'Please share your thoughts with Lieutenant Donadze, Lado.'

Jojua sat and straightened his trousers, an amused smile playing on his lips. 'We believe that Lekso Berishvili was compromised, Lieutenant: bribed or blackmailed. He was then in a perfect position to recruit Koba Brachuli at our Kazbegi Avenue branch. Other branches may also have been involved.'

'Involved in what?'

Jojua shrugged. 'Money laundering.'

'From where?'

'Russia primarily. Belarus as well, we think. We'll confirm that when the audit—'

'The point is, Lieutenant,' Maier interrupted. 'We're certain this infiltration was *attempted* by only a small number of individuals, possibly with Russian involvement. But—thankfully—our robust *security processes* ensured that the main perpetrators were quickly identified before any more damage was done. It's just a pity the police allowed Berishvili to be killed before he could tell us how he became involved.'

'Very tidy,' Donadze said.

Maier smiled. 'How so, Lieutenant?'

'A Russian plot: that's sure to get people excited and on your side. And it's something our government can get behind as well. Everyone will be grateful that your *robust security* identified the plot early on. And your customers will be grateful you kept their money safe. A small number of people died but that's hardly your fault. The police should have done better. You'll be a hero, Herr Maier.'

Maier smiled again, his eyes crinkling. 'That's very good, Lieutenant. And remarkably close to the truth.' His smile dropped. 'Did you have anything more to discuss?'

Donadze turned to look at Jaqeli.

She shook her head.

'No,' he said. 'Not today.'

'Then, thank you for coming.' He turned to Kesaria. 'Emzar, show these officers out.'

Kesaria accompanied Donadze and Jaqeli down the Bank's central stairway, watching them as they walked to the door.

'Thank you,' Donadze said to the receptionist as they passed her desk, receiving a surprised but sincere smile as his reward.

'It's not that hard, is it?' Jaqeli said.

'But not my greatest strength.'

'Something for you to work on then.'

They left the Bank and strolled along Marjanishvili Square, the late afternoon sun reflecting dazzling light from the creamy, stone facades of the graceful nineteenth century buildings.

'I need coffee,' Donadze said. 'And something to eat.'

Jaqeli pointed to a cafe on the opposite side of the road. 'That place looks okay.'

She went inside to order while he chose a shaded outside table, moving the overflowing ashtray to a neighbouring table before sitting.

Jaqeli returned and took a seat beside him. 'So, what do you think, Ramaz?' she asked.

Donadze's mouth turned down. 'I think Herr Maier is laughing at us, he thinks he's won. Everything's tied up nicely and his bank keeps its reputation intact.'

'Right, but it's not our job to worry about the Bank's reputation. Our job is to find Sophia Brachuli and Vano Chedia's killers.'

'And whoever hired them—and that's someone from the Bank.'

'You're sure of that.'

'Yes, it has to be.'

'Who?'

'How long has Maier been in post?'

'He told us two years.'

'How long would it have taken to set-up his money laundering scheme?'

'*His* money laundering scheme? You really don't like Christoph Maier, do you, Ramaz?'

'He's not a likeable man. How long?'

Jaqeli shook her head. 'I don't know. A year? Maybe a bit longer?'

'So the timing's right.'

'But how would that have worked? Did Maier come to Georgia and see an opportunity. Or was he approached in post? Or maybe he was recruited with that job specifically in mind.'

'Yes, all these scenarios are possible.' Donadze paused while the waitress brought their sandwiches and coffee, throwing a look at Jaqeli as she lifted two full ashtrays from the neighbouring table. He bit into his sandwich while she retreated into the cafe. 'So how would Maier have got himself appointed?'

'I think chief executives are appointed by the company directors, mainly the chairmen. Maier was an external recruit so the Bank may have used an agency to find him.'

'Maybe but maybe not. You would think senior banking people would know each other, wouldn't you? It must be quite an exclusive club.'

'Are you going down a rat hole here, Ramaz? Assuming Maier's behind all this just because we don't like him.'

'So it's not just me who doesn't like him?' He took a

sip of his coffee. 'But you're right. Let's not shut down other possibilities. Have you checked-in with Tina today?'

'No. I'll call her later this evening.'

'That's okay, I'll do it. I want to speak to her anyway. I'm hoping her audit's about finished.' He shook his head. 'We should never have agreed to it.'

'Yes, you've said that before. And it's not *her* audit, is it?'

'No, it's not,' he agreed. He looked at his watch. 'Any plans for this evening?'

'Misha's taking me out for a meal.'

'That's good.' He checked the bill and left a twenty *lari* note on the table. 'I'll drop you at your apartment,' he said.

TWENTY-EIGHT

The audit team's feedback was scheduled for ten that morning. Donadze arrived at Mtatsminda Station at eight and called Tina Ninua.

'Lieutenant,' she answered brightly.

'Are you coming into the station this morning? I was hoping for a heads-up before we go to the Bank.'

She hesitated before replying. 'I don't think I'll have time, Ramaz. The team's getting together soon; we've got a few things to tidy up before we see you. And Irakli asked me to put the presentation together.'

'Irakli?'

'Irakli Todua, the audit lead.'

'Okay. Can you email me the presentation when you have it?'

She hesitated again. 'I can ask but I think Irakli will say no. He'll probably want everyone to receive the information at the same time.'

'*Everyone* being the Bank, the Ministry and us?'

'Yes, the Bank, the Ministry and the police.'

'And you're clear that you're police, aren't you, Tina?'

There was another, longer pause. 'I didn't ask to join this audit, Lieutenant,' she said, her voice low and even. 'But I've done my job and what you'll hear later this morning is both accurate and fair. Or is that not what you wanted?'

'No, accurate and fair is about right. Sorry, Tina, I didn't mean to sound critical.'

'No, of course you didn't,' she said, hanging up.

Donadze smiled as he put his phone away; Tina Ninua was tougher than he'd thought.

Jaqeli and Misha Arziani arrived a few minutes later. Arziani nodded to Donadze and continued to his office. Jaqeli stood for a moment, watching his retreating back.

'Something wrong?' Donadze asked.

'Not here,' she said.

'Okay. Do you want to go for a coffee?'

'Yes, I do. One minute.'

She walked to Arziani's office and went in. Donadze glanced up a few minutes later to see her touch his face before turning and walking away.

'I'll see you outside,' she said as she passed his desk.

He stood and looked through the office window. Arziani gave him a tight smile and shook his head: he didn't want to talk about it.

Jaqeli was waiting by his car. 'I thought we could go to the same cafe on Marjanishvili Square,' she said.

'Good idea, it'll be handy for the meeting.'

They got into the car and Donadze joined the traffic on Mtatsminda Street. He glanced at Jaqeli. She was staring out the window, her mouth tight.

'What do you think the auditors are going to tell us?' he asked.

She took a moment before replying. 'Misha asked me to marry him.'

He glanced at her again. 'And you said no?'

She turned to look at him. 'No, I didn't say that. I told him there are a few things we'd have to discuss first: we both work at the same station, he's my boss. That's already a bit awkward. He didn't take it well and we ended up arguing.'

'Ah…'

'What does that mean?'

'You want my opinion?'

'Yes, why is he angry with me?'

'Well, as you asked: I don't think he's angry, I think he's hurt. I know how much he cares about you and maybe he heard your concerns as rejection.'

'I didn't reject him. I just said there are things to discuss.'

'And you're right. There are issues you both need to deal with if you want to be together. But they're not insurmountable; not if that's what's making you hesitate, not if there's nothing more to it than that.'

'There *is* nothing more to it than that.'

'Well, Misha told you what *he* wants. The question is: do *you* want the same? Yes or no—either answer is okay.'

She laughed. 'Wow. Ramaz Donadze: relationship guru. Who would have known?'

Donadze shook his head. 'Not quite a guru but you learn things when you keep getting it wrong yourself.'

She put her hand on his arm. 'Thanks, Ramaz.'

They drove in silence for a few minutes. 'Could we

return to the station?' she asked. 'I'd like to speak to Misha again.'

Donadze glanced at his clock and indicated to make a turn. 'Okay,' he said. 'We've got time.'

Jaqeli left the station and strode to Donadze's car. She climbed into the passenger seat and buckled up.

'Everything okay?' he asked.

She reached into her jacket pocket, turned and opened a small jeweller's box. 'Yes, everything's good,' she said, smiling.

'It's beautiful.'

'Yes, it is. I love it.' She put the ring on her wedding finger and held it to the light, its diamonds sparkling. 'But I'm not going to wear it yet, not all the time, anyway.' She returned the ring to its box. 'Misha and I *are* engaged, but we're keeping it to ourselves for now. Working together could be a problem; but you were right—it's not insurmountable.'

'Well, I'm very happy for you both. I hope it's okay to let Tamuna know?'

'Of course it is.'

He nodded. 'Well, now that's settled, let's get back to work…'

She leaned over and kissed his cheek. 'Thanks, Ramaz.'

They drove to Marjanishvili Square in comfortable silence, Donadze content to leave her alone with her happy thoughts. He parked outside the Bank and they entered the grand old building through its imposing doors.

'Lieutenant Donadze and Detective Jaqeli,' the

receptionist said with a charming smile. 'Welcome back.' She consulted a printed list and highlighted their names with a yellow marker pen.

They hadn't identified themselves to her. 'We must be spending too much time here,' Donadze said.

'Not at all, it's always a pleasure to see you.' She retrieved two security passes from a drawer and slid them across her desk. 'You're in Meeting Room 1. I think you've been there before?'

'Yes, we have,' Jaqeli said, lifting her pass. 'Who else is here?'

'Let me see.' She ran a painted nail down her list. 'Here we are: the audit team's waiting for you in the meeting room; Colonel Meskhi hasn't arrived yet and the Deputy Minister is with Mr Maier.'

'In the meeting room?'

'No, she's with Mr Maier in his office, I believe.'

'Thank you,' Donadze said.

'You're more than welcome,' she smiled again.

They left Reception and walked to the stairway.

'I think she likes you,' Jaqeli said.

'What's not to like?'

They took the stairs to the meeting room level. Donadze paused on the landing area. 'We're a bit early. Let's say *hello* to Herr Maier.'

'What are you doing, Ramaz?'

'The First National may be the friendly face of banking but we're the friendly face of policing. I think it'd be friendly to let Maier know we're here.'

They continued up the stairs and along the corridor to Maier's office.

Donadze opened the door. Emzar Kesaria was in the waiting area, a folder opened on his lap. Maier's personal assistant was—as always—stationed behind her desk, guarding her boss whilst viewing the world with distaste and disappointment through tortoiseshell glasses.

Kesaria fumbled his folder closed and got to his feet. 'Detectives, welcome,' he gushed, stepping forward to shake Donadze's hand. He glanced at his watch, puzzled. 'I booked a meeting room,' he said, his voice inflected as though posing a question.

'Is Herr Maier free?' Donadze asked.

'You'd like to see Mr Maier now?'

'That's why we're here,' he said, stepping forward and opening the inner door. He turned as Maier's sentinel rose with surprising speed from her chair. 'Don't worry, Nina. I won't take up much of his time.'

Maier and Deputy Minister Maka Lomaia were sitting side-by-side at his conference table, a ceramic tea set, bowl of sugar and a saucer of sliced lemon set out in front of them.

'*Guten Tag*, Herr Maier.' Donadze nodded to Lomaia. '*Gamarjoba*, Deputy Minister.'

Maier looked amused. '*Guten Tag, Detektiv.*'

Kesaria and Nina had followed Donadze into the office. Maier dismissed them with a wave of his hand. He waited until the door had closed. 'What may we do for you, Lieutenant?'

Donadze gestured towards the tea set. 'We seem to have missed our invitation.'

Maier smiled at Lomaia. 'It appears Lieutenant Donadze would like to join us, Maka.'

Donadze watched the Deputy Minister colour. 'Are you always this disrespectful, Lieutenant? Mr Maier and I may talk whenever we choose—and we don't have to justify that to you.'

'No you don't.' He gestured towards the tea set again. 'Don't rush, we'll wait for you downstairs.'

Kesaria and Nina were hovering behind the closed door. Kesaria shook his head. 'Was that really necessary, Lieutenant?'

'I thought so,' Donadze said. He checked his watch. 'Ready, Irina?'

She raised her eyebrows and shook her head in reproach.

'I'll show you to the meeting room,' Kesaria said.

'That's alright, Emzar. Stay with your boss, we'll see you downstairs.'

They left the office and retraced their steps to the stairway.

The auditors were ready to provide their feedback. Tina Ninua introduced Donadze and Jaqeli to the three-member team. Colonel Meskhi had arrived and they joined him at the top end of the oval conference table.

A few minutes passed before Maier, Lomaia and Kesaria made their entrance, Maier throwing Meskhi a look for usurping his place at the head of the table. Meskhi stood as the Deputy Minister approached and they exchanged kisses. She sat, glancing at Donadze and shaking her head in silent reproach.

The meeting started. Irakli Todua, the audit lead welcomed the attendees and took them through the Bank's obligatory safety briefing. There were no questions and he clicked a button on his laser pointer to bring up the agenda. Todua was to present on all items other than one titled, *Areas of Concern*, on which Tina Ninua would lead.

Todua explained that the purpose of the audit was to provide an independent evaluation of the First National Bank's financial processes and reports. His presentation dragged on and Donadze felt his attention drift. It was more than an hour before he reached his conclusion: that most—but crucially—not all the Bank's operations and financial reporting complied with the required international standards.

That was his cue to hand over to Tina. She accepted the laser pointer and took up position in front of the screen. She explained that all Georgian financial institutions are obliged to follow the standards set by the FATF—an international body established to combat money laundering. Unfortunately, she said, First National Bank had not met these standards.

Donadze glanced at Maier as Tina paused to allow her message to land. He was staring at the screen, his mouth silently moving.

Meskhi spoke for the first time. 'You have examples, Tina?'

'Yes. We looked for typical indicators of money laundering activity: unusually large numbers of small, cash transactions; transfers to and from shell companies in offshore jurisdictions; multiple, complex movement of money between Georgian and foreign entities. We found these indicators at Kazbegi Avenue. That led us to Liakhvi Street branch. We followed different money trails. They were well disguised but the sums involved made them impossible to completely hide.'

'Do you know how much money was involved?'

'In dollars: tens, possibly hundreds of millions. But we need to do more work to be sure.'

'And where did these money trails begin and end?'

'They began in Russia and Belarus and ended in London, Paris, Frankfurt. Possibly New York. As I said, there's more work to be done.'

Maier leaned back in his chair. 'Well, it looks like our Mr Berishvili was an extremely busy man.'

Lomaia turned to Meskhi. 'This has turned out just as we expected, Gabi. This man, Berishvili clearly corrupted a couple of Christoph's branch managers. A lot of money's been moved but I think we have it under control now.' She smiled. 'I'm sure the Bank has learned lessons; there's no need for further embarrassment.'

'Thank you, Maka,' Meskhi said, turning to the audit lead. 'And thank you, Mr Todua for your team's systematic and rigorous approach.' He paused. 'But this is a purely criminal matter now and my officers will continue their investigation without further Ministry support. Please ensure all documents and supporting evidence are turned over to Miss Ninua.' He stood and tugged his jacket straight. 'Lieutenant, I'm sure Mr Maier will wish to remain in Georgia until your investigation is concluded. He won't need his passport—make sure you keep it somewhere safe.'

TWENTY-NINE

Donadze's phone buzzed an incoming text, *Funicular 20 mins.*

He presumed it was from Tatyana Rokva and—although irritated to be brusquely summoned again—typed, *OK, on my way,* adding a smiling-face emoji to demonstrate his enthusiasm.

It was a short, steep walk from Mtatsminda Street to the funicular railway's lower station and he took a moment to catch his breath and wipe moisture from his forehead before entering the building.

Rokva was in the queue waiting for the next train. She smiled when she saw him and waved him over. He joined her, ignoring the disapproving looks and *tuts* from the people behind.

'Let me guess,' he said. 'Burgers?'

She took his arm—for cover, he assumed. 'Only if you're hungry,' she replied with a smile.

The ride up the rails to Mtatsminda Park took only

three minutes and the rise in elevation was less than three hundred metres but the air was noticeably cooler and fresher at that altitude and distance from city traffic.

Donadze paused on the disembarkation platform to appreciate the views over the city as other passengers hustled past, anxious to get to the rides and food outlets.

Rokva took his arm again. 'Let's walk,' she said, guiding him towards the park's central pathway.

'Something's happened,' Donadze stated.

'Yes. Oleg Galkin's dead.'

Donadze stopped walking and disentangled her arm from his. 'The GIS killed him?'

Her face momentarily hardened, her eyes flashing. 'No, Lieutenant, *we* didn't kill him.' She paused and softened her tone, 'Come on, keep walking.'

They continued to stroll in the warm sunshine for several minutes, neither of them speaking.

'Galkin made the mistake of trying to return to Russia through South Ossetia,' Rokva said, at last.

'That's how he got into the country in the first place. The Kaldani family is from South Ossetia. Shalva Khapava's people helped him across the border.'

'It looks like they wanted it to be a one-way journey.'

'Khapava reckoned he could make Galkin or Belov tell him who'd ordered the hit on Otar Basilia.'

'Maybe he got what he wanted then.'

Donadze waited until a family had passed. He smiled good naturedly as a young boy ran into his legs while chasing his brother, both earning a sharp rebuke from their mother. 'I always knew Khapava wouldn't hand them over,' he said.

'So you can presume Khapava now knows who had his boss killed. No prizes for guessing what he'll do with that information.'

Donadze remembered his last conversation with Khapava. 'No, there's more to it than that, Tatyana, something I'm missing.'

'But you don't know what that is?'

'Not yet.'

They reached a fountain and Rokva stopped walking.

'What about Galkin's partner?' Donadze asked.

'Andrey Belov is still in Georgia as far as we know—we just don't know where.'

'And you're still watching his mother's house?'

'Yes, of course.'

'Will you tell me if he visits?'

'Let's go back, Ramaz,' Rokva said.

'You know we could find her ourselves, don't you?'

'Yes, eventually. But Belov's FSB-trained; he'd know you were watching and you'd never see him.'

'So you won't tell me?'

She took his arm and they started walking back to the funicular station. 'No,' she said. 'Sorry. I can't.'

The big SUV's engine shut down and the parking area immediately fell silent and still. Donadze stood in the half-shadows behind a pillar. He watched Shalva Khapava slide out of the car and *blip* its doors locked, the indicators blinking to acknowledge his command.

'Shalva,' Donadze said as he approached.

Khapava stopped but didn't turn. 'Lieutenant Donadze, you should have called.'

'This *is* me calling. Keep walking.'

He followed a pace behind the crime boss as they continued towards the elevator station.

Khapava pressed the call button, paused a moment then turned to face Donadze. His hand slid into his jacket pocket, his fingers bunching as if curling around a weapon.

Donadze willed himself not to flinch. 'That would never happen, Shalva,' he said. 'It takes a certain type of man to look another man in the eye and kill him. You're a keyboard warrior—nothing more.'

Khapava smiled and removed a fob from his pocket, swinging the leather between finger and thumb. 'Elevator security,' he said. 'No access to my penthouse without it.'

'Of course not.'

The door opened and Donadze took a step forward and slammed Khapava against the elevator's mirrored wall. 'After you,' he said.

Khapava pushed himself off the mirror. 'You've just made a big mistake, Donadze,' he growled, his voice betraying more fear than venom.

'Yes, I know. And you're the latest in a long line of lowlifes to tell me that.' The door closed and he pushed the control panel's top button. 'The fob,' he ordered.

Khapava held the device to a sensor and the elevator began its smooth ascent. A thought seemed to occur to him. 'Where's Jaqeli?'

'This is between you and me. I don't want her involved.'

Comprehension dawned on Khapava's face. He fumbled for his phone. 'I'm calling my lawyer,' he said.

Donadze stopped him with a single word. 'No.'

'You can't tell me not—'

'No.'

The elevator's door opened and Donadze nodded for Khapava to walk ahead. 'We'll talk inside.'

The crime boss unlocked his apartment's oversized door and pushed it open, using another fob to silence the security alarm.

Donadze followed him to the lounge. Table lamps turned on automatically, casting the room in a warm, atmospheric glow. Floor-to-ceiling windows offered spectacular views across the city, but not a view of Kandelaki Street and his own apartment block, he noted.

Khapava dropped onto a cream-coloured chair. 'What's this about?' he demanded, back on home territory and his confidence growing.

'You intercepted Oleg Galkin in South Ossetia and had him killed,' Donadze stated.

Khapava held Donadze's stare and smiled. 'What was it you called me? A keyboard warrior? No, you're wrong, I didn't have anyone killed. But it certainly looks like *someone* got to Galkin before you. Maybe *you* should have tried a little harder.'

Donadze nodded to himself, now certain, his mind made up. 'On your feet, Shalva. You're under arrest on suspicion of murder.'

Khapava laughed. 'You must be desperate, *Ramaz*.'

'Stand up and turn around.'

Khapava slowly complied, a smile playing on his lips. 'There's no way I'm going down for killing Oleg Galkin—and you know it.'

Donadze snapped the cuffs on his wrists. 'You may be right. But I'm not arresting you for killing Galkin. You're under arrest for the murder of Otar Basilia.'

Donadze's phone buzzed as he finished handcuffing Shalva Khapava into the back of his car. He pushed the door shut and swiped to answer the call.

'Are you still with Khapava?' Jaqeli asked.

Donadze stepped out of earshot, watching the crime boss through the car's rear window. 'Yes, I'm bringing him in. I know what happened now. It was Khapava who had Basilia killed.'

Jaqeli was silent for a moment. 'I'm assuming he didn't confess?'

'He didn't have to. We were blinkered, Irina. Khapava told us he wanted Galkin and Belov found because they could tell him who ordered Basilia's murder. But that was classic misdirection—and we fell for it. They wouldn't have been able to tell him anything—because there's no way they could have known. Khapava ordered the hit on Basilia himself and it had nothing to do with the bank job.'

'So what was it—a power grab?'

'That's exactly what it was. But Khapava showed his hand when he killed Galkin. He wasn't interested in speaking to him; he wanted him dead to stop him talking to us. Because if he *did* talk, he would have told us that neither he nor his bosses had anything to do with Basilia's death. And we would have believed him—eventually.'

Jaqeli was silent for a moment. 'Khapava told us Basilia

died because he got too close to the people behind the bank job. Ruling out that scenario would leave another obvious suspect with a completely different motive.'

'Yes, the man who would inherit the empire.'

'It makes sense. And killing the Russians has another benefit. Khapava told us not everyone's happy with him as head of the family. He's young and he's not Ossetian. But dealing with freelancers operating on his turf would show he's a worthy successor to Otar.'

'And scare off anyone thinking about grabbing power themselves. All that nonsense about Basilia being like a father to him. And we believed it.'

'He was pretty convincing, Ramaz.'

'He fooled us, anyway.'

'But not anymore. And you figured all this out just from speaking to Khapava this evening?'

'No, I'm not that good. There was always something about his account which worried me and I finally worked it out after Galkin was killed.'

'So, with Galkin dead, that makes finding Andrey Belov even more important.'

'We'll keep looking for Belov. But we need to find a way to deal with Khapava without him.'

'When you say *deal with…*'

'What we have is weak, Irina. The Prosecutor would tell us it's all speculation.'

'What about going back to Basilia's prison-mates—the cons who killed him in his cell—and see if they'll speak to us now,' Jaqeli asked.

'I thought about that but I doubt if anything's changed for them. Even if they did agree to speak to us it wouldn't be easy to tie the order back to Khapava—there would be buffers between him and them. We need to do something different.'

'I'm not going to like this, am I?'

'Maybe not, but here's what I want you to do.'

Donadze pulled up outside Mtatsminda Station, opened the car's rear door and uncuffed Shalva Khapava.

'My lawyer, Donadze,' Khapava said, now composed and confident as he was led into the station.

'Don't worry, Shalva, you'll see your lawyer soon enough.'

'Who do we have here, Lieutenant?' the Desk Sergeant asked.

'Mr Khapava will be your guest tonight, Dato,' Donadze said. 'Show him to his room and make sure he's comfortable.' He turned to Khapava. 'Let the Sergeant know if you need anything: change of pillow; extra blanket; room service. And please leave a review when you check out; we always welcome customer feedback.'

'You're hilarious, Donadze.'

'Good of you to say so.' Donadze nodded to the Sergeant then turned and walked out of the station.

It was easy to spot the SUV in the empty car park.

Meskhi wound down his window. 'Get in, Lieutenant,' he said.

Donadze climbed into the passenger's seat. Classical music was playing softly through the car's sound system. The clock indicated 20:44. 'I'm sorry for the late call, Colonel.'

He glanced at Meskhi as the courtesy light dimmed. He thought it was the first time he'd seen the Colonel casually dressed, a light shadow on his normally immaculately groomed face.

'Don't be. Khapava's in custody?'

'Yes. He'll see his lawyer soon.'

'At which point it will be clear you have no case against him.'

'Yes, we'll have to let him go.'

'This idea of yours; don't you want justice for Basilia and Galkin? Why not wait and see if we can develop our case?'

'I think Basilia and Galkin have already had the justice they deserve, Colonel. If we could get Khapava into court, I'd want to do that. But we won't be able to gather enough evidence to convince the Prosecutor.'

'You know it'll be temporary, don't you. Someone else will take over after Khapava's gone.'

'Yes, but that'll take time and there will be a power vacuum until it happens. We'll have an opportunity to weaken the organisation, to shut down some of the scams.'

'You're convinced Khapava had no involvement in the bank murders?'

'I'm certain of it, sir.'

Meskhi drummed his fingers on the steering wheel for a few moments. 'Very well,' he said at last. 'You have my approval.'

He started his engine and Donadze took that as his cue that the meeting was over. He reached for the door handle.

'Donadze,' the Colonel said.

'Sir?' He stopped, his door half-open.

'We've talked before about tackling criminality through *unconventional* means. This is a good example of that approach—I'm glad you brought it to me.'

Meskhi rarely gave compliments and Donadze wasn't sure how to respond.

'We'll discuss this matter again. You're dismissed,' Meskhi said, ending Donadze's internal debate.

'Sir,' he said and got out of the car.

He crossed to the station entrance and called Jaqeli. 'Meskhi's okay with it. Did you track down Tengo Sakhokia?'

'Yes, he's still at the casino—security managers never rest, it seems.'

'How about Soso?'

'He should be with you soon.'

'Okay. Speak to Tengo now.'

Donadze disconnected and called Soso Chichua. 'How far away are you, Soso?'

'The roads are quiet. Ten minutes, I'd say.'

'And the Major?'

'Right here with Soso, Donadze,' Gloveli growled. 'This couldn't have waited until morning?'

'I'll be outside,' Donadze said, ignoring Gloveli's gripes.

He returned to the station and found the Desk Sergeant making coffee.

'Do you want one of these, Lieutenant?' he asked.

'Maybe later. Do you remember Major Levan Gloveli, Dato?'

The Sergeant looked puzzled. 'Major Gloveli? Of course. Why do you ask?'

'He's on his way in. I'm taking him to speak with Khapava.'

'I don't understand. Gloveli's been retired for, what, five years?'

'Something like that. We just want an informal chat with Khapava before his lawyer arrives.'

'He's not called his lawyer yet.'

'I know, it's being taken care of.' Donadze looked at his watch. 'Gloveli will be here soon. Finish your coffee and we'll meet you at your desk.'

'You know I'm responsible for prisoner welfare, don't you, Lieutenant?'

'Yes, Dato, I do. Don't worry, we just need a moment with him.'

Donadze walked to the station entrance and waited until Soso Chichua pulled up. He opened the passenger door and Gloveli got out, wincing and holding his lower back as he straightened.

'Thanks for coming, Major,' Donadze said.

'I'm not going to say it's a pleasure.'

'Do you need me, Ramaz?' Chichua asked.

'No, we'll be okay, Soso. Thanks.'

Donadze pushed the door shut and raised his hand in farewell as the car pulled away. 'Did you make the call, Major?' he asked.

'Yes, as you requested.'

'Good. Then let's speak to Khapava.'

Donadze resisted an impulse to offer Gloveli his arm as the old policeman limped into the station.

The Desk Sergeant had returned to his desk, instinctively coming to attention as Gloveli approached.

The old policeman smiled and offered his hand. 'It didn't take you long to earn these stripes, Dato,' he said.

The Sergeant blushed and Donadze suppressed his own smile; he had briefed Gloveli that Dato was on duty and had been recently promoted.

'Lead the way, Dato,' he said.

The Sergeant hesitated a moment then snatched up a ring of keys. 'Okay, if it's only for a minute.'

There were eight holding cells in the custody suite with two occupied that night. The Sergeant pulled down the observation hatch on Khapava's cell door and peered inside. Satisfied, he unlocked the door and pulled it open. 'I'll be outside,' he warned.

The cell was long and narrow with a wooden bunk and a plastic-covered mattress dominating one of the long sides. Khapava was on the bunk, his back resting against the white-tiled wall, his eyes closed.

'Comfortable?' Donadze asked.

Khapava opened his eyes, looked at Gloveli then closed them again. 'I don't know you, old man, and I don't care why you're here. What I do want, Donadze, is my lawyer. When do I get my call?'

'We've organised that. He should be on his way.'

Khapava opened his eyes and sat forward on the bunk. 'You don't know who I want to represent me.'

'That's why we contacted your security manager. We thought he'd know.'

'You told Tengo Sakhokia to call my lawyer?'

'Not exactly. We told him you'd been arrested and charged with the murder of Otar Basilia.' Donadze paused. 'Tengo's from South Ossetia, isn't he? Probably related to Otar, somehow—maybe a distant cousin. Of course, there are a lot of South Ossetians in your organisation.'

Khapava smiled. 'You're not as clever as you think. I didn't kill Otar. But even if I had, you'd never be able to prove it.'

'Well, we both know you *did* kill him. And Oleg Galkin come to that. You're right, though, it wouldn't be easy to prove. But the people in your organisation who were *disappointed* when Otar chose you, the South Ossetians; how much proof will they need?'

Khapava's smile was forced this time. 'I think we're done talking, Donadze. Let me know when my lawyer is here.'

'Of course.' He turned to Gloveli. 'Let's go, Major.'

'Doesn't Mr Khapava want to know who *I* called this evening?' Gloveli asked.

'I don't know. Do you want to know who Major Gloveli called, Shalva?' Donadze asked.

Khapava leaned back against the tiles and closed his eyes again. 'Why not?'

Gloveli took an unsteady step forward. 'You're right, Shalva, I am an old man,' he said. 'But being old isn't all bad. One benefit is that I was around during the old Soviet, when there was a single police force operating across all the republics.'

'The KGB in other words,' Donadze said, smiling.

Gloveli frowned at the interruption. 'Yes, Donadze, the KGB.' He turned his attention back to Khapava. 'Now, things haven't gone well with Russia and its old empire—with Georgia and Ukraine, for example. But comrades remain comrades even when their countries go to war.' He patted the pocket holding his phone. 'I called one of my Russian comrades this evening. We shared information, as we often do.'

Donadze glanced at Khapava. He kept his eyes closed, feigning indifference.

'You miscalculated,' Gloveli continued. 'Oleg Galkin wasn't an *active* FSB operative. But he was important to certain, powerful individuals in Russia. And these individuals won't be happy when they discover you had him killed.'

'So you say. I didn't do it, but even if I did, it would be impossible to prove. Georgian police have no jurisdiction in South Ossetia.'

'Yes, but it's not the police you have to worry about. How much proof do you think the FSB will need to come looking for you? Do you think jurisdiction is something *they* worry about?'

'The thing is, Shalva,' Donadze said. 'It looks like you're in serious trouble. With your own people, with Putin's billionaire friends and with the Russian secret service. You're a dead man walking and that doesn't leave you many options, does it?'

'Can we go now?' Gloveli asked. 'I never did like police cells.' He looked at Khapava. 'Or maybe it was the people in them I didn't like.'

'Yes, let's get you home, Major.'

Khapava's shoulders slumped. 'What do you want from me, Donadze?'

'From you: nothing. I know you'll run—what else can you do? I won't stop you. And who knows, you might get lucky. A few months, a few years? Maybe the FSB will get tired looking for you.'

Gloveli shook his head. 'But I wouldn't count on it.'

'I'll see if your lawyer's here,' Donadze said, leading Gloveli out of the cell.

THIRTY

Donadze lifted his phone to read the text, *By your car, come out.*

Coming, he replied.

Jaqeli looked at him expectantly.

'Back in a minute,' he said and hurried out of the station.

Tatyana Rokva was waiting in the car park. 'Happy birthday, Ramaz,' she said, smiling. 'I'm here to give you your present.'

'It's *not* my birthday.'

'Okay, so I'm a bit early.' She paused. 'We've got him, Ramaz.'

'Who? Andrey Belov?'

'Yes. He's got his faults but at least he's a good son. He wanted to see his mother before leaving town.'

'That's great, Tatyana. You said she's the only one he cares anything about. Can I talk to him?'

'Better than that. You can have him. But he's FSB-trained, he won't tell you anything he doesn't want you to know.'

'Well, maybe there are things he *does* want us to know.' Donadze hesitated a moment. 'Why are you giving him to us, Tatyana?'

'Politics. It seems that this isn't a good time for us to be going head-to-head with the Kremlin. Better for the police to have him.'

'Do *you* think that's better?'

'No. I would like to have sent the FSB and Putin's pals a message. But maybe I'm not seeing the bigger picture. Anyway, I've got my orders. Can you pick him up?'

'What's the address?'

'We're holding him at his mother's house, 15 Ushba Street, Didi Lilo. I'm going there now.'

'Do you need a lift?'

'No, I've got one. Get going, Ramaz. Take him before we change our minds.'

Jaqeli was already putting on her jacket when he returned to his desk. 'I'm guessing we're going somewhere,' she said.

'Didi Lilo. We're picking up Belov.'

'Really? Should I request a patrol car to come out with us?'

He lifted his own jacket from the seat back. 'Not yet. I want to speak to him first. Could you bring the case file.'

'Why do we need that?'

'It's just an idea.'

Donadze drove quickly on the Kakheti Highway then dropped his speed on the broken, narrow road running uphill to Didi Lilo.

The houses on Ushba Street were all single level and most needed maintenance their owners probably couldn't afford. Donadze pulled up on scrubby grass behind a black saloon, guessing it belonged to the Georgian Intelligence Service.

A man in his early thirties was leaning against the car, his face turned to the midday sun. He straightened and removed his sunglasses as Donadze approached. 'Ramaz,' he said. 'It's been a while.'

'Yes, it has. Irina this is—'

'Gia Pataraia,' he interrupted, turning his smile on Jaqeli. 'Ramaz and I did some work together a while back.'

'Where's Belov?' Donadze asked.

'Straight to it, eh, Ramaz?' He patted his car. 'Right here,' he said.

Donadze glanced inside the saloon. 'You've put him in the boot?'

Pataraia winked at Jaqeli. 'We do things a bit differently in Intelligence.'

'Is Rokva here?' Donadze asked.

'Inside with Mrs Gogia.'

'Gogia?'

'Maia Gogia. She married a Georgian after old man Belov died.'

Donadze thought for a moment. 'Could you give us five minutes then bring Belov in?'

Pataraia looked at his watch. 'I don't know, Ramaz. Our work here is done. We were told to hand him over to you then get out.'

'It won't take long. Irina can help if you need her to.'

Pataraia laughed. 'Am I supposed to see that as a

challenge to my masculinity?' He looked at his watch and nodded. 'Okay, Ramaz, five minutes.'

'Thanks. Let's go Irina, bring the case file.'

They walked past fruit trees, vines and vegetable plots, scattering a brood of scratching hens hunting for morsels in the rich soil. The front door was unlocked and they went into the house.

A woman was sitting in a beat-up easy chair in the living room, her head in her hands. She looked up as they entered. Donadze guessed she was in her late fifties or early sixties but her lined face and thin, unruly grey hair spoke of a hard life lived.

'Who are you?' she said, her voice firm and surprisingly deep.

Tatyana Rokva was standing beside her. She placed her hand on the older woman's shoulder. 'Maia, these are the detectives I told you about. They're here to take Andrey into custody.'

Maia Gogia looked at Donadze with hard eyes. 'My son's done nothing wrong.'

'Do you know how your son makes his living, Mrs Gogia?' Donadze asked.

'Of course I do. He's a security advisor.'

Donadze looked at the woman, conscious her life would never be the same after today. 'No, that's not what he does. Andrey is a spy and a professional killer.'

Mrs Gogia laughed. 'Don't be ridiculous,' she said, although Donadze sensed her first stirrings of doubt.

'Well, let's see,' he said.

He heard an angry exchange at the front door and Pataraia came into the room a moment later, walking a careful pace behind a big, red-headed man whose hands had been secured behind his back. A weeping cut and bruising on his face attested that his arrest had not been peaceful.

Mrs Gogia rose from her chair. 'What have you done to my son?' she demanded.

Belov had grown a wispy beard but was easily recognisable from his passport picture. 'Hello, Andrey,' Donadze said, greeting him in Russian.

Belov laughed and shook his head. 'I'm sorry, *Deda*,' he said in accented Georgian. 'I don't know who these clowns are or what they think I've done.'

Donadze placed a chair two paces in front of Belov's mother. 'Take a seat, Andrey,' he said.

'No.'

'This is your mother's home. Should I ask my colleague to make you sit?'

Belov shook his head but dropped onto the chair, stretching his legs in studied indifference.

'Good,' Donadze said. 'Let me have the file, Irina.'

He extracted several photographs and sorted them into the order he wanted. 'We're going to look at pictures, Andrey. You get to see them first.'

'Ramaz,' Jaqeli warned.

'It's okay, Irina. Andrey can stop this any time he wants. He just has to admit what he did and who he was working for.'

He showed Belov the first image. 'This is the bank you and Galkin robbed.'

Belov smiled and Donadze crossed to Mrs Gogia and showed her the same image. 'It's a small branch, Mrs Gogia. Not a lot of cash. But Andrey didn't rob it for the money.'

Donadze returned to Belov. He showed him two photos of Vano Chedia. The first was from the Bank's personnel records; a young, serious looking young man beginning his career in banking. The second was the same man lying in a pool of blood in his branch manager's office.

'Should I continue?' Donadze asked.

Belov didn't respond and Donadze turned to his mother. 'Andrey wasn't acting on his own. His accomplice was another spy and assassin called Oleg Galkin. Galkin killed a man at the bank. His name was Vano Chedia. Vano was married. His wife's name is Eliso. She's pregnant. She told us that Vano was very happy they were having a son together.'

Donadze looked at Belov. 'Do you want your mother to see these images?'

Belov attempted to stand but was pressed back in his seat by Pataraia. 'That wasn't me, *Deda*,' he stated, his voice low and even.

'Okay,' Donadze said and showed the woman the two photos in sequence.

'No,' she said, glancing at her son and reaching to touch the second image with trembling fingers.

'Andrey knows how to make this stop, Mrs Gogia.' He looked at Belov. 'Shall we continue?'

Belov sat back in his chair, appraising Donadze, calculating his options.

Donadze glanced at Jaqeli and looked away, ignoring her horrified expression.

He turned his attention back to Belov's mother. 'One other person was killed that day, Mrs Gogia,' he said, speaking softly. 'A young woman called Sophia Brachuli. She was married to Koba, the manager of the bank Andrey and Oleg Galkin robbed. She had a six year old son: Zaal. *Your* son handcuffed Sophia to a radiator in her own apartment and shot her in the head. Zaal was there. We think she knew what was going to happen and sent him away—a mother's love, I suppose. She tried to protect him from the horror of her own murder—but couldn't. Zaal was only six but old enough to understand that your son had killed his mother.'

Belov looked away as Donadze held the last photo to his face: Sophia Brachuli lying on the floor of her lounge, one hand cuffed to the radiator, her blood sprayed on the wall and pooled beneath her broken body.

'Do you want your mother to see this picture?'

Belov lifted his head to stare at Donadze, hatred sparking in his eyes. 'You're a dead man,' he hissed in Russian.

'I've been threatened before, Andrey,' Donadze replied, also in Russian.

He crossed to Mrs Gogia. 'This is what your son—'

'Don't show my mother that image,' Belov commanded.

'Are you ready to talk?' Donadze asked.

'Tell him, Andrey,' Mrs Gogia said, her voice firm.

'*Deda*?'

'Tell him everything you know.'

'But if I do, he'll—'

'Tell him.'

Belov hesitated then nodded once. His eyes reached across the space between the two chairs, pleading for understanding, for forgiveness, for continued, unconditional love from the woman who stared back in disbelief at the son she no longer knew. 'I'm sorry, *Deda*,' he said.

Donadze slammed the patrol car's door closed, slapped its roof and stepped back to watch it accelerate away with Andrey Belov locked in the rear.

There was a moment's silence before Gia Pataraia said, 'Wow, I've never seen that approach before.'

Tatyana Rokva placed her hand on Donadze's arm. 'Are you okay, Ramaz?'

He shook his head. 'I've been better.'

'I know that was difficult for you. But Maia would have heard everything about her son at his trial. It's not something she could have been spared.'

'She wouldn't have heard it like that though. And she wouldn't have seen these photos. She's a mother; she didn't deserve what I put her through.'

'Well, Ramaz,' Pataraia said. 'The thing to ask yourself is this: would you do it again—if you had to?'

Donadze thought for a moment before replying. 'Yes. I knew what I was doing.'

Pataraia grinned. 'Then don't worry about it. What that old lady *really* doesn't deserve is a son like Andrey.'

'No, she doesn't. Anyway, it's done.' He turned to Rokva. 'Could you check on her before you leave? I'm pretty sure she doesn't want to see me again.'

Rokva kissed him on his cheek. 'Take care, Ramaz.'

'You too.' He shook hands with Pataraia. 'Let's go, Irina.'

They got in his car and took the steep, bumpy road back to the Kakheti Highway.

'I'm sorry, Irina,' he said after several minutes of silence. 'I knew you weren't happy back there.'

'It didn't have to be like that, Ramaz.'

'How else could it have been? Belov would have been released just like Khapava was—no trial because we had no real evidence. Either that or we would have traded him to the Russians. You heard what Rokva said about not wanting to go head-to-head with the Kremlin. And how about Sophia Brachuli and Vano Chedia? How would they have got justice?'

'So the end justifies the means? How often have we heard that before? That's why there are rules, Ramaz.'

'I know. But sometimes, especially in cases like this, no rules apply.'

Donadze slipped onto the Kakheti Highway, picking up speed to merge with traffic racing to the city. He glanced at Jaqeli. 'I think Colonel Meskhi is going to offer me a different job. That would be a good time for you to get a new partner.'

'Did I say I want a new partner?'

'No, but we'll always be having these conversations. You'd find it easier to work with someone new.'

'I think you should let *me* worry about that.' She shook her head. 'I'm trying not to judge you, Ramaz.'

'Don't you think I judge myself?'

'I know you do.'

'Let's leave it for now,' Donadze said. He glanced at his clock. 'Fifteen minutes.'

They continued their journey to the city in silence and Donadze pulled up behind a patrol car on Marjanishvili Square.

'Okay?'

She nodded. 'Yes, I'm okay.'

A uniformed officer got out of his car as Donadze approached. 'Where do you want us, Lieutenant?' he asked.

'Wait here. We'll bring him to you.'

Donadze and Jaqeli entered the Bank through its heavy wooden doors.

The same young woman was on the reception desk. 'We really *are* spending too much time here,' he told her.

She rewarded him with a dazzling smile. 'Not at all, Lieutenant.' She picked up a sheet of paper and scrutinised it, looking puzzled.

'We're not on your visitors list, Mirtsa,' Donadze said, reading her name tag.

'But we would like to see Mr Maier,' Jaqeli added.

'Mr Maier,' she said, looking doubtful. 'Let me see.' She consulted her screen. 'He's holding his weekly call with London. I can check if he has some time free after that?' she suggested.

'No, sorry, Mirtsa,' Jaqeli said. 'We have to see him now.'

The receptionist allowed herself a slight frown. 'One minute,' she said, lifting her handset. She spoke a few words, smiling as she listened to the response then returned the handset to its cradle. 'Mr Kesaria is coming down,' she said triumphantly. 'I'd suggest you take a seat but…'

'Thanks, we'll wait here.'

'Absolutely!'

Donadze and Jaqeli stepped away from the desk to watch the stairway. 'You're enjoying this too much,' Jaqeli said.

'Absolutely!'

A few minutes passed and Emzar Kesaria appeared on

the landing area above them, waved and quickly moved down the stairs to greet them, his hand extended. 'Lieutenant, Detective, welcome.' He dropped his hand, raising a puzzled smile as Donadze declined to take it. 'We didn't expect you back so soon. Has there been a development?'

Donadze turned to Jaqeli. 'Would you say there's been a development, Detective?'

She sighed. 'Yes, I would, Lieutenant.'

'So would I. Turn around, Emzar. You're under arrest for conspiracy to commit murder.'

'What do you have against bankers, Ramaz?' Misha Arziani asked, his face deadpan.

'Nothing—if they stick to banking.'

Arziani raised his coffee cup in salute. 'Seriously, great result. Well done, to both of you.'

'Thanks, Misha.'

'We're celebrating this evening,' Jaqeli said. 'Can you and Tamuna join us?'

'Celebrating closing the case?'

'Our engagement. Something low key: dinner at your favourite restaurant if you like. Misha's buying.'

'Thanks, I think that should be okay, let me check with Tamuna.'

'When are you interviewing Kesaria?' Arziani asked.

Donadze glanced at the wall clock. 'Soon. When he's finished with his lawyer and Meskhi gets here.'

'He must be pleased.'

'I think so. We've been in the spotlight this time. It's just as well he's good at managing the politics—and the politicians.'

'Speaking of politicians, Maka Lomaia is going to be embarrassed, isn't she? It's her job to regulate the banks, a big financial scandal won't do her career prospects any good.'

'Don't be so sure. She'll find a way to spin it to her advantage.'

'I'd like to listen in with Irina if that's okay.'

'You're the boss, Misha...'

'Just filling in, Ramaz.'

'No, you'll get the job.'

Donadze lifted his coffee and carried it to the station entrance. It was the hottest day of the year so far, the almost unbearable heat and stifling humidity of high summer approaching fast. He leaned against the building's warm brick wall and closed his eyes, allowing his mind to drift.

His involvement in the investigation was ending. Tina Ninua and her colleagues would do more work to identify the extent of money laundering through the First National Bank: how much money had been moved and who else was involved. But he had been looking for killers and they'd been found.

It nearly hadn't happened. The investigation had turned in their favour when the GIS captured Andrey Belov and he'd been made to confess. Tormenting Belov's mother had been cruel but Donadze knew he'd do the same thing again to stop killers going free. Sometimes, he believed, the end really does justify the means.

'Are you waiting for me, Lieutenant?'

Donadze hadn't heard Meskhi approach. He straightened. 'Yes, sir. I thought you'd want to discuss our strategy for Kesaria's interview.'

'I'm not sure we need a *strategy*. You lead and I'll listen. Our case is compelling enough—even without Andrey Belov's testimony. Let's go in.'

Kesaria didn't stand or offer his hand as they entered the interview room. His eager smile had been replaced by a condescending smirk and he slouched on the metal chair; relaxed, confident, bored.

Donadze recognised Kesaria's lawyer: Keti Topuria, partner at one of Tbilisi's most prestigious and most expensive law firms. She sat cross-legged and elegant, drumming her fingers on her notepad. She nodded to acknowledge Meskhi but ignored him.

Meskhi looked at the two free chairs with distaste and lowered his long, slim frame onto one, pushing it as far back from the table as its restraining chain would allow. 'Let's get on with it, Lieutenant,' he said.

Donadze activated the interview room's recording equipment and listed the people present. He stated that Kesaria was being interviewed following his arrest for suspected murder, armed robbery and money laundering offences. He asked Kesaria to confirm he understood the purpose of the interview.

Kesaria looked at his lawyer and she nodded her consent.

'Yes,' he said. 'I understand.'

Donadze let the silence build. 'How could you let it come to this, Emzar?'

'I suggest you make your questions more specific,

Lieutenant,' Topuria drawled. She looked at her watch. 'Otherwise we'll be here all day.'

'Of course,' Donadze said. He placed a folder on the table, extracted a document and slid it to Kesaria. 'Can you tell me what this is, Emzar?'

Kesaria glanced at Topuria. She nodded and he pulled the document closer. 'It looks like a cash transmission record. Two million US dollars deposited with us then sent back out a few days later.'

'Two million dollars sent from an account in Russia to your Kazbegi Avenue branch then split into smaller sums for onward transmittal to six different accounts in London and Frankfurt?'

Kesaria glanced at the document again. 'That's what it says.'

'Is it the case that your company requires central authorisation for international transfers of this size?'

'No comment.'

'You don't know your company rules?'

'No comment.'

Donadze placed a stapled document in front of Kesaria. 'This is a section from First National Bank's manual detailing financial authority requirements for—'

'I think we can accept you've done your homework regarding the Bank's rules,' Topuria said.

'Whose signature is on the bottom of the transmission record?'

Kesaria nodded. 'It looks like mine.'

'Looks like yours?'

'That's what I said.'

'Mr Kesaria, did you authorise these transfers?'

'No comment.'

'Who recruited you, Emzar?'

'No comment.'

'Was it Christoph Maier?'

'Maier?' Kesaria laughed. 'Hardly. He's what the Russians call a *useful idiot*. He—'

'Emzar…' Topuria cautioned.

Kesaria sat back on his chair. 'No comment.'

'You seem very relaxed considering the seriousness of the charges against you, Mr Kesaria.'

'Is that a question, Lieutenant?' Topuria asked.

'Tell me how you met Andrey Belov and Oleg Galkin.'

'No comment.'

Donadze placed a voice recorder on the table. 'This is a recording of an interview I conducted with Andrey Belov yesterday,' he said. He pressed the play button and sat back to observe Kesaria as his own voice and Belov's filled the room. The recording lasted less than twenty minutes. Belov had followed his mother's instruction and told Donadze everything he'd wanted to know. He and Galkin had been contacted by a former FSB colleague and told they had a job in Georgia. The job had been to kill Sophia Brachuli and Vano Chedia under the guise of a bank robbery. Lekso Berishvili had been their point of contact but they knew someone was directing him. They realised that was Kesaria when he'd ordered them to kill Berishvili.

The recording finished and Donadze pressed the stop button. 'It's all here: the robbery; Sophia Brachuli; Vano Chedia and Lekso Berishvili,' he said.

There was a moment's silence. 'I'd like to speak with my client, Lieutenant,' Topuria said.

Donadze looked at Meskhi and he nodded, standing to leave the interview room. He was waiting for Donadze at the end of the corridor. 'Topuria is going to recommend Kesaria cooperates in return for us giving him a deal,' he said. 'He's got others he can give up, people we might not identify without his help.'

'Yes, but—'

'We're not going to do it. I've heard enough. Bring Jaqeli in. Listen to what Topuria has to say then charge him with everything you've got. But he gets no deal from us.'

THIRTY-ONE

Donadze squinted into the bright sunlight reflecting off Amelia Nanava's apartment block, trying to identify which apartment was hers. But there was little point in doing so he concluded as the tall, tinted windows guaranteed near-total privacy for the people living behind them.

'She said she'd wait in for us, Ramaz,' Jaqeli said.

'And Zaal?'

'I don't know, he should be at school by now.'

'Let's hope so.'

They showed their IDs to the security guard and went into the building, the elevator whisking them to the fifth level.

Amelia opened her door, nodded by way of greeting then returned inside, her stockinged feet padding across the wooden floor.

Jaqeli looked at Donadze, her eyebrows raised. He shrugged and caught the door as it was closing, holding it for as she entered.

Amelia strolled into her lounge and sat. 'I don't have long,' she said.

Donadze glanced around the room: the framed pictures and ornaments he remembered from previous visits were gone and several packing boxes were stacked against the walls. 'Berlin,' he suggested.

She smiled. 'No, London. My company held the job open for me. We leave next week.'

'You and Zaal?'

'Yes.'

'How is he?' Jaqeli asked.

Amelia shook her head. 'I don't know. He seems okay most of the time—but even that's a worry.' She seemed to remember her manners. 'Please sit,' she said. 'Would you like a coffee?'

'No, thanks.' Donadze turned to Jaqeli, inviting her to continue.

'I'm glad we caught you before you left for England,' she began. 'I told you we arrested the man who killed Sophia.'

'Andrey Belov. Yes, and I saw it on the news. You're sure it's him?'

'Yes, he confessed. We know exactly what happened now. Are you okay talking to us about it?'

Amelia nodded slowly. 'I hope so.'

'It was a money laundering scheme,' Jaqeli said. 'Very large sums of Russian money were sent through Koba's branch: tens, possibly hundreds of millions of US dollars from Russia and Belarus were moved to various western cities. The stakes were high and the people involved were ruthless.'

Amelia raised her hand to interrupt. 'And Koba was part of that?' she asked, her voice small and tight.

Jaqeli hesitated. 'I'm sorry. Yes, he was. He was recruited by another Bank employee called Lekso Berishvili. But corruption at the Bank ran deeper than that. Berishvili was taking his orders from a manager called Emzar Kesaria. There may be others involved, we're still looking.'

'I don't remember Koba mentioning either of these names.'

'No, he probably wouldn't have.'

Amelia wiped away a tear, her eye makeup smearing. 'But why did Koba get involved? He had a good job, good prospects...'

'It wasn't that simple. The Mexican cartels have a term for it: *silver or lead*. Koba was told to accept payment to do as he was told or he—or someone close to him—would be killed.'

Jaqeli paused, waiting for Amelia to signal her understanding.

'Koba handled the illicit transactions himself,' she continued. 'But Kazbegi Avenue was a small branch and one of the tellers grew suspicious.'

'Vano Chedia?'

'Yes. Koba didn't have a deputy and Vano was close enough to realise something strange was going on. But he took his suspicions to the wrong person. He told Koba and Koba passed it on to Lekso Berishvili.'

'Koba must have known he was putting Vano at risk.'

Jaqeli nodded. 'Yes, he must have known that. Vano had to be silenced and the robbery was staged for that reason; it was never about the money.'

'But then why kill Sophia? Koba did what was expected of him.'

'He was sent a message, Amelia: stay in line or lose someone even closer than his wife.'

She closed her eyes. 'Oh, my God—Zaal.' She took a deep breath. 'I feel sick.'

Donadze stood and brought her a glass of water.

She took a sip and placed the glass on the floor. She looked at Donadze. 'Zaal must never know what his father did.'

Donadze shook his head. 'He'll find out eventually; these things never go away. It'd be better for you to explain it to him—when he's old enough to understand.'

'I don't want him to hate his father.'

'You can tell him that his father never stopped loving him. That might help.'

'How can you say that? Koba took the coward's way out. Killed himself and left me and Zaal to deal with the consequences.'

'That's not the way he saw it, Amelia. You wondered why Koba was so anxious for you to take Zaal to London.' Donadze paused as Amelia nodded her agreement. 'It was because he wanted you to take him somewhere safe. But he realised even London wasn't safe, that Zaal could be used as leverage against him for as long as he was of value to Berishvili and Kesaria. The only thing he could do was to make himself worth nothing to them.'

'By taking his own life?'

'That's something Zaal needs to hear, when he's ready; his father died to keep him safe.'

Amelia sniffed back her last tear and stood,

straightening her skirt. 'Thank you,' she said. 'England will be good for Zaal. And for me. But I know what to tell him now—when he's ready.'

'I'm really glad you're here,' Donadze said.

Jaqeli turned to look at him, surprised. 'Oh, why?'

'You're good with people. You were great with Amelia.'

'Don't put yourself down, Ramaz. You were pretty good yourself.'

'Well, let's see how we get on with Eliso.'

Eliso Chedia hadn't returned to her parents' home in Kakheti yet. Donadze parked outside her house on Kirim Street and they walked through her garden, its fruit trees and vines thriving in the warm summer sun.

She saw them through her lounge window and waved, rising from her chair to open the door. She flashed them a nervous smile. '*Gamarjoba.* Thanks for coming.' She was still wearing her dead husband's hoodie but her eyes were clear, her hair brushed into a neat pony tail, the storm cloud of despair which had followed her, now gone.

'Can we talk inside?' Jaqeli said.

'Of course.' She stepped aside to allow Donadze and Jaqeli into the house. The air inside was fresh and perfumed, the curtains in her living room open, light flooding into the room.

'How have you been, Eliso?' Jaqeli asked.

She shrugged. 'Life goes on, doesn't it?' She placed her hands over her belly, a slight bulge beneath the hoodie. 'It has to—for him.'

Donadze nodded. 'We wanted to talk to you about Vano.'

'You've cleared him, haven't you?'

'Yes. He was completely innocent.'

Donadze's thoughts drifted as Jaqeli described how individuals within First National Bank had laundered Russian money through the Kazbegi Avenue branch, how Vano had become suspicious and how that had cost him his life—murdered by a hitman who had himself been killed while trying to escape to Russia.

'My poor Vano,' Eliso said.

Donadze shook his head. 'No, Eliso, that's not who he was. Vano tried to do the right thing and it cost him his life. He was a brave man.'

She rubbed her belly protectively. 'Such a terrible world.'

'Yes, it can be, sometimes.'

There was a moment of silence. 'How do you do it, Lieutenant? How can you experience these dreadful things and still live anything like a normal life?' she asked.

'It's not easy. We have our work lives and our home lives and we try to keep the two apart,' he said, echoing advice once given to him by Levan Gloveli.

'Well, I couldn't do it.'

'It's a pity anyone has to.' He paused. 'There's one other thing, Eliso: the thirty thousand dollars deposited with the United Bank of Belize.'

'I told you before, I know nothing about that.'

'We know you don't. We think it was put there as an attempt to implicate Vano in the robbery.'

'And it worked, didn't it?'

'What do you mean?'

'You believed it. You thought Vano *was* guilty.'

Donadze nodded his agreement. 'Yes, we did, Eliso, for a while. I'm sorry.'

She shook her head, her fingers stroking the hoodie's soft cotton sleeves, her husband still with her. 'It doesn't matter now,' she said. '*I* knew he couldn't have done anything like that.'

Donadze reached into his pocket and handed her a folded sheet of paper.

'What's this?' she asked.

'The details of your account with the Belize bank—in case you want to transfer your money somewhere else.'

'*My* money?'

'The account is in your name—that makes it your money.'

'But I told you, I don't know anything about it.'

'It doesn't matter. I said we think the money was deposited to implicate Vano. But we don't know that for certain. That means the money's yours. No one will be looking for it.'

'You're sure?'

'Yes, positive.'

She unfolded the sheet and stared at it in disbelief.

'Are you still thinking of moving back with your parents?' Jaqeli asked.

Eliso looked up and smiled. 'No, not now,' she said.

'To what do we owe this honour, *Ramazi*?' Donadze's mother asked as she held up her face for his kiss.

'What do you mean, *Deda*?'

'Being home in time for dinner. Tamuna, when did your husband last get home this early?'

Tamuna made a show of using her fingers to calculate. 'I can't remember,' she said eventually. 'It's been a while.'

'You two should be on the stage,' Donadze said. 'You'd make a great comedy double act.'

'Well, we'd certainly have plenty of material,' his mother said, giggling to herself as she stood and walked stiffly to the kitchen area.

Donadze looked at Tamuna and made a *what's up with her?* gesture to his mother's back.

Tamuna smiled and shook her head. 'She's just happy,' she said under her breath. 'You'd better have your shower,' she continued. 'Lela's joining us, she'll be here soon.'

'Oh, any reason?'

'No, we've both just been busy and not had time to catch up.'

'Well, I'm sure she'll have plenty to tell us.'

'She will. And Ramaz, please don't disturb Eka. I want her to have a nap before Lela arrives.'

'Okay.' He crossed to the kitchen area and stood behind his mother as she stirred a pot. 'I think it's burnt, *Deda*,' he said, his voice solemn.

'Nice try, *Ramazi*.' She sniffed. 'I thought you were going for a shower?'

'You should definitely be on the stage,' he said.

Donadze showered, changed his clothes and returned to the living room.

Lela had arrived and was spooning food to Eka. 'Hey, Ramaz,' she said. 'Half day?'

'Don't you start,' he said as the three women laughed.

'Open the wine, *Ramazi*,' his mother instructed. 'It's in the fridge.'

There were two bottles of *Tsinandali* chilling and he took one out and opened it. He placed four glasses on the breakfast bar and filled them. There was a small amount of wine left in the bottle and he took a drink from his own glass—closing his eyes to enjoy the tingle of the cold liquid in his mouth—then emptied the bottle into it.

Lela was watching him. 'You were ready for that.'

'You're right, I was. Do you want me to take the baby?'

'It's okay, she seems happy enough.'

'He doesn't want to say it, Lela, but he'd like to give his daughter a hug,' Tamuna said.

'Guilty as charged,' Donadze admitted as he took his baby girl and stared into her beautiful face.

The meal his mother had prepared was exceptional and the company easy. As expected, Lela had plenty of news but wouldn't deny or confirm there was a new man in her life. Tamuna was animated, becoming like a young girl again in her friend's company.

Donadze felt good. At one point—possibly during his third or fourth glass of *Tsinandali*—he relaxed on his stool to absorb the women's chat and comfortable laughter. His mother caught his expression and smiled at him. She patted his hand, telling him—without words—that everything he needed was here, right now, in this apartment. He returned her smile, replying—without words—that he had always known that.

THIRTY-TWO

Eka was awake and crying. Donadze willed his eyes open, his head throbbing from the evening's wine. The bedroom was in darkness and he illuminated his watch face: four forty. He kept still, hoping Tamuna would be first to weaken. 'Your turn,' she said.

'Again?' he croaked. He swung his legs out the bed, paused for a moment then stood and crossed the room, his hands outstretched as he reached for the door. He walked to the baby's room, listening for his mother stirring, hoping she would take over and let him get back to bed. He heard nothing and reconciled himself that his day had begun.

'What's wrong, *chemo gogona*?' he said, bending to lift his daughter from her cot. He held the little girl against his chest, patting her back as he carried her to the living room. 'Are you hungry?' he cooed.

The apartment wasn't cold but he put the heating on anyway. He used his free hand to open the fridge and retrieve a bottle of milk, warming it in the microwave while he changed the baby's nappy.

He carried the now-fragrant child to his favourite armchair. He was right: she was hungry, draining the bottle and giving two or three sicky burps before settling back to sleep in his arms.

Donadze was numb with fatigue but didn't want to risk wakening Eka by returning her to her cot. And, being honest with himself, he valued these quiet, intimate moments alone with his daughter. He settled into the armchair and closed his eyes.

He woke to see Tamuna looking down on the baby as she lay snoring softly in his arms. 'Sleeping beauty,' she said.

He shook his head. 'No, I was awake.'

Tamuna ignored his attempt at humour. 'Here, let me take her.' She reached down and lifted the little girl, shushing her as she protested being disturbed.

Donadze stood and rotated his stiff neck and shoulders. 'Coffee,' he declared.

Summer light was seeping through the balcony doors—it was only six twenty but felt much later. He made a pot of strong coffee and filled two mugs, adding extra sugar for himself.

'You should have put her back down,' Tamuna said.

'I know, but she asked me not to.'

'You're such an idiot,' she smiled.

Donadze yawned. 'It's been said before. Okay if I go for my shower now?'

He examined himself in the bathroom mirror, not liking his pale, puffy face or the red eyes that stared back at him. He shaved and spent ten minutes soaking in the shower, the hot needles stinging him out of his stupor.

He dressed and returned to the living room. Eka was back in her cot and Tamuna was on a stool by the breakfast bar, cupping her coffee mug with both hands. He was hungry and wanted to eat before going to the station. 'Isn't my mother up yet?' he asked.

Tamuna looked at the wall clock. 'No, but she was tired after last night. Probably catching up with her sleep.'

'It's not like her,' Donadze said. 'I'll just make sure she's okay.' He crossed to her bedroom and knocked on the door. 'Are you awake, *Deda*?'

There was no response and he knocked again. '*Deda...*'

He turned and looked at Tamuna.

She eased herself off the stool. 'Let me check,' she said. She knocked on the door and called the older woman's name. There was no response and she looked at Donadze, gave him a reassuring smile then opened the bedroom door and went in.

He waited outside the room, a cold dread clutching his gut.

Tamuna came out a few minutes later, drawing the door closed behind her.

'No,' Donadze said.

She put her arms around him and drew him close. 'I'm so sorry, Ramaz,' Tamuna whispered. 'She's gone.'

Donadze's thoughts were dark and dismal. Sleep wouldn't come and it was a relief when his phone buzzed. Tamuna stirred and he carried it to the living room.

His mother was there, lying in her open coffin, dressed, her hair brushed and tied with ribbon, her arms crossed and resting on her chest, serene, her worldly cares over.

Mourners, most of whom Donadze would barely know, would visit over the next few days. The women would sit, sobbing and praying on chairs placed around the coffin while the men would circle it, tight-lipped and sombre, their demonstration of respect, grief and piety helping to ease another soul into Heaven.

Donadze stood over the coffin, gazing at his mother's lifeless face in the dim light and answered the call.

'I'm so sorry, Ramaz,' Jaqeli said.

'Thanks, it was her heart…'

'I know, it's awful. How about you, are you okay?'

He felt flat, numb, devastated. 'I'm good,' he said. 'What's happening?'

'I wasn't going to call you but Soso said you'd want—'

'What is it?'

'A body's been found in Vera Park. Do you want me to take it?'

He looked at the wall clock: three forty. He would like to have answered, *Yes, you take this one, Irina.* But he didn't. 'Twenty minutes,' he said.

He heard her sigh. 'Okay. I'll see you there.'

He placed his hand on his mother's forehead, leaving it there a moment, then returned to the bedroom. Tamuna was awake, sitting up in bed as he gathered his clothes. 'Do you have to go, Ramaz? It's only been a day…'

'I know. Try to sleep, I'll be home as soon as I can.' He kissed the top of her head and walked to Eka's room. He watched his baby girl sleeping in her cot, realising she would have no memories of her grandmother as she grew. 'But don't worry, *chemo gogona.* I'll tell you all about her,' he whispered.

He took the elevator to the car park, the cold, damp air

clinging as he got in his car and pressed the start button. The engine roared into life in the still, concrete-encased void. He paused for a moment—brittle and alone—then released the parking brake and manoeuvred up the ramp onto Kandelaki Street.

It was a short drive to Vera Park. A patrol car was stationed on Nikoladze Street, its roof-mounted lightbar strobing blue and red against the dark, sombre trees.

A uniformed officer was leaning against the car. He straightened, took a last draw of his cigarette and threw the butt to the ground. 'Lieutenant,' he acknowledged.

Donadze remembered the officer had been stationed outside the First National branch on Kazbegi Avenue. 'What do we have here, Gio?'

'Young girl. Student. It looks sexual.' He pointed into the park. 'She's over there, near the kids' play area.'

Donadze could see the forensic examiner's van a hundred metres or so in the distance.

'She's one of the students they were talking about on the news,' the officer added.

Donadze shook his head. 'I didn't see it.'

'Indians. Coming here to study because it's cheap. There are about two thousand of them now. It makes you wonder, doesn't it?'

Donadze took a step towards the officer. 'Makes you wonder what?'

The officer dropped his conspiratorial grin. 'Nothing, sir. Just passing on information.'

Donadze stared at the man until he looked away. 'That's what I thought,' he said, turning and walking down a concrete stairway into Vera Park.

The park was set out with walkways criss-crossing green, open spaces. Uniformed officers had done their best to secure the crime scene, stringing tape between trees and erecting barriers across the walkways. A forensic tent had been installed near a hedge in a grassy area close to climbing equipment.

Jaqeli turned when she heard Donadze approach. She gave him a long, tight hug and took a step back to appraise him. 'Are you sure you need to be here?'

'Yes, I'm sure,' Donadze said. He pointed to the tent. 'Did I see Natia Gagua go in there?'

'Yes. She'll let us know when it's clear for us.'

'What do you have so far?'

She handed him an evidence bag. 'The victim had this in her purse.'

'Credit card?'

'No, student matriculation card.'

The park lighting was dim and Donadze used his phone's flashlight to examine the small plastic card. It incorporated the blue, oval logo of Tbilisi State Medical University, a bar code, a name and date of birth and a passport-type image of the holder. 'Hiral Modi,' he said. 'She was nineteen. The cop at the entrance said she's from India.'

'Yes, we're trying to locate her next-of-kin.'

'Was she raped?'

'It looks that way.'

Donadze shook his head. 'She came a long way just to die in Vera Park.'

Jaqeli hesitated a moment. 'Are you sure you're okay, Ramaz? Maybe you should take a few days' leave?'

'Yes, maybe. But not right now,' Donadze snapped. He took a breath. 'Sorry, Irina.'

She touched his arm. 'It's okay…'

A man wearing a white protective suit and mask ducked out of the forensic tent, Natia Gagua's technician, Donadze remembered. He looked around for a moment, his eyes adjusting to the park's weak lighting. He spotted the detectives and crossed the grass towards them, taking off his mask and nodding to Jaqeli. 'Natia said you can come in now.' He looked Donadze up and down. 'Wait there, I'll get you some kit.'

They pulled on suits and masks and followed the technician to the tent. He held the flap open for them to enter.

Gagua was bent over the body. She wrote something on a notepad and straightened. 'Irina told me about your mother, Ramaz. I'm so sorry, such a terrible thing to lose a parent.'

She stepped away from the body.

The girl had been small. Her sad, slight corpse lay sprawled beside the hedgerow, naked, her long dark hair lying lank across her face, shoulders and breasts, her eyes wide and staring.

'Dumped over the hedge,' the technician said. 'Not been here long, though.' His eyes crinkled above his mask. 'The fresh ones are the best.'

'Hiral Modi,' Donadze said, his voice flat.

'What?'

'Her name was Hiral Modi.'

The technician's eyes narrowed. 'I know that. It was me who gave Irina her ID.'

'We're almost done here,' Gagua said to the technician. 'You can start taking the equipment back to the van.'

She waited until he'd left the tent. 'Give him a break, Ramaz. He sees this kind of thing every day. Speaking like that—it's only his way of insulating himself from it all.'

'Yes, maybe that's what it is.'

Donadze looked at Gagua, silently requesting permission to approach the body.

She shrugged and he crossed the damp grass and crouched beside the murdered girl. He stared into her lifeless eyes: everything she had or would ever be, taken from her. The rage—when it came—was an old, familiar friend, restoring meaning to his world, removing all doubt. Donadze knew why he was here, what he had to do. He looked down on the broken body. 'Hiral,' he said. 'I'm going to find who did this to you. I promise.'

End

ACKNOWLEDGEMENTS

I'm extremely grateful to the following people for their kind and generous support in helping me write and develop this book.

My wife, *Jacqui Liddle*, my greatest supporter and most stubborn critic for reading every scene many times, advising what did and what didn't work and for putting up with my moods when the dreaded writers' block struck.

My 'beta readers' for reading my manuscript and offering their constructive and valuable feedback: *Annette Rose; Fiona Macdonald; Tom Stewart; Fiona Russell; Mary Puttock; Douglas King*; *Evelyn Halliday*; *David Main*; *Brian McKinstry* and my daughter, *Kirsty McMillan.*

I was again advised by my Georgian friends, *Sandro Chitadze* and *Nino Meladze.* Knowledgeable readers, they kindly offered their feedback on the quality of my writing and on how well I had captured various aspects of Georgian life and culture, thereby ensuring—I hope—an authentic read.

Ruth Sherpa was an incredible proofreader. I thought I'd nailed every annoying typo but, inevitably, I hadn't and Ruth flushed out the few survivors.

I am indebted to my author friends who read and provided their assessment of my completed book. *G.R. Halliday; Marion Todd*; *Mark Wightman; Craig Robertson; Marsali Taylor and Emma Christie* are all successful authors whose work I deeply admire and their advice and encouragement was gratefully received.

ABOUT THE AUTHOR

Alistair Liddle is a former ships' captain, business advisor and operations manager in the oil and gas industry. *No Rules Apply* is the third novel in his series featuring Lieutenant Ramaz Donadze.

Alistair is married with two grown children, a granddaughter and a grandson. His interests, when not writing, include travel, walking, cooking, supporting Heart of Midlothian FC, swimming in Scotland's beautiful lochs, playing guitar badly and writing occasional songs for The Grumps.

After a lifetime of travel, Alistair has settled in Stirling, Scotland.

ajliddlebooks.com

AUTHOR'S NOTE

I was privileged to have lived and worked in Georgia for more than fifteen years. It's a wonderful country, its people friendly and genuinely hospitable.

The war between Russia and Ukraine was grinding on when I wrote *No Rules Apply.* All war is tragic but the devastation of Ukraine and the attempted terrorisation of its people is beyond awful. I was particularly saddened that my Georgian friends had become fearful of hostilities widening in their region. I hope by the time you read this book that the war has ended and that a just peace has been achieved.

I owe Georgia so much and, as always, I hope my writing has piqued readers interest in this amazing country. You should visit if you're able, you won't be disappointed!

Made in the USA
Las Vegas, NV
08 November 2024

11378610R00204